The
Condo

Peter Hassebroek

Upbound Solutions

Also by Peter Hassebroek

Upbound

Melange and Other I. T. Stories

The Dancer's Spell

Greenplays

Thylacine

The Journal Keepers

The
Condo

The Condo

Published by
Upbound Solutions
Whitby, Ontario, Canada

ISBN: 978-0-9866640-9-0
E-Book: 978-0-9991815-0-5

www.peterhassebroek.com

The
Condo

August

The Condo

That gurgling sound again, so loud it might wake Harold. It's behind the walls, out of reach, so it's got to be the corporation's responsibility. Good thing, can't afford a plumber and Harold's Aricept. Heavens, where did I put that cane? Ah, there it is, where you left it, as my dear spouse would say. Now gently turn the deadbolt, pull the handle, and great, no squeak. Maybe I won't lock it. Should be all right, being next to the elevator, just be a minute . . . oh that ting was sharp. Maybe I should rehearse what to say to the property manager. Gary. Don't like talking to him. Too stern. "Hi, I'm Marjorie Gibbons, I live in unit three-zero –" Ground floor already. Gosh, so empty and silent in the lobby – what? Office closed. I'll knock anyway. No answer. Just my luck, he's only here half a week, today would be one of his days at his other site – no, today's Tuesday. According to this sign, Gary should be here all day from nine. It's already ten-twenty. Probably stepped out, heavy smoker I think. Suppose I can wait it out. Might be easier if we had some online way to get things done. Though it'd take time to

*figure out, everything on computers always does. But at least it would
save — wait, someone's entering the lobby. Gary? No, it's the man who
moved in last week, the one Harold calls reclusive — he's a fine one to
talk. And how did Harold conclude that in such a short time? Wonder
how old this fellow is. Younger than us, to be sure, most of his hair in
place still. But not young. I'd guess sixty. Seventy if he's one of those
who takes good care of himself. Friendly nod, cheerful enough, in tune
with the others here. So glad we bought this condo instead of settling
in a home. Can't imagine dying in a place like that. Here we remain
independent, but still looked after. Eventually. Maybe I should go back
to lock the door, then return to wait until Gary does show up. If he
does. I think others have complained about this.*

Raymond Tibbett removes a pricey Barossa Shiraz from a paper
LCBO bag and ceremoniously sets it at the centre of the granite
island. A treat to celebrate, at last, being able to enjoy the condo.
And its amenities. To exercise in a fully outfitted gym, take laps
in a narrow but long pool — as many as his sixty-four-year-old
body can complete — or relax by shooting a game of pool in the
Social Room. A room equipped with a basic but full kitchen and
sitting area with sofas, chairs, tables, a makeshift library, a flat-
screen television. A place to mingle with neighbours such as the
elderly lady in the lobby with the kind face. A non-judgmental
face, possibly concealing a suspicion that Raymond, entering
with a liquor store bag, just after the store opened, in scrubby
shorts and sandals, is a run-of-the-mill wino.

She would be wrong to assume the worst for Raymond is
more teetotaller than lush. Albeit for fiscal reasons rather than
an aversion to alcohol. In fact, back when money was not such a
concern, he developed a fondness for more expensive craft beer,
to the point where he'd rather go without than drink the plain
lagers and ales of old. This discretion coincides with an overall
thriftiness that spurred Raymond to invest in this condominium
four years ago, bought from a colleague who was transferring
to Calgary. He barely knew Craig, but mutual friends ensured a

trusted private sale that avoided the cost of a real estate agent. Raymond got a great price and a chance to leave downtown for the suburbs, an idea he'd contemplated for some time. Craig left behind the tasteful IKEA furniture, of which Raymond kept all but a few pieces, donating the rest. It left little else to do beyond several changes of address, such as for the online grocery store, which he was happy to learn delivers out here.

Only then he lost his job, forcing Raymond to keep the tiny but cheap apartment and rent out the condo. It took just over a month to land a contract position, but the anxiety of those idle weeks spooked him into designating the condo as a retirement investment he could rent to supplement his income.

Now he's retired, several years earlier than intended. That became unavoidable once the increasingly sporadic IT contracts dried up and forced a choice: pad his retirement kitty by selling the condo and continue living in the drab and drafty, albeit rent control protected, basement apartment; or adopt a more frugal existence in a comfortable, spacious, tall-windowed condo.

He took it as a sign when his tenants—a delightful Korean couple—had a baby and decided to buy a house. So reliable, he was fortunate to have found them and couldn't count on such luck again. If that wasn't enough to convince him, a career site reconnection with an old colleague did the trick. Terri's asking Raymond to take on a contract to analyze and document legacy code he'd written decades ago heralded a safety net to mitigate his financial concerns. Best of all, he'd be able to work at home. As long as he met corporate standards for a fast, secure Internet connection. When it took over ten minutes to email acceptance of the offer it was evident the one provided by the condo would require an upgrade.

The sun is bright and shines through the vertical blinds in a pattern that enlivens the grey granite kitchen island. He looks out over the open concept living and dining room, out the floor-to-ceiling windows to the lake where white caps of waves chop the water, while sailboats in the marina to his right, to the west, bobble rhythmically. Last night the wind got so violent it made the windows rattle; the fear they might shatter kept him awake for two hours. That was followed by a persistent rain pelting at the glass with an acute tapping. Which ruined another hour of sleep. These are sounds he'll have to grow accustomed to, along with the train horns, sirens, and other traffic noises that come with living near a major intersection.

It's tempting to open the bottle to celebrate, but he needs to get busy to reclaim the suite as his. While the Lees kept it clean and left no sign of their cocker spaniel, and while the cleaning lady did a fine job making it look as new as possible, his suite still has an aura that makes him feel like a visitor. Maybe it's the unidentifiable odours. An aromatic residue of Asian cooking, mixed with those of the vinegary, ammoniac cleansers used by the cleaning service he hired. It doesn't smell bad, just off, and he can't pinpoint the source. Sniffing the walls and furniture up close reveals nothing. He drops to his knees. The laminate floor has a pleasantly clean lemony smell. Is it in his head? Raymond shuts off the air conditioning, opens the balcony door. The incoming breeze is humid, but brings fresh air. He opens all the windows in the master and second bedrooms too.

Now for the dishes. He opens the cupboards, hesitates. Is it really necessary to wash them? He takes a porcelain bowl, rubs his fingers along its light grey surface and up along the powder blue and black trim. Smooth. An unexpected surge of nostalgia comes over him, recalling Corinne making the identical motion while unwrapping this gift from an aunt, smiling in a charming way. One of the pleasanter moments of their six-year marriage. Is this how it will be in retirement: blasts of memories surfacing in the vast idleness? Would that be so bad? Raymond ponders this while taking down dinner plates and slotting them into the dishwasher. It's full when he realizes he has no detergent. Why would he? There was no dishwasher at the downtown place, he did it all by hand. He laughs: such luxuries could take getting used to. Instead of putting the dishes back, he runs a rinse cycle, which will confirm the appliance still functions.

The whir of the machine fills the silence with a background noise that blends with the traffic outside. Raymond tackles the master bedroom next, checking the dresser drawers are empty, then removing the plain grey bed linen. It's in good shape. Same with the pillows, still fluffy. It would feel weird to keep them,

6

even if he washed them. He's not in the mood to do laundry. He tosses it all in plastic bags, then inspects the en-suite bathroom. Spotless. He digs through his packed box of linens, selects a set of geometrically patterned sheets, and makes the bed. It appears smaller than the one in the city, though it's also queen-size. He plugs in the vacuum cleaner—the old beater, another wedding gift—to suck up thin layers of light-coloured dust on the dark floors. Dust will be an ongoing concern, he fears.

Raymond gathers the garbage into several grocery bags that he ties and takes down the hall to the chute. His hands are full so he opts not to lock his door. A troubling thought as he drops the bag with the sheets: were they the ones Raymond bought to prepare the unit for his tenants? Did they choose to use their own instead? If so, these would still be new. What a waste. It's too late, but not for the pillows, still back in the condo.

As he approaches his door, a sharp yelp from a dog startles him. It's coming from inside. He enters slowly and almost loses balance when a white Pomeranian launches its tiny body at him and starts licking while Raymond holds on.

"Don't let Buster out in the hallway."

The dog yelps several times, apparently realizing Raymond is not who it thinks. All four dark paws scramble to get away. Raymond doesn't let go. Then he recognizes the dog as one he's seen leashed to a cheerful, sociable woman who for some reason is now inside his home, her unleashed and rather slippery beast challenging Raymond's one-handed grip as he tries to shut the door behind him with the other.

The dog relaxes once they clear the narrow foyer and are in the living room. He sees the woman up close for the first time, stretched languidly across his couch, her medium-length blue plaid skirt draped over her knees, which are draped over two of the four cushions. Her patterned blouse matches the frumpiness of the skirt. A mane of the blackest tousled hair he's ever seen falls to her elbows. She is unprepossessing: wrinkled eyes; an absence of makeup; a formless body; an utter lack of vanity. Yet she exudes a beguiling charm from another era, despite being engrossed in a Smartphone, madly texting at someone.

"I got him. I got your Buster."

"Ah!"

Her scream incites Buster to resume his battle for freedom, causing Raymond to release his hold temporarily, but regaining it to gently lower the animal onto the floor. The drip-drip sound preludes a warm liquid streaming down his shin. The dog starts licking again while the woman puts down her phone. Raymond is paralyzed momentarily when she approaches.

"Buster, what have you done? I'm sorry, but who are you?"

"I think, as the owner, that's my question to ask."

"Shoot, that's right, Kim and Min were moving out. I had no idea it was this soon, though. I'm awfully sorry, what you must think of me just coming in — oh, and Buster — let me clean that."

She rushes to open the cupboard under the kitchen sink but can't find what she's looking for. Raymond points to the far side of the long counter.

"I have paper towels over there."

"Stay put, don't spread the puddle."

She grabs the entire roll and brings it over, pulls off a bunch of sheets for herself, then a few for Raymond. As she wipes the floor, he dries his leg. The faint odour of urine remains after all is dried. She smiles, then asks he wait a minute, before leaving without Buster who is as confused as Raymond, but just as still, obeying her order. She returns with a damp cloth she runs over the floor. A fresh scent overwhelms the urine smell. Combined with the fruity fragrance coming off her, it generates a pleasing aroma. He looks down at Buster.

"Guess you don't have to go for your walk now."

Her smile when she looks at him erases all the indignation a situation like this might otherwise stir up. An almost alchemical process converting his irritation to joy, anger to cheer. Only this makes her frown.

"I'm so embarrassed, this is so awful."

"It's okay, it's okay. My name is Raymond Tibbett."

"Nice to meet you, Ray. I'm Kayla Slaske."

Her strong grip impresses Raymond and distracts him from making his usual request for people he meets to not shorten his name. Or it's her friendly tone, one that could never devolve to the "stink-ray" epithet kids used to tease him with at elementary school: "What's that smell? Is it a fish or is it just that same old Tibbett stink-ray?"

"I assume you knew my tenants, the Lees, well?"

"Met them at the potluck last year on the roof. They brought a delicious kimchi. My grandmother and I loved it. They made too much, they always do, so ever since they give us their extra. I came by to see if they had any. I forgot they were moving."

Kayla still seems rattled, but also sad. Raymond invites her to sit, to stay, and is taken aback when she readily accepts. It's rare for him to have a woman in his home, too self-conscious of his humble downtown abode. He excuses himself to change his pants. He returns to find Kayla reading the wine bottle label.

"Special lady coming over later?"

"No, that's for me to celebrate. It'll last me a few days."

"What are you celebrating?"

"My retirement."

"Get out. You can't be old enough to retire."

"I am."

"I don't know. I mean, it's true men can get better looking as they get older, but I'm wondering if you're just rich."

"I'm sixty-four, certainly not rich. Just normal. "

"Good for you. What are your plans?"

The big question, the one he's put off, posed by an intruder in his home. There's no psychology behind the procrastination, he simply has no clue. Retirement for Raymond isn't so much a choice as an inevitability for which he is prepared in survival terms, but clueless as to how to fill the days. Light travelling, perhaps, getting out to the lake or other recreational options in the vicinity. Is that enough? The danger of retirement boredom has preyed on him since he was compelled to enter the lucrative but volatile freelance portion of his career. The eternal months between contracts were retirement dry runs but could not give a true sense of the expanse of free time. Now this charmingly impertinent woman is exposing this stark reality, pulling apart the curtains of his wilful ignorance.

"Just waiting for the phone guy to install my Internet."

"Oh? Okay . . . why not just use the condo WiFi?"

"Not reliable enough, or secure enough for my needs."

"Works fine for me now, after the guy came and helped me set up a box of something."

"A router?"

"That's it, a router."

"Well, for me, since I'll have some freelance projects, I need a high bandwidth. The best they can do here isn't even close to what I'm required to have."

"You know they're improving it."

"Is that right? Do you know when?"

"This year or next year, whenever the contract's up, I've lost track. It's been discussed for so long now."

"Discussed? Where?"

"At the AGM, of course. I'll bet they have news this year."

Raymond flinches, as he does every time he hears about the AGM, the Annual General Meeting. He's endured them all. Two hours of boring prattling to which he pays scant attention, alert only for financial surprises and, once it sounds okay and one or two or three directors are elected, he tunes out, longing for it to end. He knows he should engage more. Maybe this year.

"I'll check into it."

"You should. Though that's not what I asked. I asked about your plans for your retirement. Beyond odd jobs."

"I guess we'll see."

"You know, if I was retired, I'd bike around here all the time and lose weight. Though you don't need to lose any weight."

"That was my plan. I hoped to get a decent bike, but saw the updated the condo rules prohibiting them in the units."

"Sorry, that was my grandmother probably. It's tough to get in and out of elevators, even the lobby, with her scooter. If she has to share it with bikes. You could use the stairs."

"I'm eight floors up."

"There is a bike room. Bruce, the security guy, he showed it to me once. You have to rent it and get a key."

"That's an idea. You seem to know a lot about what goes on around here."

"I pay close attention, I have to. My grandmother is terrible at these sorts of things. And I like to talk to people."

"Some quite well, I see, like the Lees. Well enough to—"

"To barge in? No, don't shake your head, that's what I did, barge in. Don't let me off the hook. It was extremely rude."

"But didn't the Lees ever lock the door?"

"Didn't have to, Min was always here. Except to take out the garbage, recycling, or check the mail, you know?"

"Min? I thought the wife's name was Jasmine."

"Min is Jasmine's mother. She moved in when Jasmine had her baby. I helped set up her bed in the second bedroom."

"There is no bed in the second bedroom."

"They must have taken it with — wait, didn't you know they had her living here?"

"No, but I guess it doesn't matter. Not anymore."

"Don't be angry with them. If not for Min, this place might not look as good as it does now. I'll miss them but between you and me, the younger Lees were not the tidiest people."

Raymond reassures her he's not angry but checks himself to not sound too eager to forgive and expose his elation at having met such a charming neighbour. How old would Kayla be? At least in her thirties. Early forties perhaps. A generation younger than him at least. Does it matter? He enjoys her company, wants her to stay, get to know her, learn from her how things work in the building, things not covered in the scanty guidebook.

Kayla's Smartphone plays a song. After a brief exchange, in a foreign language Raymond's heard before but can't identify, Kayla says she must leave to attend to her grandmother.

"Before you go, can you tell me how to get a notice put up on the lobby bulletin board? Is there some sort of process?"

"What are you selling?"

"Not selling. Leasing. My parking spot."

"No way, are you serious? I'll take it, if it's an indoor spot. I have been wanting one for months. How much?"

They agree on a price and she tells him she'll drop by later with a cheque, and a form for property management.

Raymond locks the door after her. The bottle of wine stands alone on the kitchen island, as if to chastise him for not offering to share it with Kayla in the evening.

Above the microwave is a narrow cubby where he stores all his condo documents in chronological order in a black binder.

He pulls it down and opens it on the small round dining table. What Kayla said about the WiFi tweaks his interest. The phone company package is costly, even when bundled with a landline and television on a two-year commitment. It'd be a waste to pay for the same thing twice if they're going to improve the quality soon enough.

He flips through the pages, in chunks at first, skipping thick batches of real estate documents and condominium declarations until he finds one from two years ago that references the WiFi, as part of the financial addendum. It says:

> *Three years left until the contract with ForageX for WiFi services ends. Currently, the monthly fee is $4,100, which includes all taxes and scheduled increases.*

The same section from last year repeats this, except with a higher price and that it's two years off. But there is another note further on, as part of the finance director's report.

> *I know we are all tired of the WiFi that was initiated by the developer. As we are nearing the end of our obligation at last, your Board, with the aid of Property Management, has begun the process of talking to alternate suppliers who can provide an improved package, potentially at a lower price, when this contract expires.*

Now he recalls it being discussed last year. Specifically how the treasurer implied the sooner the condominium got out of it, the sooner owners could save on condo fees. Raymond searches for the minutes from last year until it hits him they aren't sent until the next AGM, ten months later. What's the point of taking minutes if they're not shared for a year? By then it's impossible to connect what's written to one's oral memory.

The phone rings, the call coming from the lobby, the phone company service man pulling Raymond back to today's reality. He presses * to let the man in. A knock coincides with a swoosh of hot air from the balcony. Raymond turns the air conditioning on before opening the door.

The man works fast at running the wires before connecting, then testing a router and television box. He demonstrates their operation with a complex remote control unit before setting up the WiFi connection to the desktop computer. Raymond signs a work order and at last he's ready for his assignment from Terri.

Alone again, Raymond goes to the balcony, looking around on the off chance he'll see Kayla and Buster. Minutes pass with no sign. He then splays himself on the sofa, breathes in a whiff of humid air, turns on the television. This is the aura he wants. Now he can consider the condo reclaimed as his own.

An hour passes before boredom sets in. Raymond takes the stairs down to the mezzanine to inspect the Social Room or even play a game of pool. Only he encounters a sign indicating it's in use for a condo board meeting.

-2 -1 G **M** 2 3 4 5 6 7 8 9 10 11 PH R

"Ran into Marjorie Gibbons this afternoon. Guess the plumbing issues on that line might be coming up again, so to speak."

"Lorie, you know everyone. Who is she again?"

"Nigel, you ought to get to know the people here better."

"You know her, Dennis?"

"Of course. The sweet lady on the third floor, the one whose husband, Harold, isn't well."

"Good for you, but I'm a director on a board that represents over a hundred and fifty suites. I can't get to know every single one. My consulting business takes up — wait, is her husband the guy with the walker that sparkles?"

"Yes he is. So you do notice, Nigel."

"All right, if there's no new business, can we talk about the upcoming AGM before I go home?"

"Just a second, Gary. The reason I mentioned Marjorie is she says she came to see you this morning."

"That's right, waiting in the lobby, as I came in. I wish I had a less public way to get to — never mind — okay, she has an issue with her toilet."

"And?"

"I gave her the name and number of a plumber."

"She seems to think it's not a plumbing issue, but something behind the walls we need to investigate."

"I know you mean well, Lorie, but it's impossible for me to investigate each and every sound a resident hears. Usually it's a waste of time. Better to get a professional. Ideally a professional we recommend and therefore can trust to confirm it first."

"I suppose you're right. But plumbers aren't cheap."

"If you own a unit in this building, you can afford a couple of hundred bucks."

"What do you think, Stacie?"

"Let's defer to our property manager . . . okay, anything else before moving on? Lorie? Nigel? Dennis? Good. I want to look ahead to the AGM. Specifically, getting a fifth director as no one has volunteered to fill the vacancy yet. That means it'll happen at the AGM. Yes, Lorie?"

"Ned Esposito is hoping he'll get it. He wanted to join when Cynthia quit but has to complete his therapy first. The timing of the AGM is perfect for him."

"Ned. Is that the heavy set fellow with the curly blond hair, the one who walks with a limp?"

"Yeah, that's him."

"Doesn't he seem rather young and inexperienced?"

"Sure, he's young, but he says he had IT experience when he was working. I think he'd be an asset. At the same time it'd help his self esteem."

"Being on the board isn't a hobby, or therapy."

"Ned is perfectly ready to take on responsibilities."

"Sounds to me like a good fit. Have him submit his letter by the deadline. I'm convinced we'll get enough proxies for him."

"Is there an issue, Lorie?"

"Truth is, Stacie, he'd rather just stand up at the AGM."

"Gary, you're shaking your head."

"If he waits for the AGM, with no proxies, and someone else stands for election, it'd be a toss-up. Meaning the likelihood of someone unfamiliar joining the board increases."

"Why can't he at least submit a letter?"

"He would rather not submit anything just now."

"Maybe he's not suited for this."

"It's not that, Nigel, that's just silly."

"You must admit, it's a little strange. You're close to the guy, Lorie, what's his concern?"

"He's on disability and hasn't worked in over ten years. He's afraid it'll show poorly."

"Just get him to list the jobs he had until he stopped. Until he was . . .?"

"Twenty-four."

"Until he turned twenty-four. Stretch them out and present it on his résumé the way I did."

"How's that, Nigel?"

"Leave out the dates."

"Mine isn't nearly as full as any of yours, I still got elected."

"You were the only one running, Dennis."

"That's not my point."

"Which is?"

"Which is Lorie's got a tax department background. Nigel is a business consultant who I'm sure worked in many industries over all those decades. And Stacie, she's an executive recruiter. I'm a homemaker, for my Tim, and proud of it. It takes all kinds is what I'm getting at. By the way, you're all sweet to not point out I didn't bring my butter pecan cookies. "

"Right. Back to Ned. He sounds like a good candidate. What do you suggest, Gary?"

"If you're fine leaving it to chance, get someone others know to nominate him. We'll see how it goes. Ideally no one else steps up to be a candidate before I send out the notice . . ."

"What is it, Gary?"

"It is pretty straightforward this year but next year, three of you are up. We could end up with a rogue board. Something for us all to think about. So you kind of do want this Ned guy."

September

The Home Office

-2 -1 G M 2 3 **4** 5 6 7 8 9 10 11 PH R

Gosh those drills are noisy, and the hammering. Wonder how loud it is for the other suites. Must be bad considering the looks the workers told me they get whenever they encounter anyone on the floor. Regret not writing a little note for my neighbours, regardless of Gary's insistence it's unnecessary, after he unequivocally said he wouldn't do it for me. I'd want to — now they're drilling and hammering simultaneously — I would want to know, it would give me a chance to plan an escape for the day. Pretty sure someone will complain, maybe even knock at my door. Would love to get away too, but they need me here for questions. Wait, is someone at my door or is it the hammering echoing? Can't see anyone through the peephole. Maybe if I step out to see how it is on the other floors, maybe it's not as bad as . . . wow, the stairwells echo with it . . . fifth floor, can't hear a — oh, there it goes . . . sixth floor, a pause, no, still bad . . . seventh, not much better . . . embarrassing . . . try the roof . . . muffled here. These building acoustics are awful, can't recall

16

having an issue in my city condo. Sign of the times, nothing built with quality. Really not much I can do about it. I mean, the work will get done eventually. Just another week, as long as there are no delays, then it'll look nice. Then I'll be able to go shopping for some new furniture. Maybe even get a puppy.

Raymond's home office is terrific, better than any of the dozen or so cubicles he occupied during his career. The L-shaped desk is large enough for a thirty-inch monitor while leaving ample space for manuals, scratchpads, mini-speakers, a lamp, a caddy for his pens, pencils, and stapler, with plenty of elbow space to confidently drink from his treasured Expo '67 mug—filled with hot mocha caramel coffee—without fear of accidentally swiping it onto the desk or floor. His ergonomic chair rolls left and right, back and forth, with ease, even over the laminate floor grooves. It was worth dedicating the entire second bedroom as an office, to create an inviting space that's not only conducive to heads down analysis of legacy code but also participate in video calls in comfort. The fast, reliable WiFi from the phone company tops it off.

It made financial sense to commit to a two-year contract for his Internet service because it came with a plethora of television channels. At his downtown apartment he was content with the Canadian over-the-air channels, getting the occasional one from Buffalo on clear nights. He'll become addicted if he's not careful. He's already recorded dozens of hours of Sopranos, Breaking Bad, Game of Thrones, those water cooler shows people at the office talked about. When not watching them, he finds a music channel to match his mood, be it classical or classic rock, jazz or easy listening, even new wave and retro. All that's missing is an assignment from Terri.

He wants to call her directly, not wait for the email as she asked him to do. Even if there's no work yet, it would help to know when it will come. He could offer some free advice on the legacy system, help identify approaches or potential shortcuts, at the same time reacquainting himself with the code.

Except he can't call from here due to the constant drilling and hammering in the building from some unknown place. He's walked up and down the stairwells, crossed various floors. He can never determine the source of the noise because it starts and stops intermittently throughout the day, every day, starting at precisely nine, ending at precisely six. Whenever there's a long pause and he starts a call, a heavy drill will start up, usually the instant he presses the last digit. No sense when it'll end, if ever. A courtesy notice would have been nice.

Raymond exits his suite and once again makes an effort to discover the source, only for his pinpointing effort to get cut off by another sudden silence. A bait and switch that activates once again back in his suite. He grabs his keys, heads to the elevator, which plunges him to the ground floor.

The property management office is adjacent to the security desk and Raymond finds its door open. The narrow workspace inside resembles more a disorganized utility closet than a place of work. An awkward setting for the thin man wearing a pair of Dockers and yellow golf shirt, sitting at a narrow, cheap desk. A few sets of mismatching binders lean against each other on top of a precarious shelf overlooking a balding head. Envelopes and papers strewn about almost conceal the laptop. A lunch bag lies partly open next to a pack of cigarettes with a red lighter on top.

Raymond's first episode with the condo property manager, Gary, was frustratingly inauspicious. The money from renting a parking spot to Kayla prompted Raymond to go for a nicer bike. After finding one he liked, he came to Gary to rent a spot in the bicycle room where it would be more secure than keeping it in the general racks in the garage. Bruce at security confirmed the two spots were still unused. But when he asked Gary, Raymond was tersely informed none were available. Gary's explanation of the unused spots was confusing. It left Raymond with the sense the guy just didn't want to do the work, evident by his bristling at the suggestion he create a waiting list. The issue became moot when Raymond opted for a less expensive bicycle he can lock in the basement for free. No problems so far.

Raymond takes a position in the narrow doorway.

"Hello. Gary?"

The property manager peers up, straight ahead, as if rudely interrupted, before turning to the doorway. He seems to make an effort to affect a smile, only to abandon it upon recognizing Raymond.

"Yes?"

"That drilling noise . . . where's it coming from? I mean, it's really loud. It's disturbing."

Gary's expression abruptly shifts to a procedural defiance of a type Raymond experienced often during his career. Yet this version is distinctly primal, a mix of white collar entitlement, blue collar martyrdom, blended with a street smart savvy and resourcefulness to ensure any questioner feels instantly in the wrong. Concealing his distaste makes it a struggle for Raymond to describe the noise. He fumbles his words. Then Gary's voice unsettles him further with its tender musicality.

"One of the residents is doing renovation work, which they are allowed to within the prescribed hours."

"And how long is it supposed to go on? How many days?"

"I really can't say."

"Which unit is it? I'll go ask them myself."

Gary frowns, the first indication of emotion, but composes himself quickly with an impenetrable grin that makes it clear he has no intention of providing an answer.

"The noise is so loud, wouldn't it make sense to let the other people living here know, so they can make other plans?"

"It's not a requirement."

"Maybe not, but perhaps a courtesy notification? I mean, the noise can be heard on all floors. Haven't others said anything?"

"It's up to individual residents, if they wish."

"Maybe it's something to consider incorporating as part of a process for renovations. You could send out a notice."

"I'm here to enforce the condo declaration. Beyond that, you can bring it up with the board of directors."

A sharp yap from a dog throws off Raymond. It's coming from the elevator and stops quickly at the tinkle of a little bell. He wants to look in that direction, to wave at Kayla and Buster, to follow them out into the open space and sunshine and escape this closet of an office and the company of this obstinate fellow. But he can't. He must finish the discussion. Gary, unaware of or indifferent to Raymond's uncertainty, peers at his laptop, acting as if the conversation is over.

"And how do I go about doing that?"

"Doing what?"

"Bringing it up with the board?"

Gary merely shrugs, conveying what? That he isn't willing to answer? That he isn't sure? That Raymond ought to know? So maddening. In similar situations at work he could always find a way to coax an answer out of such people. Gary's bureaucratic facade is different. With people at the office one could generally suss out an agenda. With Gary there doesn't seem to be one, his resistance belying a weakness that's hard to pin down beyond a sense this is not how someone ought to behave with clients.

The encounter leaves an unpleasant after-taste Raymond is unable to eradicate, compounded by a mental replay of the bike room scene and a slew of other issues that could be attributed to the property manager: Kim's complaints about the annual fire alarm inspections that don't follow the schedule; resending the budget notice and condo fee increase because he mistakenly re-sent last year's; the condescending nagging behind many of his messages — "Stop speeding in the underground, we know who you are" — and underlying it all a conspicuously silent board of directors that apparently condones this. Seeds for the same sort of indignation that arose within him at the end of his career.

A lengthy bike ride along the waterfront trail might provide an escape from this negativity. Unfortunately a brisk wind, a slight but persistent drizzle, and low grey clouds filling the sky, eliminate cycling as a viable outlet. Instead of going to his suite, Raymond takes the elevator to the mezzanine, to play a game of pool. Highly unlikely there's a board meeting on now.

A waft of chlorine from the swimming pool catches him by surprise. He pauses at the Social Room entrance, then waves his fob at the sensor and opens the door. The empty space is dark, clouds tinting the windows. He stops upon hearing the squeak of chalk against a pool cue. Damn it.

The pool table is usually available in the daytime. He thinks of retreating but then the drilling starts again, though it's fainter than before. He proceeds quietly to see someone in jeans and white t-shirt lining up a bank shot. This person knows how to play; even a hack like Raymond can tell. He's mesmerized by the cue elegantly pulling back to strike. The white ball hits the first bank firmly but softly, then a second, before kissing the eight ball and causing it to roll straight along the rail into the corner pocket. The player rises, a thick mass of black hair tumbles down her shoulders. His clap startles Kayla. When she turns around, she smiles coyly.

"Hello, Ray. Grab a stick."

"I'm not very good."

Kayla nods to a rack of cues on the wall. He takes one, eyes it as if he knows how to measure straightness, then rolls it along the table as he's seen others do. This amuses her but she doesn't offer help. He tries to decline her insistence that he break, but without success. Fortunately, his break is strong. He manages to sink one ball. The only one he sinks, because she soundly routs him in a quick, silent game.

"Good thing we're not playing for money."

"I wouldn't do that to you, Ray. Otherwise, I'd have done it for your parking spot."

Ray. A little tug of annoyance still exists with Kayla calling him that, but it's receding. In fact, he kind of likes how she says it, the last letter slightly extended, the first enhanced by a subtle higher-pitched trill that at times sounds seductive.

"Guess that came in handy, today."

"Yeah, that storm followed me all the way from work."

"What do you do?"

"I fill in looking after a property for family friends."

"You're a property manager?"

"Not exactly. My site is nothing like this one. It's not even a condo, only eight rental units. A dump, to be honest. But I like it, I like taking care of things, of folks. Since we're on the subject, what were you talking to Gary about downstairs?"

"Nothing, really."

"Tell me. I'm interested in this stuff."

"All right, I was asking about the drilling noise."

"Loud, isn't it? Even at four floors down from you."

"You don't seem bothered."

"I'm used to it. Besides, I know the owner, André. He's been itching to redo his unit for a long time."

"How do you know who it is? Gary wouldn't tell me."

"André and I are friends. We play pool. I've gotten to know a lot of people in the building."

Kayla's tone is matter-of-fact but with a detectably coy taunt for him to ask follow-up questions. Her charm is undeniable, it easily counteracts her physical shortcomings, enough for him to declare her attractive. Yet it's easy to stem his curiosity about a theoretical rival. It's not her age; he has dated younger women before, it's that he cannot envision a romantic relationship with Kayla who is more like a niece, or a daughter. Raymond adopts an avuncular tone.

"You'd be a good property manager here."

"Another game, Ray?"

He suspects the game is a diversion to avoid talking about herself, but couldn't be more mistaken. She's chatty and direct, immediately addressing his query by explaining she detoured her career to care for her grandmother who, it turns out, bought her condo only a month before Raymond bought his.

Her grandmother, her Babcia, like his own mother, is over ninety years old. Unlike his youthful mother, the woman cannot get around without her scooter, which has to be transported in a special van everywhere. She hates public transit so Kayla has to be her chauffeur. The van occupies her grandmother's parking spot, that's why Kayla needed one for her Civic. An interesting tidbit: Her parents seem to not approve of the attention Kayla gives Irena Slaske who likewise is not fond of Kayla's father.

"We Poles can be so stubborn."

"So Slaske is a Polish name? I have a Polish heritage."

"Really? Tibbett doesn't sound —"

"My biological father died in Europe when I was a baby. My mother came to Canada with me and met Ronald Tibbett on the ship coming over. He adopted me after they married."

"What a story. Like the Titanic, with a better ending."

"Never thought of it that way."

"But what happened to your real father?"

"I don't know."

"What do you mean you don't know?"

Raymond shrugs, not wanting to reveal his ignorance is due to a defiant refusal to grant the existence of another "Pop" when his mother and Ronald told him on his fifth birthday. Why they chose that particular day to inform him always puzzled him. But an attempt to solve the puzzle would mean acknowledging a fact he was resolute never to acknowledge. So he never made one. His mother and Ronald obliged. Over time the topic faded. He feels silly about it now.

"All I know is, after he married my mother, he was sent to Siberia but arranged for her to escape to Canada, with me."

"That's fascinating. He was a real hero. I'm shocked that you wouldn't know every detail."

She's right. Raymond feels his face turning red, a sickening feeling in the pit of his stomach as it now clicks in why they told him when they did. She had received word his real father, Leo, died in Siberia, and that after she and Ronald married, Ronald would adopt Raymond and become his legal father. Good news for Raymond, but his little mind was too stunned at learning Ronald wasn't his real father to grasp its significance. He spent his entire childhood denying it by ignoring it. Understandable for a kid, unforgiveable for an adult.

"It was a sensitive subject to my parents, not to be discussed around the house."

An obvious lie Kayla ought to see through, but one he still hopes to get away with. To his surprise, she nods.

"My Babcia is a concentration camp survivor."

"Where? Auschwitz? Dachau?"

"I doubt you've heard of it. It's a labour camp. Connected to one called Gross-Rosen. Babcia hates whenever I ask about it so I treat the subject as off limits now."

Raymond watches Kayla sink another eight ball for her fifth straight win. This is getting out of hand, he thinks, referring to her dominance at pool, but perhaps too to the obscure link they share, especially as his part is predicated on a lie.

He likes Kayla. She isn't like anyone he knows. An anomaly in his world, as much an anomaly as he is himself.

An awkward silence ensues before they share a few smiles but no more talk. Then Kayla sneezes before she starts pulling up balls from the pockets and sliding them to the middle.

"All right. Rack 'em up. Let's play again."

"Now that you've finally agreed on the minutes from last year's AGM, everything is lined up for the meeting next month. Lorie, Gary just needs you to submit your financial letter to include in the package and head office can mail them out."

"I'll have it ready tomorrow."

"As usual, I may call upon Gary but the rest of you need not say a thing. I'll field all the questions."

"No need for a message from the board president?"

"Not really, Stacie. I mean, if you wish, but no."

"Okay. That's a relief. To be honest, Sheila, I'm never sure if it's best to say something or just let things be."

"Just let things be. If you're in doubt."

"Yeah, the less you say, the quicker it's over."

"That's true, Nigel. Not only does it take up less time, it also reduces opportunities for confusion and questioning."

"Sheila, I don't mind acknowledging again how grateful we are to have Omnirez chair our AGM."

"Forget it, Stacie. I've chaired many owner meetings, I enjoy it. I also know how to handle a crowd's animosity — what's that, Dennis?"

"Animosity? In our building? This is a nice building."

"It is, I agree. But in my experience, one needs to be alert to unexpected changes."

"New people move in every year, new personalities."

"Oh Gary, I'm sure they're all fine."

"So you're not nervous about the AGM, Dennis?"

"Of course not."

24

"Wow, I'm board president and I'm nervous every year, and relieved when Sheila gets us through it as smooth as possible."

"Why should I be nervous? These are our neighbours. What do you find so amusing, Nigel?"

"Because it's your first one. I felt the same last year only to discover it's different on our side of the floor."

"Different? How?"

"With each raised hand you feel as if you're about to come under attack. It keeps you on edge the whole meeting."

"It's hard to maintain your poise at times."

"Stacie's right. Poise is of utmost importance. Which is why it's best to let me field questions before they become challenges. Trust me, they can come from anywhere at anytime. How many new owners since the last AGM, Gary?"

"Nine new owners, six now renting their suites or who have new tenants."

"Last year's minutes? Any potential red flags?"

"Nah. It would have come up by now. However a resident from the eighth floor came to complain about the fourth floor renovation noise."

"Was he the only one?"

"No, but he had that willing-to-challenge attitude I often see in new owners. Except he isn't a new owner, just a new resident as he was leasing it previously. It's the same guy who pestered me about the bike room."

"Who is it?"

"His name's Raymond Tibbett."

"I don't know him. Anyone?"

"Anyway, he might take issue over those unused spots."

"Are they paid for?"

"No."

"Sorry?"

"The issue, Sheila, is they're reserved for another unit?"

"But they're not paying to keep those spots?"

"They don't have bikes but intend to. One day."

"So why can't they be given to someone else until then?"

"They're reserved for that suite."

"Let me have a crack at this, Stacie."

"Be my guest, Nigel."

"It sounds like once a spot is allotted to a particular suite, it stays with that suite. If not used, it stays empty. Meaning, Lorie, no revenue for those spots. Am I right?"

"You got it. Stacie, you still look confused."

"That sounds a little . . . inflexible."

"That's how it works. When we build the additional storage lockers to rent out, it'll work the same way."

"If you say so, Gary."

"I have a suggestion. As long as you concur, Stacie."

"Whatever you suggest, Sheila, I'm sure it'll be good."

"Let's bury the budget line item for the bike room income and include it in the general income line item. If it comes up at the AGM, I'll intercept. Got it?"

"Works for me."

"What about the WiFi?"

"That's covered in the AGM package, right Gary?"

"I just copied last year's message how we were looking into options. What I think Lorie is referring to is this is the last year of the contract. They may expect us to say more."

"Is there more? Nigel, this was your baby, right?"

"It's not 'my baby' as you say. I've got no time to lead it."

"So you've got nothing to add."

"Correct."

"Then Lorie, I suggest you cover it in your section the same as previous years."

"I hope it's enough, it could generate discussion."

"Discussion is fine. It can even be good in giving a sense of involvement, as long as the issue stays in your control. But you still have a year, if I'm not mistaken, right Stacie?"

"Correct, Sheila."

"But we will need to address it promptly after the AGM."

"Of course. Maybe your friend, assuming he's elected, will take it on. Didn't you say he has an IT background? Like Nigel?"

"He would most certainly take it on. He is rather bored, the dear. It's a shame to be unable to work at such a young age."

"Youth is good, youth should help. And he is kind of cute in a roly-poly way."

"Dennis, you're married."

"A fellow can look, can't he? Besides, I have a soft spot for the chubby ones. I keep baking and baking, trying to get Tim to put on a few—"

"That's nice, Dennis. I think we're in good shape. Possibly even farther ahead than I thought."

"As long as Ned gets elected."

"No one's submitted any intention to run to me. A shoo-in."

"Unless someone convinces the crowd otherwise."

"Might be wise to accumulate some proxies, just to be sure."

"Good idea, Gary, though don't put that in the minutes."

"Duh. Now I definitely need to get home. Since this meeting was longer than usual, I'll be leaving early on Friday."

"Understood, Gary."

October

The AGM

-2 -1 G M 2 3 4 5 6 7 8 **9** 10 11 PH R

Just fill out the proxy Arnold, Tanya says, just put Ned's name down, and you can skip the meeting. Not sure it isn't shirking responsibility, but she's right in how dreary those sessions have become. Half asleep through most of it anyway – two hours the last one. And what really happens? Nothing. Except this residue of used car slickness giving the feeling the board and Omnirez are trying to get away with something. Even though there's no inkling in the numbers or notes. Then again who reads them? Or listens, for that matter? Not sure about this Ned. Being a bachelor and all. Kind of withdrawn, seems immature. Didn't someone tell me he's a video game junkie? Is he actually running? No letter, no résumé, nothing to indicate it. Unlike Nigel who's up again. Another oddball. He seems too old, but he does look shrewd. Bizarre, his résumé contains no dates for the various jobs he's had – hey, look at that, I do notice details. At least he provided something, indicating he wants it. What if this Ned kid has no one nominate him? Won't be

28

me. And what if he backs out? I'd feel silly having put his name down, feel obligated to nominate him if no one else does — the hell with that. Tanya did say that Lorie assured her he was running, so maybe she'll nominate the guy, though that'd look funny, her being a director and all. Probably safer to write Nigel — wait, two openings, two directors. Okay, that solves it, I can put both names down. Ned — don't recall his last name — first name should suffice. Then Nigel Khan. Should I have written Nigel's name first? Oh well. What's done is done.

-2 -1 **G** M 2 3 4 5 6 7 8 9 10 11 PH R

"Thanks for lunch, and driving me home, Terri. You can pull up there to turn around, that's fine."

Raymond's old colleague steers her BMW towards the wide lane marked with diagonal yellow lines and backs it in. As he moves to open the door, she clutches his other arm to hold him back. She rolls down the windows, turns off the engine.

He first met Terri three decades ago when she was a co-op student on a university work term; they shared cubicle pods. A time when his current sexagenarian age was only a variable to calculate what salary percentage to contribute to what then was a distant retirement. A time he found Terri very good looking, when such a touch might have carried romantic significance. At this stage of their lives, she married twenty-plus years, a recent granny, he set in his bachelor ways, the touch is only nostalgic.

"I'm sorry, Raymond, I wish I had better news to give you. I am trying to get this done."

"I know, out of your control. While I appreciate you telling me in person, I feel my home office is wasted."

"Don't abandon hope. Funding is suspended for all projects, not just this one. The budgeting for next year, with new money, will begin soon. You can be sure I'll keep at it."

"I guess that's the way it goes."

An odd turbulence goes through Raymond's gut. It's telling him something precious, something he's held onto all his life, is being torn away, but also that it's important he let go and not try to hang on. Terri releases his arm.

Raymond looks to his condo entrance, wishing for the glass doors to open and suck him inside. A door does open. Buster emerges, followed by Kayla. In this light, she looks terrific, even with her big brilliant hair tied back. She's wearing leggings and a turquoise t-shirt that complements her pale skin. She makes Buster wait while she puts on her sunglasses and adjusts her baseball cap. Which is when she sees Raymond and waves. He sticks his head out the window.

"See you at the AGM tonight."

Kayla puts a hand to her ear for him to repeat but Buster is pulling her away. Terri gives him a playful slap.

"Good to see you smile. Who's that?"

"Oh, Kayla. A neighbour. I'm renting her my parking spot."

"Okay . . . she's sort of cute. Seems bubbly."

"She's twenty years younger, at least. More like thirty."

"I seem to recall you preferring younger ones. Besides, you could pass for mid-forties. Easily. Avoiding IT work appears to be good for you."

"Nice try. I'd prefer the income."

"You can use the companionship of a lovely girl. Ever since you and Corinne split—didn't you learn something from that?"

"I learned to appreciate being alone."

"All right. Have it your way. Enjoy your retirement. Take it easy. I'm envious as I'm still a few years away."

The full weight of his disappointment at Terri's update hits him when he's inside his suite. She's optimistic about next year but he suspects the opportunity is lost to him forever. An urge to skip the AGM is countered by a desire to see Kayla there. The latter wins out as he organizes the documents to scan through while he eats a grilled cheese sandwich.

His prime interest is the WiFi. The AGM package he got last week reveals little more than the previous ones and contains the same description of the contract and a more subjective note. Its tone this time is a little stronger.

I know we are all tired of the WiFi contract initiated by the developer. At last we are nearing its end. I expect this to be a lively topic at the AGM. Be assured your Board, with the aid

of Property Management, is in the process of reviewing
alternate suppliers who can provide an improved package,
potentially at a lower price, when this contract expires.

Nothing else, no update, nothing in the minutes that bear a resemblance to his own, albeit poor, recollection. It may not be a concern, there is still a year left in the contract. But if Raymond had his druthers, the package would have provided an estimate of when owners can expect an announcement, a sense of what's involved, if only to demonstrate the board has a solid grasp of the situation.

It does bring to mind that board member, Nigel, elected two years ago. The one who confidently put forth a strong business background, an awareness of the market, a willingness to lead. The guy was smug but his message was encouraging. Though Nigel has had two years to provide some sort of update.

What will it mean for his two-year contract if a resolution is announced? Probably not a lot. The phone company service will act as a hedge in case of delays or issues and there are generally delays when dealing with vendors, especially if a changeover is involved. It's worth it to pay more to protect himself from such potentialities. Ideally they'd let the current service expire so that owners can fend for themselves, and deduct that portion of the cost from the monthly fees. Then owners could bundle Internet with phone and television as they please, or upgrade to higher speeds instead of settle for a one-size-fits-all solution.

The lobby is busy, over a dozen owners clutching envelopes like Raymond, gathering to carpool to the meeting. The drizzle outside—it always seems to rain on AGM nights—explains the hesitance of most to walk. Raymond doesn't recognize anyone, no imminent ride offers for him, so he'll brave the weather. He squeezes past two couples talking to Bruce at the security desk.

"Hey, Ray."

He hardly recognizes Kayla, who's wearing a pleated dress and beige long-sleeve blouse. She looks elegant standing behind a blue electric scooter. Its occupant, an old woman, appears to be dozing, but seems to have a spasm when he speaks.

"Is this your grandmother?"

31

"Uh huh, Babcia had to undergo a bunch of tests in the city so she's exhausted. Say, are you going to the meeting?"

Raymond nods. Kayla hands him a sheet of paper.

"We came down to give it to Gary but I suspect he left early to prepare. You'd be doing us a big favour if you took it."

"You're not going?"

"Of course not, I'm not an owner."

It sinks in. All this time Raymond assumed Kayla lived here and was his neighbour when, in actuality, his neighbour is the old woman. Kayla watches him, as if tracking his thoughts.

"So can you take this and hand it in?"

"Of course."

He takes the proxy. Without thinking, without realizing it's a private document, he spots a name, Ned, handwritten on one of two blank lines for board positions. Nigel Khan's name is on the second line.

"Who's Ned? I don't remember a Ned as a candidate."

"Beats me. Some guy Lorie told Babcia to vote for."

"Who's Lorie?"

"Lorie Winstanley. You've seen her. She's the treasurer. Tall and thin, she was a college volleyball star. Her husband passed away last year."

"You should go, Kayla. Especially if you're interested in this property management business."

"Thanks, but no. I went to one and almost died of boredom. Besides, my grandmother is exhausted from the tests. It's better if I watch over her until bedtime."

Raymond pockets the proxy and Kayla startles him with an appreciative clasp of his hands. She pulls him close to whisper:

"Meet you for some pool after?"

As she says this the old woman stirs, looks up at them, then makes eye contact with Raymond. Her eyes come alive, but it's impossible to tell from what. Fear, anger, drugs? Whatever it is, Raymond finds it unnerving. To counter this, he moves to shake the woman's hand, only for her to instantly shut her eyes again. Kayla doesn't notice because her attention is on a man in his thirties in jeans and an argyle sweater.

"André."

The man comes over. Kayla averts his hug to introduce him to Raymond. André du Bois, perpetrator of the renovation noise several weeks back. A handsome, beardless metrosexual, André is much closer to Kayla in age than she is to Raymond, not the octogenarian of his imagination. André's handshake is firm, his voice low, his demeanour affable.

"Pleased to meet you, Raymond."

The old woman gazes at André while he apologizes for the noise, his Quebecois accent adding sincerity.

"Now I wish I had warned my neighbours. Gary said not to bother, it wasn't necessary. Can I make it up to you by offering a ride to the meeting?"

"No thanks."

Raymond explains he prefers walking, not disclosing a need to be alone a few minutes to ponder how well André and Kayla know each other.

Only the encounter with the grandmother is uppermost in Raymond's mind on his way to the marina. The image pierced him deeply; it isn't going away. There was terror in her look, or rage, or both, plus another element. Shock of recognition? That would be insane. He's never seen the woman before.

These thoughts dissipate upon entering the marina parking lot as he passes boats on racks, others still in the water awaiting winter storage. He imagines owning a boat at this marina and it being located where he can view it from his balcony. That was a key factor in his deciding to buy the condo.

He registers at a desk, hands over the proxy, gets his voting form, and sits in the last row of chairs in the large room with massive windows. He removes the can of ginger ale he brought, opens it, and slowly sips it, not wanting to agitate his bladder.

While he waits for his fellow owners to take their seats, he again skims over the meeting documents, once again dismayed by a set of skimpy minutes that may or may not represent what was said last year. How could they if they come out just before the next one? It's bizarre. Ten months of raw, potentially un-transcribed notes sitting idle. The temptation to sculpt them to fit a current context with the benefit of hindsight to make Gary or the board or others look good would be difficult to resist.

The notes from the treasurer have more substance, and are more readable than anything else. The WiFi note, including the expectation of discussion, is promising. It seems the treasurer is keen to save money. Not enough money to put the boat in the marina, but enough to sustain the dream. The treasurer is Lorie Winstanley, the name Kayla mentioned, and she is indeed a tall woman who, even sitting, is almost a head taller than Nigel, the director who made the auspicious election speech targeting the WiFi. Seeing them bookend the other two seems a good omen.

The seats around Raymond fill up, save for the empty chair separating him from a young, obese fellow on his left who, like Raymond, is by himself. His tight blond curls are magnificently yellow, the naive grin on his peach fuzzed face cherubic.

In contrast a gaunt woman with silver hair, centering a row of people at the front faces the owners, clears her throat before she starts to speak. Her voice is lucid but drones in a monotone that instantly incites boredom but demands alertness because it sounds slickly obsequious, like a used car salesman.

"Hello everyone, good evening. My name is Sheila Mathers. I'm Senior Vice-President of Operations at Omnirez. We are the folks honoured to manage your lovely condominium building. Once again, your board of directors has respectfully invited me to chair your Annual General Meeting. Before I go further, does anyone here object to my doing so?"

This is met with a silence made odd by a simultaneous turn of heads at the front. It tempts Raymond to say something. Not necessarily to object but to ask why the president of the board is letting an outsider take charge of his most important meeting.

"Good. Please let me introduce everyone at the front table."

On Sheila's right is Wayne, a studious-looking man exuding the type of confidence one wants to see in an accountant; then Gary, leafing through papers. On her left are the four directors. Nigel Khan, completely bald, with shrewd intense eyes hidden behind dark, scholarly glasses. He's sporting a trim millennial beard, despite being at least sixty, and desultorily nibbles at his fingernails. Dennis Jones, tall and flamboyant, with a room-brightening multi-coloured sweater, glances left, right, then at the owners, as if suddenly summoned. Stacie Costas is the slim, unsmiling board president who sifts through a stack of papers, her hands moving in sync with Gary. Finally, Lorie Winstanley, in her fifties, too thin, gangly. She does not resemble an athlete whatsoever. Her librarian glasses alternately give an impression of motherly concern and a grimness ready to shush the crowd. Sheila then points to an empty seat next to Nigel.

"That was for Cynthia until she resigned. Her position will be filled with tonight's election."

There's little to be gleaned from the expressions on the faces at the front, all neutral, all glum. It again strikes Raymond how odd it is to have a vendor taking charge of a meeting for owners on behalf of a board that consists of owners. Isn't that a conflict of interest? And why does the board president meekly look like an observer, not a participant? It's like a family gathering, or a wedding, in which the church custodian emcees the reception, because no one else can be bothered.

Raymond's instinctual dislike for this emcee grows into all out enmity the more she prattles on in her patronizing manner. It's silly, irrational, because he doesn't know her. If anything, his frustration ought to target the board that thinks this is okay, or the owners who don't protest, and accept it. But those people, to extend the wedding analogy, are family, hence exempt.

He does enjoy listening to the accountant, Wayne, walk the owners through the financial statements. His voice is direct and his manner professional in describing the various categories of expenses and income. Strange. Raymond is sure there was a line item for bicycle room revenue last year. It's not here. He thinks of asking but it's a dead issue for him. Wayne then removes his reading glasses to encourage owners to take greater interest in how their building is run, to participate, going so far as to hint at how everyone will benefit from variety on the board.

The tedium returns when Sheila takes over again to review the minutes from the previous meeting — undoubtedly forgotten by all those there and so unchallenged — and runs through other items that seem bureaucratically necessary but inconsequential. Raymond can't help but get a sense this Sheila purposely makes the meeting as dull as possible, putting people asleep, deterring them from contributing, let alone raising concerns.

Things pick up when an owner questions the maintenance of the swimming pool, specifically the chlorine content. He adds he could arrange a free, independent test. But he's shot down by a defensive Gary.

"You're wrong. Our technician is here every morning at six o'clock to test the water and adjust it if necessary."

A condescending response with an equally condescending tone from someone personally offended anyone would question one of his vendors. But Raymond, as well as his fellow owners and the board, offers no support. The issue drifts away. Though Raymond can't be sure, he thinks he noticed other hands raised for concerns earlier. Now there are none.

It's the treasurer's turn to speak. Lorie basically repeats the content of her documents. Her solemn manner exudes a mix of competence, humility, trustworthiness that keeps her audience's attention. It's the first time Raymond has gotten any sense of the board speaking to the interests of owners. Her recap ends with a section declaring potential conflicts of interest, of which there are none. Lorie sighs.

"Now, for a matter of concern to many of you."

At last, the WiFi is brought up. Several owners relate their displeasure but, to Raymond's surprise, several are satisfied.

Then an owner across the room stands up. His voice and its distinct Quebecois accent identifies him as André du Bois. It's a voice that grates on Raymond until it declares it would be better for the condo to get out of providing WiFi, pointing out how the trend is to bundle Internet, television, and phone offerings. This concurs with Raymond's desire the condo drop the service and all its associated costs and complications and have owners shop for Internet as they do for television. Not only would it save on monthly fees, it would save on other media. If nothing else, it provides a choice. Raymond rises to add his support, spurred by an unexpected admiration for Kayla's friend.

While they are in accord, and no one disputes anything they say, something seems missing, even more than the muteness of his fellow owners. Nothing is resolved, the topic gets changed.

The time comes to elect two directors. One to serve a term of one year, the other for two years, the candidate receiving the most votes earning the longer term. Raymond feels an impulse to nominate himself, bolstered by the pep talk from Wayne, the accountant. Another hand raises, belonging to André du Bois, who nominates himself. A relief.

Then Raymond notices the overweight man sitting next to him. He's fidgeting, bobbing up and down, looking towards the directors. His gestures get sillier as he hisses, "Lorie, Lorie," and when there is no response his waving gets animated. Up at the front, the treasurer looks uneasy but then raises her hand.

"I would like to nominate Ned Esposito."

Lorie points to the man next to Raymond, causing heads to turn their way. The waving calms and the man sits back down. It seems clumsy and fishy at the same time.

The candidates each give a speech but Raymond's already decided to vote for Nigel and André. It surprises him when Ned wins the most votes, garnering the fidgety man a two-year term. Maybe people like Kayla's grandmother are unconcerned about a clique forming on the board. Meanwhile, poor Nigel will have to do it again next year if he wants to retain his seat.

"Motion to destroy ballots immediately after the meeting. Is there a second? All in favour . . . motion carried."

This agitates Raymond briefly, but then the WiFi comes up for discussion again. Listening to Nigel makes Raymond regret voting for a man who pledged to apply his professional acumen to the matter. Only to discover, contrary to past AGM notes that implied an active search, they've done nothing. All talk. Nigel's every word makes Raymond cringe.

"We need a solution to enable smart homes, a solution that will operate our lights, doors, hallways, all our energy systems. A solution that supports video conferencing and enhances our communications abilities. A solution for the future."

Okay, Nigel. You expect this within a year? At what cost? It gets so infuriating Raymond waves his hand to interrupt.

"Excuse me, but isn't it too late to talk of features?"

Raymond stands up as heads turn his way.

"To replace what we have within a year, let alone entertain such ambitious goals, takes time and demands a degree of effort and coordination. I think you guys need help. I have experience and skills in IT project management that I'm willing to offer to help you stay focused on the issue at hand."

There is no verbal response, for or against, though the vibe feels supportive of what Raymond said. What else can he do?

Raymond feels a tap on his arm, from Ned Esposito, who is nodding at him. Ned hands Raymond a pen and paper and asks for his contact information. Raymond obliges, feeling inspired, and ironically amused: he wants to inhibit Nigel—the man he just voted for—to assist Ned, who he voted against.

The meeting ends and people start to leave. One man comes up to Raymond to concur with his perspective, but also to warn that ForageX is well-entrenched and removing their equipment will be a challenge. There is nothing more from Ned who moves on to talk to other people, including André du Bois. Good time to escape.

In his suite, Raymond is pumped from the meeting, but also uncertain. Did he make the right choice in volunteering? He's about to turn on the television when he remembers Kayla.

He finds her playing pool by herself, playing well, as usual. A shark even when she forgets to bring her own cue, which she left in her grandmother's suite.

"I was wondering if you'd forgotten about me."

"I'm sorry, I almost did. That meeting was more animated than I expected."

"Uh huh."

"The WiFi? The board hasn't done a thing about it. No clue what it involves. I said as much at the AGM. But there may be hope with Ned."

"Who's Ned?"

"The one your grandmother voted for on the proxy. He got elected and asked for my contact information. Meaning I might get involved with the board of directors."

"Ooh, look at you, on the board of directors."

"Not on it, just assisting. But I'm having second thoughts."

"Why?"

"I don't know. Just a hunch. How long can you play?"

"As long as you like."

"Don't you have to get back to your real home?"

"I'm staying here tonight."

"Everything all right?"

"Actually, no. My Babcia's in a bad way. She got spooked by something earlier, I have no clue what it was. I had to make her take a sleeping pill, man how she fights me on those. I'll be here for as long as you care to play."

-2	-1	G	**M**	2	3	4	5	6	7	8	9	10	11	PH	R

"Now you've met everyone, I just want to say, congratulations, Ned, welcome to the board."

"Thanks Stacie, I'm honoured. And anxious to help on this WiFi business. A couple of owners are willing to help too."

"Good, as long as they don't get in the way."

"In the way of what, Nigel? Nothing's been done yet."

"You're looking at me as if that's my fault."

"Relax, you two, I'm sure Ned didn't mean it that way. He'll soon realize being a director is a lot more involved than just the WiFi issue."

"Of course, of course, I wasn't implying anything."

"Good. Lorie can show you how we do things next week. A good AGM overall, I think, glad it's over. Good job, Lorie. I can tell the owners appreciate your reports."

"Thanks, Stacie."

"How do you like my cookies, Ned?"

"Yeah, they're nice."

"They're butter pecan. I developed the recipe myself."

"About the WiFi. I'm thinking we establish a committee that includes these owners."

"You sure are eager, Ned, which is great. But it's been a long day and night. It can all wait until our meeting next month."

"The sooner we get going, the better."

"If Ned wants to take charge in my place, then by all means, let him have at it."

"Are you sure, Nigel?"

"As long as I'm kept in the loop."

"You wouldn't have it any other way, right Ned?"

"Absolutely, Lorie. I'll get right on contacting these people. See what they can bring to the table."

"Whoa there. We ought to run this by Sheila and Gary. They may have concerns. One thing I've learned, and you'll learn this too, is to trust Omnirez and utilize their guidance."

"I suppose, but can we wait for the next meeting? Lorie, you agree with me we need to start sooner, right?"

"Yes, dear, but Stacie has a point. Stacie, how about you and I go see Gary tomorrow at his other site and run it by him."

"Generally I prefer not to undertake condo business outside our formal meetings."

"If Gary hadn't rushed off, we could deal with it now."

"Point taken, I'll make an exception. When are you available tomorrow, Lorie?"

"Anytime, I'm always here."

"You want me to join you? I'm at home too."

"No, Ned, Gary doesn't know you so well yet."

"I could swear Gary said he was joining us earlier."

"He did say that, Dennis."

"What are you implying, Nigel?"

"Nothing, nothing at all. What did you think I meant?"

"I have no idea what you meant, just that it sounds as if you don't fully trust our property manager the way Lorie does."

"That's your opinion."

"If Gary couldn't make it, I'm sure there was a good reason."

November

The WiFi Committee

-2 -1 **G** M 2 3 4 5 6 7 8 9 10 11 PH R

Pretty good gig. Nice building. Modern, still looking new. Fantastic neighbourhood. People friendly, most of them, not all. Incident reports are rare, thank goodness. Most interactions are for service people, real estate agents, receiving packages, getting signatures, a little chit chat. Superintendent nice guy, property manager a bit grim, many are. At least Gary isn't fussy about me being a few minutes late. In fact, he's more annoyed if I'm early, meaning waiting in the car on the days he is here. Looks like he's leaving early, if the hours posted on his office door mean anything – none of my business. Guess he only comes in half the week. Is he part time? Probably manages another property. Yeah, good gig, nice career-end landing spot. Boring but pleasant. For a security guard, at least an old-timer like me, boring is good. There he goes, guess he's leaving me to lock the office, leaving me alone. Not for long. Soon a parade of dog walkers will strut past, from the elevators, or from outside returning from long walks. Joggers too, power walkers as this crowd likes to say. A few couples, many widows or widowers, going out twice a day, rain or shine, they claim. Good for them, taking care of their bodies while I sit like a lump. They do distract the hours before dark, but then it gets too quiet. So quiet it's tempting to follow Gary's lead and skip out before midnight. Except the cameras would provide evidence, if anyone complains. They surely would tonight, with that party. Like the guy I see approaching the entrance. Don't see him as much, though I remember him talking to Kayla the night of the AGM. Weird how Irena acted asleep in her scooter while glowering at him as if he was the devil set on exploiting her granddaughter. It was intense. He's too old for Kayla. Though he looks too young to be a retiree. Unless he's one of those who grey early. In his fifties, at least. What was it? Freedom Fifty-Five? Can't blame him for trying with Kayla. She's a sweet girl, always up for a chat. Not beautiful but in the right light — I wouldn't say no.

| -2 | -1 | **G** | M | 2 | 3 | 4 | 5 | 6 | 7 | 8 | 9 | 10 | 11 | PH | R |

Raymond waves his fob at the sensor and opens the lobby door. He smiles at Bruce at the security desk, who smiles back with a wink. Weird guy but friendly, chatty. A little too chatty on some days, but this time Bruce doesn't interrupt Raymond's path to the mailbox. Election appeals, realtor postcards, a letter from his MP, fast food coupons, and bulk mail addressed to Resident. He drops it all in a nearly overflowing blue bin. Waste of paper. He presses the call button for the elevator, then notices one is at the roof, the other at P2. Could be a while.

"Hey Bruce, elevator's busy tonight."

"Yeah, bit of a mix-up. Someone's having a party on the roof despite the cold, and there's a fiftieth birthday bash in the Social Room, for Lorie. People keep going to the wrong one, then have to get to the other. Hope it doesn't end up with anyone stuck if the elevator gets overloaded."

"Does that happen often?"

"From time to time."

A young couple enters through the front doors, stops at the directory, finds a name, punches in a number. A click precedes the man pulling the door and holding it for the woman. She has her hands full with two bags that don't look as heavy as the one he's carrying. They stroll to the elevators. The man presses the button, one comes right away. Raymond considers joining them but decides to stay with Bruce.

"I guess Lorie's pretty popular."

"Oh yeah. Always says hi to me. Very caring. Ever since her husband, Sam, passed, she's been doing a lot around here. She's kind to that Ned guy too. He's a bit of a loner."

It's surprising Raymond's heard nothing from Ned since the AGM. Disappointing too, at a lost opportunity to invest himself in his building, in his neighbours—not just Kayla who isn't a neighbour technically—and get to know them. The accountant's inspiring words at the AGM still resonate. As does a dream he had that night of Sheila and the board behind closed doors in a dark room. Raymond was watching them through a glass floor from above while they made arbitrary, foolish decisions he was powerless to stop. Now the dream makes him wonder about the accountant's pep talk, whether it was more of a warning than a hero's call to get involved.

Bruce grabs his coat and walkie-talkie to begin his rounds. Raymond tries the elevator again; this time it arrives instantly. Only it stops at the mezzanine where the doors open to a burst of noise coming from the Social Room. Since it's adjoined to the pool room there will be no games with Kayla tonight.

The same couple he saw in the lobby joins him, but they do not recognize Raymond. They're laughing. The man nods before pressing the button for the roof. They shift and now he sees the notice for Lorie's birthday pot-luck party, and that all residents are invited. He saw it last week too but forgot about it, except to mention it to Kayla. A hint. However, she said she avoided such events, unless her grandmother insisted on going. That put it out of his mind until now. Maybe he ought to reconsider.

Participation would infuse a welcome degree of sociability in his life. The latest funding delay for Terri's project intensified Raymond's sense of alienation from the IT world. Yet he's just as much an alien outside that world. The dearth of human contact—admittedly one motivation driving him to purchase a condo in the suburbs — is depressing him. It's likely a phase in the retirement process. This notion is reinforced upon exiting the elevator and leaving the happy couple by a sense of relief at seeing an empty hallway and a clear run to his suite. There he opens a can of beer to relax. But instead of relaxing, an impulse to go to the party takes over and only passes with an unrealistic but pleasantly agreeable hope Kayla might drop by.

He unlocks his door.

During the next hour, as he nurses his beer, a renewed urge to be with people grows. It is possible Kayla could be there. She and her grandmother are friends with Lorie aren't they? Maybe her grandmother insisted. At least he assumes they're close with Lorie; he's never heard Kayla say so explicitly.

His beer gets warm. He finishes it, opens another, and goes to the mezzanine via the stairs. Much quieter now outside the Social Room. He taps his fob at the sensor, pushes the door. The room is empty, save for several seniors at a table playing bridge, sharing two bowls of popcorn. The kitchen is messy with dishes and a pervading smell of microwave popcorn.

"Hey, guy. You just missed Lorie's party."

The male voice comes from his right, by the pool table. It's Ned, standing with a pool cue in his hand. It appears he's had a few beers and is brimming with self-assurance.

"Hi Ned."

"Was about to email you. Still interested in helping out with the WiFi?"

"Yeah, you bet."

The words come out automatically. Just as well as it shields the instinctive hesitation accompanying them.

"Good. You got a minute now?"

"I do."

Instead of taking a seat at a table, Ned points at the stand of pool cues. Raymond searches for the one he uses with Kayla as Ned collects and racks the balls. It's not there. But it's not gone, it's in Ned's hands. Raymond selects the one Kayla uses when she is without her own. Ned motions for Raymond to break, which he does well, without sinking any, leaving a clear shot on the three-ball, which Ned sinks.

"How far along is the board on the WiFi?"

"Just starting. Clean slate."

Ned says this with a degree of pride, baffling Raymond as he sets up the six-ball after Ned misses a bank shot. He makes it but inadvertently sinks one of Ned's balls.

"So you haven't considered any solutions?"

"Not much to do until we rid ourselves of ForageX. They're bad, I mean really bad, as I'm sure you know."

"Actually, no, I use the phone company."

"Because they're bad, right?"

"So you've already determined you want to replace them?"

"Absolutely. No brainer. Soon as the contract terminates in September, they're outta here. Gone. See ya. Good riddance. All those complaints about poor service, we'd look like idiots if we didn't find an alternate."

Ned's assuredness ought to assure Raymond but he finds it troubling. There's less than a year left on the contract, less than that to select and test another vendor with enough confidence to replace ForageX, regardless of how they perform. It's too hasty. That they need help was obvious to Raymond at the AGM; that they need it this urgently is painfully evident to him now. And it scares him.

Then again, maybe it need not be so urgent. For Raymond, and André du Bois as well, if he understood that man correctly, the best solution may be to let the contract expire and leave it to owners to provide their own WiFi needs, as he, Ned, and André have done. Time is less a concern then. Still, it's not as simple as doing nothing. Removing an entrenched vendor—ForageX has been here close to a decade—can be complicated, albeit more in terms of communications and process.

"When did you last talk to ForageX to share our concerns?"

"Don't need to. Gary deals with them."

"So we raise issues with Gary that he passes to the vendor?"

Ned, in the middle of lining up a shot, pauses.

"Gary deals with the contract we have with them. Anyone who has issues with the service calls ForageX directly. Which is another issue. They're across town. Often people have to wait until evenings or even weekends."

"That's not good."

"Don't worry about that. They're gone, that's the only thing that's important. We're focusing on a new solution."

As Ned sinks a series of balls—he'd give Kayla a run for her money—he explains his intent to form a special WiFi committee consisting of three of the five board members—himself, Lorie, and (reluctantly, it sounds) Nigel—along with the two owners, Raymond and André du Bois, who expressed interest in helping out at the AGM meeting.

The card players finish their game and proceed to cleaning the kitchen area, only rinsing the dishes, taking the dirty plates and cutlery and pans back to their suites in a bin. They are gone before Raymond finishes his beer.

The committee idea sounds great and Raymond is excited both at the prospect of getting involved and taking on a small but potentially largely rewarding project. If project-managed in a proper way, using reliable methods, it would prove beneficial to himself, as well as his fellow owners. That would put him in good stead with his neighbours.

"Ned, let me put on my project management hat to come up with an approach you can take to the board."

"That'd be great. Maybe you can address the board."

"It would be best to keep the two entities, the board and the committee, distinct throughout this. It makes sense if you're the point person for everyone."

"But they'll have to come in at some time. For me, the key to all of this is getting Gary's buy-in."

"Gary? He's not on the board."

"Of course he is, he's a key member."

"He's involved as a stakeholder, and may provide input, but he's not on the board. And I'm not sure how key he is."

"Very key."

"Okay, but he's not a board member. He may attend board meetings but he doesn't have to and he'd only attend as a guest, to advise. He's certainly not a director. He can't be a director, he isn't an owner."

"Not sure I see it that way. Gary has a say in everything we decide as a board."

"As an advisor, not as a decision-maker."

"Let's leave that for now and get our committee going."

With that, Ned sinks his last striped ball, lines up the eight-ball, and sinks that too. He puts out his hand for Raymond who shakes it weakly, not comfortable letting the discussion end if there's a chance this new director isn't convinced there are five directors, not six.

It might be better to leave it to Ned's fellow board members to correct the misconception and to target instead what is in his control. This is a clean project with a clear goal, unobstructed by consultants, middle managers, and bureaucratic clutter. This is an endeavour that can help pass time as winter approaches.

A brief email from Ned sent to Raymond and André about the committee the next day prompts Raymond to put together a high-level assessment and rough plan of approach that he sends to both men:

Problem / Opportunity (assumes ForageX out):
- *Replace WiFi or remove, as cable and phone companies incentivize TV subscribers to buy Internet packages*
- *Assess / plan removal of verified ForageX on-site assets*
- *Work with new vendor on changeover – user conversions*
- *Coordinate with other property management software*
- *Less than 1 year*

Impacts / Stakeholders:
- *Disruptions to WiFi service*
- *Train on use of new equipment / interfaces*
- *Acquaint property manager with new vendor processes*
- *Train security guards and all (potentially) transient staff*
- *Unknown impacts for ForageX (or how they'll react)*

Approach:
- *Clearly define steps to be taken; determine whether to terminate ForageX or consider renegotiating*
- *Adopt project management methods to meet timelines – this is where I can add value, given board support.*
- *Have subset of board assume project ownership.*

Note: this could be farmed out to Omnirez to manage as they might any other bid process. However, technology is volatile. As an owner I would be hesitant entrusting this task to them because their recommendation might restrict our leverage at the next contract renewal with them.

An unusually warm autumn day brings an email from Ned suggesting they get together to discuss Raymond's notes, which Ned says are full of good ideas. He suggests meeting at a bar nearby instead of the Social Room. Raymond likes this idea and joins Ned in the lobby to walk there.

The temperature is lower than Raymond expected and their slow pace, due to Ned's girth and limp, doesn't help. Ned is in the middle of telling him how he shared a drink with André du Bois the other day, but hasn't heard from him since. Ned pauses to wave at a car travelling the other way.

"Who's that?"

"Gary."

Raymond glances up in time to wave and see Gary smile, a sight he's not seen before. It mollifies his misgivings except for one: does Ned still believe Gary is a board member? Will they argue about this?

Ned appears to be a regular at this bar. He takes a seat and flags down a waitress with whom he flirts innocently, allowing her to ruffle his curls, before ordering a large glass of Chablis. Raymond opts for a craft pale ale.

"Lorie and I reviewed your points with the board members. We have decided to form a WiFi Committee that includes you if you're still interested."

Ned is jittery in general Raymond concludes, as his meeting partner twitches, glances away, drums his nose and shoulders, puckers his lips in a rhythm. Like a poker player who, aware of his tell, rather than trying to stem it, attempts to camouflage it behind a series of deflecting tells. It's off-putting and distracting at first, but Raymond finds himself getting used to it.

"What about André?"

"He and I shared a drink the other day, had a good chat, but he's no longer responding to my emails."

Raymond can't help but be curious, can't help but wonder if it has anything to do with Kayla. That knowing it was Raymond working with Ned turned André off. Otherwise, why wouldn't the guy just say he's no longer interested? Not something he can ask Ned or André or Kayla. He may never find out.

The waitress returns with their drinks. The wine glass looks odd in Ned's flabby hands as they raise a toast when Raymond confirms he'll join the committee. Raymond then expands on his email points. Oddly, despite saying he's worked with IT before, it doesn't register the way one would expect. Then again, Ned is young and possibly unaccustomed to Raymond's approach. He may be a harbinger for what to expect if Terri comes through.

The conversation drifts to personal matters as they consume more alcohol. Ned's fidgetiness diminishes while Raymond gets comfortable enough to ask Ned about his leg, and whether he is forced to telecommute. Ned shakes his head.

"Nasty accident some years back put me on disability. Can't work anymore. Which means I got lots of time on my hands."

"You seem to get around okay."

"You mean the walk here? That's my therapy for the day. I'll get back and I'll be out for good until tomorrow."

It's a pleasant conversation. The only troubling thing is the ease with which Ned gossips about other directors. He is close to Lorie, the treasurer, needlessly stressing it's not romantic. He respects the president, Stacie, but despises Nigel. It sounds as if the feeling is mutual. Of Dennis he is unequivocally critical.

"But he insists on being called board secretary."

Ned arranges a meeting to formalize the committee. A good start, clouded by a setback. The corporate lawyer, after looking over the condo declaration, deems they cannot legally alter any major service without a two-thirds vote from owners. He deems the WiFi to be a major service. Hence, no killing it easily.

Ned is sitting next to Lorie at one of the sad tables near the windows when Raymond arrives in the Social Room. He takes a seat across from Ned who is twirling and tapping a pen. Lorie is watching apprehensively, unlike the confident woman from the AGM. She looks slimmer and more attractive up close, and with her long brown hair let down.

Other than to play pool, Raymond is rarely here and this is the first time he's taken notice of the room. It's dark, with dark furniture and poor lighting. Possibly it looked better a decade ago, now it's out of date. The leather is crinkling too, with a few tears showing in the seats.

Nigel enters. Ned stiffens. Raymond finds himself doing so too. Nigel says hello, takes a seat, and the tension lowers.

They begin a discussion that to Raymond indicates they are on the same page. The three board members cover several other issues first, some Raymond thinks would be best kept for when he's not around. Including the startling revelation Gary's laptop was infected with a virus last summer. It happened while Gary was on vacation and his Omnirez backup clicked an email link. It still hasn't been fixed. Could this be the "email problems" on which Gary blames all of his recent mistakes?

All three board members are in sync about ForageX and this universal dissatisfaction unites them to form a WiFi committee, comprising the four present. They agree to the recommendation Raymond offers to adopt his project management approach and acknowledge his lead role in that. Even better, they are open to consulting owners via information sessions. They concede most of the issues with ForageX are anecdotal and so the sessions can ensure facts come to the surface, along with a sense of what owners want and where they are willing to compromise.

Raymond doesn't reveal his true wish is to convince owners to drop the WiFi altogether and garner support to meet the two-thirds vote minimum. Lorie's reluctance to spend five hundred dollars to conduct a formal vote is silly, as at the sessions a case could be made to show that investment would be worth it.

Ned issues minutes that evening. They require corrections but the promptness is impressive. Raymond feels good about it. To complete his action item, he drafts a letter for the owners:

Nearly a decade ago the developers of our condominium entered into a long-term contract with ForageX for WiFi service. That contract expires at the end of September, next year. As indicated at previous AGMs, your Board of Directors will seek an alternative solution.

*The impact of this will vary with individual owners and a
committee has been formed to help the board manage those
impacts. A first step is to coordinate two-way information
sessions in January for owners to better understand the
impacts, and for the committee to gather owners' wishes that
can be used to determine effective solutions that, in terms of
cost and function, best fit the needs of owners.*

*The sessions will be informal. Owners are encouraged to
participate so they can fully understand the situation,
including factors behind the decision not to renew. More
importantly, this is a chance for owners to contribute to the
direction taken as no commitments have yet been made. We
have various options, each with varying impacts on service
and, of course, condo fees.*

*The Board of Directors urges all owners to make their
concerns and wishes known early to allow as much time as
possible to ensure a seamless transition. The dates and times
of the sessions will be announced before the new year.*

Lorie augments the letter, modifying a few words that don't
alter its general thrust, and inserting it into a file with the condo
letter head to prepare for distribution via Gary, once it receives
board approval.

-2 -1 G **M** 2 3 4 5 6 7 8 9 10 11 PH R

"Gary and I spoke, and then followed up with Sheila about your
committee and these so-called information sessions."
"Lorie and I both think they'll be helpful."
"How about you, Nigel?"
"I concur with Lorie and Ned."
"Really. I'm glad to see you're all on the same page. I too can
see how this could be of assistance."
"But Stacie."

"Relax, Gary. However, I'm afraid Gary and Omnirez, and I, feel it would be best to defer such an action. The work involved in setting up the sessions will be overwhelming, especially with the holiday season approaching."

"I think we can handle it, right Lorie?"

"Yes."

"You also need to consider the potential issues."

"What issues, Gary?"

"Ned, you're still new, you haven't dealt with ForageX."

"I don't understand."

"The letter definitively says we are choosing an alternative."

"We are choosing an alternative. This is what we've told the owners. What's the big deal?"

"The big deal is the sessions will confirm ForageX is on the way out. Since they deal directly with residents, one is bound to let the cat out of the bag. Once it's out, they have little incentive to support their product."

"But they have to support it."

"Why, Nigel, if they're going to be fired?"

"Professionalism? Fulfilling a contract?"

"Don't be naive."

"There must be a way to deal with that."

"Be my guest, Ned, in figuring that out. But until then, we'll have to proceed without that."

"Fine, Stacie, but what do we tell owners? What do we tell someone new to the building who, seeing how bad the service is, enters into a long-term contract with another company?"

"That's their problem."

"That's rather harsh, Gary."

"Like I always say, there's no obligation to ask or to consult. They elected you, so your choice is their choice."

"Welcome to the board, Ned."

"I think we're all agreed then? We hold off such sessions at least until we have a firm grasp of what solutions are available."

"It's for the best, Ned."

"That may be, but where do I go next with this?"

"I'm confident, we're confident, you'll figure it out. For now, be thankful your holidays are freed up."

"Does everyone agree? Obviously you do, Gary. How about you, Dennis?"

"Yes, of course, Stacie."

"Nigel?"

"Sure, whatever."

"Lorie?"

"I'm concerned about the lost time, but you and Gary raise valid points. So yes, I agree."

"Ned?"

"Guess I'd be outvoted if I didn't. What do I tell Raymond?"

"Share with him our concerns about how ForageX will react, that we're opting for a low-key approach."

December

The Low-Key Approach

-2 -1 G M 2 3 4 5 6 7 8 9 10 **11** PH R

This isn't a bad deal, especially the first six months, but even after that the prices are reasonable. The two-year minimum is the troubling part. It'd be nice to know what's going on with the WiFi. All I have is last year's AGM minutes saying the contract expires next fall. Implying a new provider. Really, the simplest option is the best option, which is to let it run out and leave it to us owners to figure out. The less they need to manage, the better. It's been a distraction too long. That'd be great. I could scoop up this offer and not rely on an in-house version. If only I knew. That property manager is no help. "It's a board matter, they're addressing it." That's all Gary tells me. Reminds me of the guy who mismanaged my condo in the city — wait, there it is in the Resident's Handbook . . . it is the same firm, Omnirez. How did I miss that? This property manager is Gary Lewis, the other was a Darryl, Dean, Don, or something like that. Real fatso too. Even fatter than the guy who just got elected to the board. They all act the same. Bet they teach this *deflect, deny, delay technique to subdue owners. Imagine a career in which you spend most if not all of your energy covering up lies caused by avoiding straight answers? No wonder they look so haggard. Can't feel sorry for 'em for that. Why didn't I catch this when I was buying the place? I had meant to avoid Omnirez. Am I becoming complacent Is it contagious? Is it silly to avoid a good condo because of a property manager? No, it's not. Only it's too late now. Guess I can treat it as a devil-you-know situation. At least that can prevent me pounding my head against a wall when I don't get responses. In a way, this gives me an answer: there is less risk committing to a cable company offer than trusting building management not to fail.*

<hr>

-2 -1 G **M** 2 3 4 5 6 7 8 9 10 11 PH R

It's been nearly two weeks since the committee meeting and the memo he crafted that Lorie finalized to distribute to owners still hasn't gone out. Not even a peep from Ned. Nothing. Raymond, unable to get it off his mind, happily accepted Kayla's invitation for a game of pool, abandoning a lopsided Champions League game to suffer his own pounding at the hands of a woman who is kind, except when holding a pool cue. He hopes Kayla can offer a hint about the silence. When he tells her about it, though, she seems detached, disinterested, contrary to her enthusiasm about this topic when it came up at other times.

"The board is slow at the best of times."

Kayla lines up to sink the eight for another win. The white ball strikes it sharply but her aim is off and the black ball misses the corner and comes to rest for a clean shot into the side pocket for Raymond. A chance to beat her for once. Yet he remains still, as if Kayla missing a shot is a mirage not to be altered.

"Your turn, Ray. Finish me off."

"Don't you think it's strange — oh, you mean my shot."

He makes it. Kayla smiles as she gathers the balls to rack up for another game. It seems to cheer her those rare times he wins. In a way that's insulting, patronizing, but she does it with such guileless sincerity, it actually cheers him up.

"What's strange?"

"Pardon me?"

"You were about to say something's strange."

"Right. It's that WiFi thing. Like I said, we all agreed on the letter, so why the delay? There's not a lot of time left."

"There's like nine months still, isn't there?"

"Nine months is probably enough for the installation once a vendor is selected, which itself is an involved process."

"How so?"

"Because it requires a substantial analysis to first determine what is needed, to find vendors that can deliver the solution, to put in place an objective process that includes a solid evaluation plan and selection criteria. Everyone has their prejudices, their favourites. It's why the parameters must be defined and agreed to beforehand. Then they should be shared with the candidates so they grasp the situation accurately and equally to ensure the responses are consistent and how we want them. Even then, it's a dreary task slogging through the bids because, believe me it's always apples and oranges, before we can apply the evaluations fairly. The payoff after all that is you can choose a winner with confidence due to your diligence. Then if anyone challenges or questions your choice, it can be explained."

"It sounds complicated."

"That just covers the selection. After that, it will take a great deal of coordination and communication to remove the existing vendor before implementing the solution from the bid winner."

"Wouldn't it be easier to stick with ForageX?"

"Easier, sure, but it seems they wore out their welcome long ago. We do need to talk to them and I would have no problem including them as a candidate. But the board is dead set against them, wants them out, they see no point even engaging them in discussion."

"Won't they be involved even if you're getting rid of them?"

"I told them that. Just as I told them to consider getting an option to extend the current contract, just in case."

"Sounds like they should have started this a year ago."

"At least. Each AGM, I got the impression they had it under control. If it was, I wouldn't feel a need to get involved."

"Before you sounded like you were enjoying it."

"I was. Now I'm concerned. I mean, this is just the letter. It's not the sessions themselves."

Kayla wraps the triangle around the balls to position them, then pauses before removing the triangle.

"Sessions?"

He explains his effort to involve owners in the process. This animates Kayla more.

"You know, Ray, Babcia's biggest complaint is not knowing what's going on in the building, never hearing anything from the board. She thinks that they shirk responsibility by inserting Omnirez as their agent, their middleman, while staying mute at the AGMs. That's the real reason she stopped going."

"I thought she liked Lorie, respected Lorie, thought she was her friend."

Kayla pauses to break. Two solids sink and she proceeds to go after the others, speaking between shots.

"I don't know if I'd say friend. Not like they play bridge or anything. To be honest, she thinks Lorie is weak for kowtowing to Gary and enabling his laziness. Lorie's an officer on the board yet does trivial tasks like posting elevator notices or overseeing the guy painting parking spot lines or other stuff Gary ought to be doing or overseeing. Lorie's a lackey, sad to say."

"Maybe she does it to save the corporation money."

"She's not saving the condo any money. I guarantee you no vendor, least of all Omnirez, is losing revenue. She isn't doing it for that reason, or at least I hope not."

"Then why is she doing it?"

"For kicks? Babcia suspects these board members see being on the board more as a hobby than as a responsibility. It used to infuriate her but now it amuses her."

"She doesn't think much of Lorie then?"

"As a nice person, not much more."

"Wow, I thought everyone revered her. What about Gary?"

"It's funny, Gary treats Babcia very well—your shot."

He sees a table scattered with stripes, several adjacent, and a single solid precariously dangling at the far pocket. Any shot he takes could knock it in unintentionally and set her up for the eight ball lying conspicuously in the centre. She set him up well.

"What's so funny? My shot situation or Gary or Lorie?"

"Maybe all of them."

His efforts to get her to elaborate fail; she's too engaged in the game now, intent on beating him. Raymond makes a valiant run but it's not good enough to win. The next break, Raymond sinks a blue ball. He goes to identify it.

"It's the ten, striped."

Raymond inspects the pocket anyway, confirms that it's the striped blue. He lines up for an easy side pocket shot on the nine. Kayla lets out a sigh. Her impatience, subtly present since the first game, is escalating. He glances up to see her nibbling at her fingernails as her pool cue slightly bounces up and down, as if it's resting on her shoe and she's stomping her feet. He misses.

"These WiFi sessions, Ray, you going to be there too?"

"Of course."

"Maybe I'll check them out."

"You should. I know what information we need and how to explain the process. Your Babcia will appreciate the clarity."

"She won't go."

"Why not?"

Kayla shrugs and prepares for a bank shot to sink the seven, almost too deliberately. Raymond suspects she's holding back a thought. He waits for her to finish the shot, which only seems to delay her more. Finally she shoots, and misses an easy shot.

"Is that why you agreed to play pool with me, Ray? To talk about this WiFi thing?"

She gives him a strange look in which her eyes sparkle but her mouth is in a frown.

"What do you mean? I thought it would interest you."

Kayla leans her pool cue against the table, but then the wall when it keeps rolling away. She approaches Raymond, takes his cue and does the same.

The hug catches him by surprise but it's the kiss that shocks him. He almost suffocates before she relaxes her grip. Instead of pulling apart, she wraps her hands around his neck and kisses him again. Now she retreats, taking several steps back, her foot undercutting her cue, which crashes to the floor, generating a brief clatter that seems to echo.

She inspects her cue, sees it's fine, gives him a shy smile.

"I'm sorry, Ray, but I've wanted to do that since I saw you carry Buster in your suite. Hope you don't mind."

No words come to Raymond, the unexpectedness of it being beyond his imagination. He has been circumspect around Kayla lately, fearing she would get the idea he was attracted to her in a romantic sense. He's ruined promising friendships in the past crossing that line. Never did he imagine Kayla crossing it.

"I'm too old for you, Kayla. I don't see us—"

She chuckles. Raymond senses the strained aura that's been there since they started playing wash away in a wave. A wave of what? He wants to identify it before he too gets swept up. It's been ages since the prospect of a true romance presented itself to him. Is this what he wants?

"Relax, Ray, it's all right. I wanted to kiss you, yes, but don't think I'm presumptuous enough to assume you did. And let me declare that you are not too old. Not for me. I prefer older guys. Maturity appeals to me more than muscles. Besides, for the time being, until I settle some things, you are off limits."

"What are you talking about?"

"It's Babcia. She forbids me to spend time with you."

"With me specifically? Why would she care?"

Then Raymond recalls the look from the lobby prior to the AGM meeting. Those piercing, frightened eyes out of a horror film, so vivid it dilutes the shock of what Kayla explains.

"You remind her of someone at the concentration camp who tormented her, made life more awful than it already was. Seeing you in the lobby sent her off. She's convinced you're the man's son or kin and is afraid you will come after her."

"But that's preposterous."

"Not to her. Not if you see how she is when she talks about it. Only you won't. See her that is."

"She doesn't know you're here with me now?"

"Oh no."

"Why did you kiss me, in that way, if this has no chance of going anywhere?"

"For you to ask that must mean you care about me."

"I do care about you, but didn't in that way."

"Didn't? Could you see it in that way? Someday?"

"We can see what happens. But still . . ."

"Look, I'm an open person. I'd rather embarrass myself that way and be clear with people than play silly games. I don't like to play games. I want you to be open too."

"All right, here it is: I adore you as a friend. My attraction to you is your company, your conversation, nothing more. Not to say that can't change. I just haven't given it a thought because of our age difference, true, but primarily because I believe you and I can be very good friends. I don't want to risk that."

"Fair enough, Ray, nicely put."

"Good."

"However, unless I can convince Babcia, beyond any doubt, you can't be related to that man—I mean, really, that would be some coincidence—even a friendship will be challenging, if not impossible."

"I'm not German. I told you, I'm Polish."

"But you also told me you don't know anything about your biological father. So you can't really deny it is possible."

"I suppose there's no way to be sure about anything."

"How about a DNA test?"

"What would that do?"

"Ideally, confirm beyond a doubt you're father's not a Nazi."

A DNA test. A bit of spit sent to a lab to extract your code to compare to a database. Certainly easier than the traditional way of ascertaining one's ancestry by searching record books that are not necessarily accurate. But are these tests accurate? He points this out to Kayla, who smiles.

"Accurate enough for my Babcia. The less she understands a technology, the more she trusts it. I'll set it up."

"Are you getting one too?"

"Did it last year, no mystery there. Besides, my Babcia is as Polish as can be, we have tons of pictures. Just as Luc, the man she married after arriving in Canada, can trace his Métis lineage to the Riel Rebellion. He was Jewish too, by the way."

Raymond suspected Kayla was of mixed race but would not have guessed those three. It could explain her exotic, not quite Asiatic eyes, as well as the contrast between her pale face and pitch black hair. Kayla's assuredness and pride in her heritage is infectious. It transforms what was a moderate interest into true curiosity. An odd bell interrupts, causing Kayla to rush to her purse and pull out her phone to read a text message.

"I've got to go, but I'll drop by tonight. Better yet, let's go to the pub in the plaza."

The pool room feels ominously empty after Kayla's gone. Raymond leaves the balls in disarray, his cue on the table, and returns to his suite. To take his mind off of Kayla he emails Ned for an update. The response is instantaneous, asking Raymond to meet in the pool room.

Mere minutes after leaving it, Raymond is standing over the pool table once again, watching in déjà vu dismay, as Ned sinks shot after shot while divulging the board's decision to take what he calls a low-key approach.

Raymond's not clear on what that means precisely, the only interpretation coming to mind is the absurd conclusion they've decided to do nothing, putting themselves back at square one.

"So when do we hold the sessions?"

"There will be no sessions."

"Why not?"

"Ray, Gary fears that if ForageX learns about these sessions, they could cause trouble."

"Gary?"

"Yes, Gary."

"What kind of trouble?"

"Service disruptions, that sort of thing. Which is why a low-key approach is best."

Does Gary, of all people, believe a vendor would sabotage a customer in the middle of a contract and risk their reputation? That a tiny company like ForageX would enact a scorched earth policy? If anything, the fear would motivate them to investigate issues and address them before the contract ends.

What does this say about Gary, or about Omnirez? Is this a hint Omnirez would behave that way if they felt in jeopardy of losing their contract?

Ned's update injects bitterness in Raymond. What makes it worse is he genuinely likes the kid, the only board member who

61

is taking action. Correction: was taking action. Raymond wants to shake Ned to say: you have no time for a low-key approach. If this is low-key, what do you call the last few years? No key? Compounding Raymond's indignation is a sudden patronizing conciliatory board-knows-best tone Ned adopts, echoing that of many dysfunctional middle managers Raymond worked with at the tail end of his career. Yet, almost magically, his frustration dissipates with the interruption of a recent memory.

The lingering sensation of Kayla's kiss is an antidote that's opening a world of possibility, one Raymond long ago deemed unattainable: romance. Even love. Now he no longer feels she's too young for him. Not at all. She doesn't have the best body, and isn't the prettiest, yet in this time and place, Kayla might be the best woman he's ever met and will ever meet. The best thing to happen to him in this condominium. Does he need this WiFi complication to save him and his fellow owners a few dollars a month and forego the chance to do something for himself? He keeps quiet, happy for every shot Ned makes.

It's when Raymond's back in his suite, taking a shower, that the full impact of Ned's news sinks in. By taking — correction, by avoiding — this next step, the board just surrendered. Whether they're aware of it or not, they are quitting. There will never be a solution. The board will continue to procrastinate under the delusion they are up to the task, until they run out of time and are left with no option but to crawl to ForageX to buy time and renegotiate, after having squandered all their leverage.

But Raymond doesn't care, Raymond has a date.

Yet when he emerges from the shower the bitterness is back and uppermost in his mind, not Kayla. It vanishes again with a knock. Kayla is with Buster but doesn't enter. Instead, she tells him it's raining and Buster hates the rain. So she'll just take the dog out to do his business and they'll meet in the lobby.

Bruce isn't there, instead it's the taciturn security guard who predictably ignores Raymond as he waits in a lobby that's much brighter now that the rain has stopped and clouds have shifted.

The elevator opens. Kayla emerges, wearing a pair of tight black jeans and a thin blouse he's never seen before. Behind her is a man. Kayla hesitates approaching Raymond until the man exits via the back door. Her inhibition continues upon greeting him and all the way to the bar she's quiet. Does she not want to be seen with him? Is she having second thoughts? A more likely reason, one she probably assumes he'll assume, is not wanting others to see them together and tell her grandmother.

This fills Raymond with another fear: what if Ned is at the bar? The issue isn't Ned discovering him with Kayla, but that Ned's presence will create an unpleasant distraction.

The bar is full but, luckily, Ned-less. A couple is leaving just as they arrive so they get a window booth that looks out across a wide stretch of baseball fields beyond which is his building. A few new clouds appear, lighter now; through them he can make out the crescent moon hovering over the marina. Kayla taps his arm to hand him a small tube. He looks at it.

"Go ahead, spit into it, as much as you can."

"Before they think I'm an alcoholic?"

"Just do it."

He obeys and returns the tube to Kayla. She looks at it for a moment, before inserting it into a little baggie she seals shut.

Just then a server arrives. She holds the baggie beneath the table while they order. It turns out Kayla's a beer drinker and they share a pitcher of Moosehead. A compromise between her simple ale and his craft beer.

When the server is out of sight, a couple passes by. They're holding hands like a couple but, in the reverse to Raymond and Kayla, the woman is almost twenty years older than the man. It makes Raymond feel queasy in an agreeable way. When they're gone, Kayla puts the vial in her purse.

A pleasant silence passes until the beer arrives.

"You know, Kayla, all my life, I've never dated anyone more than a couple of years younger than me."

"That's funny because ever since I graduated high school, I haven't been with anyone less than ten years older. But let's not count our chickens — "

"Right. How long will it take to get the results? To put me in the clear?"

"Six to eight weeks."

"That long, huh?"

Her accompanying laugh sounds less amused than nervous. She smiles at him.

"The way you say that, Ray, makes me feel less embarrassed about doing what I did earlier."

"Don't be. It caught me by surprise but I did mean it about being open to what may happen. It's unfortunate having to wait to dispense with this little matter."

"It'll be fine. The time will fly. My family's having a reunion in Winnipeg for Hanukkah. I'll be away for that. We leave next week. Until then you and I can still play pool."

The holidays. He always enjoyed going to the office during that period, as it was quiet. Other than an overnight visit to his hometown to see his mother, he'll have little to do. The time will pass but it would be nice to have her company for some of it.

Unfortunately, he only sees Kayla twice the ensuing week, and only briefly each time. Organizing the Manitoba trip proves far more complicated than anticipated. It falls on Kayla to make the special arrangements for her invalid grandmother, as well as the simple ones for her parents and twin brothers.

Despite that, it's evident her romantic interest in him hasn't waned. It's just as clear nothing can develop between them until the new year and the DNA results to convince Babcia he's not a monster's offspring. Maddeningly, the longer he has to wait, the greater his desire for this relationship with a terrific woman to go beyond friendship. What else can he do but be patient?

The call from Terri couldn't come at a better time. It appears she found a little end-of-year money for Raymond to take on a small exploratory analysis project. He happily accepts.

-2 -1 G M 2 3 4 5 6 7 8 9 10 11 PH R

"My goodness, the snow is awful, my car slipped twice coming here this morning."

"Bet you wish you were back in Cuba."

"You can say that again."

"We missed you, Gary. Back in the groove?"

"Unfortunately, Stacie, my laptop is still out of whack with that virus. Which is why we don't have much to cover today."

"Do we need to get someone in to look at it?"

"Appreciate it, Nigel, but Sheila's getting an Omnirez techie to come by to demonstrate the fancy new property management software we're recommending. He'll look at my laptop then."

"We should consider getting a new computer for Gary, or at least subscribing to a cloud-based application package to ensure our data is protected. They don't cost that much."

"I agree with Nigel, it would be worth the expenditure. And there is money in the budget to cover it."

"Look, everyone, I'm comfortable with this one. Also, I use it at my other site. I'd rather not manage two machines."

"Good point, Gary. Let's table this for discussion in the new year. I don't think we need to elongate this meeting. At least not the business part of it. It's holiday season and time we exchange our gifts."

"Me first. Here you go, everyone."

"Let me guess, Dennis. Cookies?"

"Not till you open it, Ned."

January

The DNA Test

-2 -1 G M 2 **3** 4 5 6 7 8 9 10 11 PH R

All that the property manager said makes sense. I'm convinced we'd be better off to keep the unit, renting it out, despite Kenny's insistence we not be landlords. When I argued Gary's point that pretty much all the third floor is renting, all Kenny could come up with was a fear of renters taking over the building one day and the guilt he would feel for contributing to that. Why is that our problem? If Gary doesn't have an issue with it, why should we? Once Kenny hears what the old guy next door gets per month, he'll come around. Condos are in demand, always a market of people who'll pay a premium for a modern building such as this, especially one so close to the train station and highway. Best part: no rent control. Kenny is the first to whine about a condo fee increase but by renting, it's irrelevant. Whatever the increase, that is how much we increase the rent, maybe rounded up a tad. Of course, if that new WiFi solution they keep promising materializes and knocks the fees down a notch, no reason it needs to go the other way. Another bonus: renters tolerate fussbudgets like Kenny who harp about dogs barking and noisy arguments and smelling marijuana and the tiniest collections of dirt on the hallway or elevator carpets. His conscience may be troubled at saddling neighbours with an unpredictable renter, especially sweet Marjorie. But that'll pass. No doubt about it, we must keep the unit. Kenny'll come around.

-2 -1 G M 2 3 4 5 6 7 **8** 9 10 11 PH R

What are they doing? It's five-thirty in the morning as Raymond is awakened by a pickup truck with a wide plough scraping the parking area below his balcony, despite the snow having been cleared for the past several sunny days. The idiocy would have gnawed at him months ago, would have sent him downstairs to say something the moment Gary got in. But now, realizing the futility of complaints, he lets it slide, praying the noise subsides soon. Too many other matters to occupy him, not least of which is Kayla who just came back from Winnipeg. It's been a lonely holiday season, one he's glad to see end, just as everyone is glad for a break from the winter storms.

The work Terri gave him didn't involve any pure analysis, just an assessment of the documentation she found for their old legacy system to help build her business case. Scanning through logic he described long ago would have been dull if not for the pride he felt at seeing how clever he once was. One thinks they improve over time but for Raymond, if honest, that was the apex of his career. When he was called upon to be creatively productive, not creatively bureaucratic as was the norm after he diverted his technical path to project management. While Terri's task paid well and provided nostalgic pleasure, it only lasted a week, not the duration of Kayla's absence. However, it did bode well for a chance of future work, based on Terri's feedback, and her wish to discuss it today.

At last the unneeded snow removal truck departs, leaving a pleasurable silence to catch some sleep. Until he's woken again by the faint alternating grinding rings of fire alarms. He forgot today is the day that includes his floor's annual inspection of all smoke detectors. Alarms constantly going off above, below, and beside him. Good timing, Terri, he thinks, as he readies himself for his excursion downtown. It'll be good to get out. He is wary of a growing agoraphobia the more he's cooped up in his condo.

Today is a cold, pleasant day. The morning rush is over, the commuter train car nearly empty, making for a leisurely hour-long ride into the city. The calm lake glistens as gentle waves nudge chunks of ice that seem impervious to the warm sun. The gentle roll on the rails lulls him to doze off.

Raymond wakes as the train eases into the city terminal and is swallowed between new condominium towers, all requiring boards of directors, property managers, etc. Really a crapshoot, isn't it, the quality of people a building might get to fulfill those roles. He's read horror stories of corrupt boards taking millions from owners then forced to engage in expensive legal battles to get it back, if they catch it. He's fortunate with Ned, Lorie, et al. They lack the ability or initiative, though incompetence inflicts its own erosive damage over a longer period.

Construction dominates the station, forcing Raymond to detour along unfamiliar improvised subterranean pathways to an exit. Here too, as he emerges at the top of the steps, he finds himself disoriented in a city he's lived and worked in all his life. A mild claustrophobia threatens to envelop him among swarms of urbanites whose pace he struggles to match. Despite the cold, his neck is perspiring underneath the greenish shirt and silver tie he dug out from the back of his closet. His legs feel clammy against the wool slacks. It's uncertain when, if ever, he last wore this combination. No choice, because his other dress shirts were too wrinkled. Which made for a struggle to look presentable for Terri, who always dressed smartly, even on casual Fridays.

It's odd approaching the old office tower without stressing about a meeting with an overbearing project manager, paranoid director, delusional vice president, or intractable team member to get a status update. Never mind the deadlines. He's free of it now and arrives feeling as light as those vendors who take an hour to convince an executive their offer is superior to anything his staff could build. Only to scurry off with the executive to a golf course, leaving the presumably inferior staff to deal with the omitted side effects of what they sold.

Raymond laughs. He may feel light, free, but it seems those old frustrations can still rile him up. He's able to brush it aside as he approaches the building. Glass doors slide open to a lobby where he sits to text Terri he's arrived.

As he waits, he looks out for anyone he knows. All the faces are unfamiliar, all younger than even Ned. Terri escorts him to a floor where she presses a badge to a pad just as he used to. A nostalgic expectation is obliterated by the image that awaits him beyond the frosted panes. Instead of a bland farm of fabric cubicles, Raymond observes long, low rows of close knit desks, beyond which is a splendid skyline view, frequently blocked by ear-budded people speaking into cell phone microphones, large drink containers in hand. The lack of privacy is unsettling.

Terri leads him past empty meeting rooms to sit at the end of a long table filled with people in front of laptops typing away or reading screens. The vibe is of newness and freshness, totally bereft of nostalgia.

"You don't have your own office?"

"Much has changed, Raymond, since your time."

"Can't we use a meeting room? How about I buy you lunch, and we can talk there?"

"I take it you're uncomfortable here?"

Terri chuckles, but underneath Raymond senses uncertainty or even disappointment. As if his reaction to this environment is an unforeseen setback for her.

"Relax, most of your work will be done at home."

"So tell me about it."

"Do you know what blockchain is?"

"Blockchain? I'm not sure. Is it . . .?"

"Relax. Neither do I. But they all do, or think they do."

As her finger arcs to encompass the floor, he notices all her colleagues are under thirty years old. His observation is met by a corresponding nod from Terri. She smiles.

"You and I, we're the parents here. Grandparents even. I bet some of them think you're my husband."

"So what is this blockchain?"

"Basically, a method to de-centralize data and transactions, kind of like the distributed applications and databases we toyed with in the early nineties, but with the data protected by heavy-duty encryption to ensure security and independence."

"As I recall, we ended up centralizing more. Just like many of the other places I've worked."

"In a sense. I might say we never got off the ground, never got the momentum, or funding, needed to do it properly. Which made us retreat and continue enhancing legacy systems. Until it became necessary or aesthetically desirable to focus on the front ends. So instead of re-engineering the legacy systems, we added new layers on top of outdated ones, ignoring or never realizing we were steadily concealing the functionality at the core."

"I know that story well. Like old civilizations buried under rock and sand by progress. And as the original builders die out or move on, the mystery deepens."

"Precisely. Which is why I need your help. To unravel it."

"There's no one left?"

"Our legacy systems are all outsourced now. We still have a few programmers who've maintained them—you'd recognize a few names—but no one involved in the original design. You can count on a lot of ruined but workable code, Raymond."

"My role then is to be an IT archaeologist."

"You could say that."

"So what's different about blockchain?"

"Blockchain is not about optimization but about addressing trust, security, and integrity of data via complex computer logic that is theoretically impregnable and can't be hacked. It requires computing power we could only dream of before. It's behind Bitcoin's ability to ensure secure transactions by storing each on thousands of hosts within minutes, each host logically having to verify itself. Corrupting a transaction would entail having to modify it on most if not all hosts. No single entity could muster the computing power for that. Case in point, Bitcoin hasn't been successfully hacked yet—oh, Stan."

Terri motions for a lean youth in jeans and a Croatian soccer jersey to join them. He introduces himself as Stan Krevic. Stan's accent is thick but his enunciation is perfect and his voice has an appealing sing-song quality. His handshake isn't limp and some deep wrinkles belie maturity from experience.

Terri goes on to explain they're contributing to a marketing endeavour to exploit blockchain technology, ideally to eliminate dependence on the mainframe by embedding the functions of those systems into distributable applications. Stan glances off occasionally, squeamishly, as if listening to his elders talk about mainframe systems is akin to listening to hypochondriacs talk about their ailments. Or parents about sex.

"That's massive. Beyond my capacity if you're looking to me to do the coding."

Terri shakes her head.

"We are contractually bound to outsource the coding. I am looking to assess the feasibility of using blockchain, of getting a sense of what it might cost and involve. Stan's putting together a prototype for a blockchain that we hope will eliminate trust issues between our silo systems, that will get them to interface without all the middleware. I liken it to renovating a house and making it open concept by removing the walls and doors."

"How would that work with this blockchain?"

"It might not, to be honest. Raymond, these days marketing departments dominate IT, compelling us to entertain all sorts of ideas. Ideas they acquire at technical conferences they probably shouldn't attend."

"So what's my role, what do you need from me?"

"Stan needs the underlying logic behind our legacy code, so he can replicate it. Your metaphor about the archaeologist is a good one, but I see you more as the original building contractor identifying the load-bearing walls, special wiring, plumbing etc. for a new house owner."

She goes on to reveal, in a roundabout way, that she needs Raymond because she trust the outsourcing vendor to provide a reliable assessment. They might either underestimate to ensure the project is approved, to give them a boost in revenue, or, if confident of its approval, pad the estimate. He has worked with enough vendors to empathize with this fear. She is also afraid Marketing may engage a third vendor soon and so she needs to understand what's entailed quickly.

Terri leaves Raymond with Stan who talks enthusiastically about hashing algorithms, public keys, private keys, distributed ledgers, distributed apps, and smart contracts.

The more he listens to Stan, the harder it is for Raymond to correlate what the young man says to his outdated perspective. Stan reassures him, as Terri did, that Raymond doesn't need to fully comprehend blockchain. That sounds fine, only Raymond is interested and wants to grasp it. It's an enticing opportunity. He shares this with Terri who buys him lunch afterwards.

"Raymond, don't get too caught up in the technical aspect. I need you as a business analyst to guide Stan. I can't afford to let you get lost in all the blockchain minutiae."

"Right. As to that, I'll need the documentation and access to the code."

Terri reaches into her purse, grasps something but pauses to glance around before pulling it out. An external hard drive. She gives it to him like they're playing hot potato.

"I'm forbidden by contract with our outsourcer to have this, let alone share it. It's the code from our last release, which I had copied — don't ask me how."

"You really don't trust this vendor. Are they corrupt?"

"Corrupt, incompetent, all I know is this prototyping has to be well underway before they get wind of it, before they can cry to our Chief Technology Officer, who brought them in."

"What am I getting into?"

"Nothing but a little consulting work, the internals of which you can ignore. Which I need you to ignore."

"What have you gotten yourself into?"

"Don't worry about me. I'm at the end of my career. This is kind of exciting and Stan and the others appreciate my ability to shield them from the politics. I was hoping you could start right away. Stan is ready for you, unless you need to get back home."

"No, I'm downtown, I've got nothing else."

She grabs his hand and her tone softens.

"Maybe afterwards you and I can grab a drink to talk about old times. And other things."

"Everything okay?"

"I could use a friend because, well, I'm getting a divorce."

Raymond pulls his hand away more quickly than intended but Terri doesn't take offence. In fact she smiles, acknowledging the awkwardness. He points at the hard drive.

"Rather than letting Stan spin my head around more, maybe it'd be better for me to spend the weekend reacquainting myself with the legacy system."

"I suppose that's wise."

The next morning Raymond, after an evening spent reading old documents and watching blockchain videos online, sleeps in past nine o'clock, waking to dazzling daylight. His balcony is drenched in sunshine, making it warm enough to wake himself with fresh air without putting on a coat. He sees someone wave at him. It's Kayla. She has Buster on a leash.

It's been a nearly a month since he's seen her. She's put on weight, he can tell, but it makes her look more vibrant in a way. She says something but traffic drowns out her words. Now her arms move beckoningly? Does she want him to join them? She does appear to be waiting. He holds up a finger, breaks away to get his keys, wallet, and jacket. All the way down the elevator, he's afraid she'll be gone. But she's still there. Though she does deftly thwart his attempt to hug her.

"Not here."

"Right, sorry."

As if to compensate, Buster jumps at his knees. He grabs the dog, raises it, and allows it to lick him while Kayla laughs.

"That's sweet. Buster's missed you too. Did you miss me?"

"You have no idea—I mean, not like that. It was dull here, a little work, playing pool by myself. And the snow was so brutal I had to postpone my visit to my mother until later this month."

"Winnipeg was cold, but we had little snow."

After Buster does his business near a bush and Kayla picks it up, they sit at a bench overlooking the lake. It's calm, the only ripples from an occasional bird landing and a small boy trying to skip stones. An intrepid cyclist in a thick coat and balaclava rides past. Once he's gone, Raymond grabs Kayla's hand to hold it, afraid she might resist, but she lets him. Her hand is cold and she seems to appreciate his warmth.

"Your DNA test results are back, Ray."

"That was fast. I thought it'd be two more weeks."

"Yeah, I was able to get a rush done."

Raymond is curious about the results, if she's looked, but he can't ignore a sense of sadness at realizing that once they look, the pleasure of this limbo will be gone forever. Regardless of the misery of being alone at Christmas, the pleasure of their kiss in the pool room and its ensuing promise has been like a fine work of art, a still frame he can enjoy at his leisure. An image that, for some reason, he fears will evaporate after seeing the results. She must wonder why he isn't curious. Yet the way she gazes at the lake indicates she might be having similar thoughts.

"Have you opened the envelope?"

"Actually, it's online, but no, I haven't looked."

"Let's go to my suite and check it out."

"Why don't we go to Babcia's suite? She'll be at the hospital for tests until the afternoon."

The mustiness of the one-bedroom unit, half the size of his own, jars Raymond. The cloth sofa and matching chairs and the dark wood tables are shabby. It resembles the before shot from a home renovation show for an old farmhouse, not a modern condominium suite, even one owned by a lady in her nineties.

"She's very nostalgic."

Kayla's referring to shelves and tables crammed with small plants snaking around a lifetime's worth of knick-knacks, most on lace cosies. Very little dust, though. Overall the apartment is immaculate, the kitchen tiny but spotless. The white appliances look like the originals. Kayla grabs a blanket away from the sofa and it's evident she sleeps there whenever she stays over.

"This is my first time in someone else's suite."

Kayla ignores this and beckons him to sit beside her on the sofa. She opens a coffee table drawer to retrieve a laptop, but as she does so an object falls out, slides under the sofa.

"Just leave it."

However, Raymond's hands are already groping around on the floor. They touch a metallic object, a chain. He pulls it out. It's a necklace, an old-fashioned locket, its tiny door open to a tiny photograph of Kayla holding Buster as a puppy.

"That's a wonderful picture."

"I asked you to leave it."

The change in her tone startles him and he looks at her. But she's looking away.

"What's the matter."

"I'm sorry, it's just that's not mine. It's Babcia's. It should be in her bedroom dresser drawer."

"That's sweet she has a photo of you like that with Buster. I like the added sepia touch."

"It's not me. It's a photo of her, taken before the war, before she was put in a concentration camp. The dog, Dia, was shot the day she was taken away."

"That's awful."

"She takes it out when those memories begin to torment her. Not sure what triggered it this time."

Raymond feels he should say something but nothing comes to mind. He hands over the locket and takes the laptop as Kayla rises to put the jewellery away. The screen is open to an email from the DNA site, which contains a link and a password. Not wanting to be nosy, he turns his eyes away, then notices nearly all the knickknacks strewn about the unit are Pomeranian dogs. A Pomeranian-themed calendar, still on December, is on a wall, and the coasters on the table show Pomeranians at play. A large stuffed Pomeranian is in the far dining room corner.

Kayla takes the machine. Her finger rubs the mouse pad to get the cursor over the link. She presses it, then enters the user id and password. She lowers the screen to flash a suspenseful grin at Raymond.

"Ready, Ray?"

"You sure you haven't peeked?"

"I promise."

She raises the screen. It shows a report of various sections in different font sizes and colours, along with a set of graphs and a few pie charts. It takes a while to orient before Kayla points to a summary section on the left and slaps him on the arm.

"Look at that, Polish, just like me."

"Only half. The other half is . . . other eastern European?"

"Germany's not eastern, it's central. You're no Nazi."

"Right. But do these things really work? I mean . . ."

She interrupts him with a kiss that seems to have made up for their time apart. Her infectious joy sends his heart racing to handle a feverish, unbridled happiness he hasn't experienced in a long time.

"Let's celebrate."

"Later. I've got to sort this place out before Babcia returns. I can't wait to show this to her."

"You're sure she'll believe it. I still have my doubts."

"She's in awe of technology. If it looks polished, she will eat it up. When she does, we'll celebrate like this."

Another long kiss sends him away happy. A happiness that lingers all day as he ponders ways to celebrate. Along with this good feeling, though not diminishing it, a void opens up within Raymond. One of curiosity about his mother and her life before she met Ronald Tibbett.

Another void opens over the next two weeks during which he hears nothing from Kayla. The time passes quickly because he spends much of it commuting to the city to meet with Stan. He's not used to this pace, nor leaving in the dark and arriving home in the dark. It's exhausting. The days turn into nights and vice versa. While he wants to see Kayla, most of the time it's a relief just to collapse in his bed.

The project pays well but it's frustrating: Stan struggling to grasp a legacy application built when application design had to be efficient with computer resources; Raymond unwilling to let go a mindset appalled at the intentional redundancy involved with blockchain. All those computers churning away, all that electricity spent, just because humans are untrustworthy.

The Friday of the second week, Terri collects Raymond and Stan to inform them that officially the effort is suspended. Stan's lack of surprise—in fact, he declares he has enough to go to the next phase, which can't possibly be true—surprises Raymond.

"Honestly, and I'm not saying it because I want to bill more hours, I think we've barely begun."

"Raymond, if it was 1992, I'd be in full agreement with you. But I've gotten used to these new methodologies that operate on timed achievements, taking them as is, and moving forward."

"Forward with incomplete, even inaccurate information."

"But still going forward. That's what's important these days. The work you and Stan did has value, regardless of the state it's in. Two weeks value. I see you shaking your head. I understand why. The problem is no one else can. You and I can spot what's missing, what are the weak points, even where you may have to redo what's been done. All everyone else is concerned about is progress. Reportable progress, I should say."

"So this work is just as much about showing progress on a GANTT chart as it is about the actual functionality."

Terri's smile retreats.

"Maybe more."

Raymond sighs. He's seen this coming. It's no different from his latter years during which he never felt as if he accomplished anything. Except then he could look away; whereas now he has to face that reality dead on. It's not pleasant. This is one of those rare moments in which he's thankful about his advancing age, for this can only worsen.

"I guess I should just take the money and run."

"It's your best approach. Now let's get some wine."

As Terri guides him to the bar in the building's concourse, Raymond studies his old colleague. She's still good looking, still maintains a nice figure, although her drab pantsuit is anything but enticing. Did he read her wrong?

"So, how are you doing, you know . . .?"

"You mean my divorce? Yeah, Greg and I are trying to work it out, but I don't know."

"What happens next? With your project?"

"We take what you and Stan have put together—I know, I know, it could be better—add a little bullshit, and try to get the funding to either fill in what's missing or go for it full bore."

"How long will that take?"

"At least a month. Lots of red tape to get through. You'll get your money shortly."

"Good. But is there future work you'd want me to do?"

"That's the plan."

They part at the bar, with Terri returning to the office and Raymond taking the train back home, the first time in daylight for quite a while. It's odd to enter the front door without having

Bruce or one of the other guards say hello. He sees Gary in the management office, head down, staring at something, but walks by without bothering to say hello.

Two more days pass with no word from Kayla. Nor does he see her. He is tempted to knock on her grandmother's door. The fear of upsetting Kayla keeps him from doing so, opting instead to maintain balcony vigils to watch for a little Pomeranian and a familiar gait at the end of its leash.

At last he does see her. Kayla shows no indication anything is amiss. If he calls out will she respond or walk off faster? All his confidence and good feeling has suddenly transformed into self-doubt, fear. He puts on boots and a coat and rushes down the stairs to catch up. Buster sees Raymond but the dog's happy yelping doesn't get her to stop or even slow down. Neither does calling her name over and over. But then she looks back, not all the way, while continuing walking.

"I can't talk to you."

"But what happened, what's going on?"

"Please, leave me alone."

Now she picks up her pace, forcing poor Buster to move his legs faster than they're built to move.

"Can't we talk? What did I do?"

Raymond's last effort brings no reply and this is frustrating. Yet he knows Kayla is too upset to pester now. He has to hope it'll be different at another time. He withdraws.

Several more days pass during which he sees them on their walks but she never looks back, nor does he intercept her. It fills him with sadness, but also anger. What happened? Can't she at least tell him that? If not, then he has no choice.

The next day he makes a pot of coffee, gets dressed, waits by the balcony. It's a grim vista, with dark, threatening clouds that might have Kayla skip the walk. But no, there she is, earlier than usual. Probably to beat the rain. Which means she won't be gone long and he doesn't have much time.

Raymond almost spills his coffee getting off his chair. He slips on sneakers and exits, not locking his door, descends the two floors down the stairs, pauses to take a deep breath, before walking to the suite and knocking.

"It's still open, dear."

The voice from the other side is old but sturdy, not the frail accented one he expected. That she thinks it's Kayla makes him hesitate, but he enters anyway. He sees the empty scooter first, then the old woman sitting in the easy chair next to it. Her back is to him as she watches a soap opera. He freezes. He was intent on getting past the door, assuming words would flow naturally. They don't. He needs her to see him, to react. He closes the door and coughs.

"Mrs. Slaske."

Her head turns sharply with instant recognition, but it takes a little longer for the horror to show on her face. When it does, it becomes clear she is afraid. Beads of sweat fall down his brow, the act of wiping keeps him from escaping. Her voice is deep, slow, even shrewd, but also shaky and filled with spite.

"I know you, Leo, I know your voice."

"You know me? How?"

"You did those things. You should be in hell."

"You think I was a Nazi?"

"Devil. I should have . . . you are a devil."

"Didn't Kayla show you I'm not German?"

"Leo was no German. He was a Soviet. And a Kapo. One of the worst. Worse than the Germans."

The door opens and in comes Buster who, like Raymond a moment ago, freezes, his head glancing alternately at his owner and a well known intruder. Kayla follows. Buster rushes to the old lady, who ignores the dog. Kayla's glare is intense.

"What are you doing here?"

"You didn't tell him, dear? That he failed his test?"

"Failed?"

"Never mind, I told him for you. Now make him leave."

Kayla slumps, but says nothing, leaving Raymond to stand alone and wonder whether he might be better off running away from this odd situation now. The power of the old woman over Kayla disturbs Raymond, confounds him. He wants to run and lick his wounds, but also stay and protect his friend.

"Make him go."

"Kayla?"

She turns her head, not to him, but to her grandmother who remains unflinching, cold. A defence mechanism, no doubt, the opposite of how Kayla described her behaving when faced with her memories. Raymond feels awful for what she suffered, and if he is related in any way to her perpetrators he will feel worse. But not guilty. He didn't do it, after all.

"Kayla, what's a Kapo?"

"Get him out of here. That voice, that voice, it is the same."

"Ray, you have to go."

"Fine, just come with me, to talk."

"Kayla, you are not going anywhere. I forbid it. I need you."

A growl from Buster prompts her to rise, take his arm, and guide him out the door. He takes her hand but she resists.

"I'm sorry, we can never be together."

-2 -1 G **M** 2 3 4 5 6 7 8 9 10 11 PH R

"That complicates matters. Maybe we ought to consider keeping ForageX, at least for a little while."

"Not with their performance, right Gary? I mean, people are still having issues, right?"

"Complaints still come to me. The residents should know by now to call the vendor directly."

"They don't?"

"If they do, they get help. I assume. Because the complaints stop. So I can't comment on their performance."

"What are you saying, Gary?"

"That maybe Stacie has a point. They keep nagging at me to let them present their new offer to the board. Nigel has a point too, as things aren't perfect."

"Damn right it's not perfect. Without reports or any way of measuring performance, they'll keep getting away with it. And besides, we promised a new solution. A solution that brings us into the future."

"Wrong, Nigel, too late for that. It'd be better if we dropped it altogether."

"Can't do that, remember? Can't significantly alter a service already being provided. We have to do something."

"If we can't drop it and if, based on the interpretation from the lawyer that the wiring belongs to ForageX, where are we?"

"In a pickle?"

"That's not helpful, Ned, especially from the guy who wants to be the lead on this."

"Only because someone who said they knew it all has done diddly squat, leaving me to start from scratch."

"Ned, Nigel, please. What is it, Dennis?"

"I know little about this but if we get another vendor, why can't they help us with the wiring?"

"You mean like ask Coke to take back Pepsi cans from the vending machine? Come on, Dennis. You're right, you don't—"

"Ned, easy, he's just trying to help."

"Sorry. It's just we don't have much time left, Lorie."

"I think you should apologize to me."

"Fine Dennis, sorry I snapped at you."

"Okay, we don't have an answer yet and it doesn't look like one is coming tonight. We are running out of time, but it is still only January, we're not out of it altogether. Keep at it, Ned, but be constructive. Lorie, you can keep them in line, I hope. Gary, I see you getting your coat, is that about it for tonight?"

"No, I was checking for my keys. But yes, that's it for official business. I do want to bring up one item, off the record."

"What's that?"

"That gay couple that argues a lot on the third floor are no longer selling their suite."

"And?"

"I'm guessing they'll be renting it, because they have not yet cancelled their elevator booking. I'm only mentioning it because that means a whole row of suites will be renters."

"That's their prerogative."

"That's not my point, Stacie. In fact, I happen to like renters. They don't have the nerve or sense of entitlement some owners have. Not to mention the insolence."

"Who's insolent?"

"I don't want to name names."

"Let it go, Dennis, Gary's talking about something else."

"I'm pointing it out because this year three of you are up for election. To remind you of the possibility a rogue board could take over, undoing your fine work. It might be in your interest to garner a proxy before they're gone. As is often the case with owners who become landlords, they stop attending the AGM. It can make them feel better to provide a proxy vote. No reason to not lock that in, in advance."

"Okay, thanks for that, Gary. Do you know them, Lorie?"

"I do."

"Maybe you can . . ."

"Next time I run into them."

"All right, 'til next month, everyone."

February

The Real Kapo

-2 -1 G M 2 3 4 5 **6** 7 8 9 10 11 PH R

What have I done? Made my poor dear miserable, and Buster too. Had little choice, though, did I? Like Kurt says, we cannot stop being alert, or stop being scared, not till our dying day. What's this? A network upgrade? Funny, you hear nothing for months about that inane WiFi business and now here is — oh, wait, it's not from Gary, but ForageX. Let's see, changes to network to improve speed and reliability — why bother if it's going to be replaced? Not sure why it has to be replaced. Everything works fine for me most of the time. Those fellows are nice and patient whenever Kayla's not here and I call them. Another note. From Gary. Asking residents to register pets in case of emergency. Good idea to register the little fellow. I'll get Kayla to look after it, if she's not too upset with me. Poor girl. She's hurt and not blaming me even though . . . just wish I'd handled it better. Though I'm not sure I could have. She deserves a man who appreciates her sweetness, a man who can value her charms and not need her to be a beauty. Not like

83

that louse, the French fellow. She can't fool me acting like it was only a fling. It hurt her. This fellow seems nice, but it's too risky. And he's too old. And he is — after all these years, I truly thought it was over, only for this to come up. Can't tell Kurt the details, though. No, it has to be over. He won't like it but I have to release Kayla from our . . . let her do what is best for herself, live her life. I won't tell him.

-2 -1 G M 2 3 4 5 6 7 8 9 10 11 PH R

The train departs Warszawa Centralna, rumbling through many switches to get to the mainline. Once out of the city and moving at a great speed, Raymond is confident the seat next to him will stay vacant until the next stop an hour away. An hour to reflect in solitude on Kayla's grandmother's accusation that sowed the seed for this mission of truth.

A seed germinated days later on a visit to his mother at her retirement home, a visit that began awkwardly when he arrived and disrupted her euchre game. Unlike most parents in homes, his mother Julia never gets upset if he lags in his visits. She has plenty to do there, plenty of friends. More than Raymond has, he ruefully notes each visit. He had to wait until she found a replacement for her game, then again at her small dining table while she made them tea. The bars of light shining through the slats of the vertical blinds forced Raymond to squint until she brought the tea and sat down to block the shine that seemed to then dissolve into her silver hair. She listened with interest to his small talk about his condo, interrupting only to register her concern about the work he was doing for Terri.

"Don't spoil your retirement the way Ronald did."

"Mom, I don't think that's why he died."

"It's not why he died, but I'm convinced it accelerated it."

They looked at the framed portrait of Raymond's father, his adoptive father, simultaneously, causing those beams of light to force Raymond to turn his head away again. His mother closed the blinds, then switched on the overhead lamp.

"Can you tell me about Leo?"

Her eyes lit up, her mouth quivered, then her lips formed a melancholic smile he'd never seen her wear before. It frightened him when she reached across to touch his face with her fingers.

"Oh, Leo."

"Yes, my real father. I want to know about him."

She recoiled her arm, laughed nervously.

"Forgive me, just lost my senses there. You saying his name, you really look like him, sound like him, I just . . ."

"I look and sound like him?"

"The eyes. You have his eyes. You're not as thin—wait, why are you asking about your . . . your real father?"

"Maybe it wasn't worth interrupting your euchre game."

"Honey, you and I both know why you asking surprises me, so don't get defensive. Since you mention it, what does make it worth coming all this way to interrupt my card game?"

Raymond hesitated, hoping to avoid sharing the accusation from Irena Slaske, yet knowing his mother deserved more than the claim of a sudden genealogical interest that could never fool her. But instead of a questioning look, he got a warm smile. She grabbed his hands as if he was a child again. It was comforting.

"I was so devastated how it affected you when Ronald and I told you. We were scared to bring it up again but I always held out hope you'd ask. One day. Though I had given up on—what would you like to know?"

"Everything."

It began with the German invasion of Poland in September, 1939, and the subsequent surrender of her hometown, Lwów, to the Soviets. Teenage Julia was volunteering at a hospital where she developed a schoolgirl crush on a Red Army soldier, Leonid Obodovska, wounded in battle, then put in her ward to recover. She knew a little Russian, he knew some Polish. They played language games to help each other improve. It was effective until his two-week stay ended and he had to return to the army. But not without promising to come back to see her at some point. Every night she would pray for his safe return but it took nearly six years for that to happen. Then one day she got a letter from Leo, asking her to see him at the hospital, where he was recovering from a long and dangerous trek home.

"I had become a young woman, somewhat pretty, and I had many suitors. But I was infatuated with Leo, despite his gaunt face and emaciated body. I could only see the man I admired as a girl. Not the mood swings, the heavy drinking, the memory loss. Everyone warned me he was trouble. Me, I saw a war hero, a survivor who escaped one of those labour camps."

"Labour camp?"

"Gross-Rosen, it was called. That was the main camp. It was in southern Poland . . . are you all right, son?"

Hearing that camp name again, the same one mentioned by Kayla, stuns Raymond on the train now in Poland as much as it did back in Canada on that visit. The tea calmed him down then but he has none to rely on today, as he continues reflecting.

"Are you all right, son?"

"Yes, please go on. What happened to him at that camp?"

"He never talked about it. He'd get upset if anyone talked of concentration camps, violent if that person was persistent and a bottle of vodka was involved. I made sure it never came up. Just as I did with you after your reaction to finding out about Leo."

"Why do you think he was that way, Mom? Could it be he was guilty of something?"

"Guilty of . . . what an odd thing to ask."

It wasn't easy but Raymond, in that moment, elected to not share his encounter with Kayla's grandmother. If Leo had kept it to himself, his mother would have no inkling of the existence of Irena Slaske, let alone any basis for Irena's accusations. What would be the point telling his dear mother the man she adored was what he was? He felt then and feels even more on reflection now that he is better off bearing the guilt himself.

"I'm just curious."

"Forgive me, son, I'm not trying to make you feel bad. I ask because I always sensed whatever happened in Poland is what got him arrested."

"Why did he get arrested?"

"Simply the act of marrying a Polish girl from a family that resisted the Soviet takeover of Lwów. L'viv as it is now called in Ukraine. They were convinced Leo sympathized with the Nazis while in Poland, and disputed his claim he was ever a prisoner."

He wanted her to stop. Everything his mother was saying was affirming Irena Slaske's accusation, compounding his guilt. He was glad to finish that part of the story and move on.

The NKVD "interviewed" Leo several times while she was pregnant with Raymond but always let him go. During the lulls, Leo engineered their overland escape with the help of a Polish friend who arranged safe passage on a cargo ship from Gdansk around Denmark and to England, then on a transatlantic ocean liner to Canada. This was mere days prior to Leo being sent to a labour camp in Siberia. His crime? No one ever told her.

It was on that ship she met Ronald Tibbett. A kind man, the same age as Leo, he was instantly smitten with Julia. She liked him too but kept faithful to her husband. Ronald stayed patient through Leo's death in Siberia. Her desire for Raymond to have a father enabled her to fall in love with Ronald.

"How did you hear of Leo's death?"

The answer proved to be the convincing factor in a growing impulse to go to Poland to face Irena's accusation, though that's not the reason he gave his mother. She encouraged him to go but was also consciously and uncharacteristically incurious. His commenting on this drew an equally curious response:

"I trust you will tell me everything in due course."

You don't want to know, he thought at the time, and thinks now, as he double checks he has the note she gave him with the answer in the form of an address in Wroclaw and a name: Jan Kowalski, Leo's friend, who arranged the emigration to Canada. A Polish friend. Would he know or know about Irena Slaske?

Raymond peers out. The winter storms at home having just receded, he finds it ironically dispiriting to see a countryside all in white. Though it is lovely, with snow sheets spread smoothly across open farmland only daintily marred by deer tracks.

The train pulls into an old station in the centre of town just as the sun breaks the clouds. A good sign. It's still cold but the briskness clears off the stale air from the train. His hotel is only a short walk from the station. The clerk speaks decent English, thank goodness. She provides a small map and shows where he might want to go, assuming he's a tourist.

"How would you recommend I get to Gross-Rosen?"

"I am sorry, what is that?"

"The concentration camp . . ."

She shakes her head, no doubt having reached the limit of her English. It's not a big deal, he's researched ways to get there, though a little local affirmation always helps: it is a complicated route. She does know the address his mother gave and points it out on the map as well as the best route to take.

Daylight wanes on his stroll towards the old town down a busy street. It crosses a wide canal before dead-ending for cars to become a cobblestoned pedestrian route. This leads to Rynek, the main square, bordered by centuries-old buildings painted in pastel colours. An elegant church with an eclectic set of spires and gables stands out but doesn't dominate the way churches often do in European cities. The vibe is lively without any sense of crowding. Bar and restaurant patios encroach into the square with tables and chairs glazed with thin layers of snow.

He circumnavigates Rynek to get his bearings, succumbing to its charms, before wandering out the other side. He stops at the river to regard a red brick castle-like structure with towers that look like chess pieces. He's procrastinating.

Twilight approaches, constellations taking shape. Raymond reaches in his shirt pocket to confirm the note places the address in the main square. He takes a deep breath, turns back to walk around the square only to find inconsistent building numbers. He circles twice before determining it must be the narrow pastel green building with unusually tall and thin windows. Inside, he finds a dark, almost medieval micro-brewery. Eight shiny tanks line the wall behind a long bar at which he takes a seat.

"*Tak?*"

"I'm sorry."

"What beer would you like?"

The bartender's tone is brusque, his Polish accent dense, but his manner cordial. He points at a row of taps with labels, none that Raymond recognizes, other than Amstel and Budweiser. It doesn't feel right ordering one of those so he studies the others, unsure what to choose, or how to ask. He points to a tap in the middle with a black and red label. The bartender pours a small glass, slides it to Raymond to sample. The beer has a nice amber colour, almost orange. It doesn't taste bad, nor as sweet as its tint would imply. His nod prompts the bartender to top it up.

"Do you speak English?"

"A little. Not much."

"I'm looking to get in touch with a Jan Kowalski."

Instead of answering, the bartender motions to another man sitting at the bar who comes over to sit next to Raymond. He's close to Kayla's age and introduces himself as Lech, icebreaking the moment by saying he is so proud of his famous namesake, he adopted the familiar moustache. Lech's English is strong, no doubt honed over time by being forward with tourists.

"You ask about Jan. How do you know Jan?"

"I don't, personally, but he helped my mother long ago. She told me she met him at this place."

"Is that so?"

"It's so long ago, I'm sure he is no longer around."

"No, he still comes here. And he likes to talk about the past. And hear about it."

"Is he here now?"

Lech shakes his head. He is amiable, but not forthcoming.

Raymond decides to share what his mother told him about her escape, but leaving out his father's Russian troubles, or any mention of Irena Slaske. Lech's smile widens as he listens. Once Raymond finishes, the Pole orders a round and makes a toast.

"A great man, our Jan. Your story is similar to that of my grandfather. He was a political prisoner who Jan helped get to the United States after escaping. Chicago. Which is where I was born and grew up, as a matter of fact."

"You're American? And you live here now?"

"After the Berlin Wall fell, I came to investigate my heritage and found I liked it better. But what is your mother's name?"

"Julia. Julia Tibbett. But Obodovska at the time. My father is the one who arranged it. Leo Obodovska."

Lech's smile vanishes at hearing the Ukrainian name.

"Jan will be in tomorrow. Come by around seven and talk to him then. I will make sure he will meet with you."

Raymond wakes up early, feeling depressingly alone, but is soon overwhelmed by the rush hour crowd at the train station, and long lines at the ticket booths. His struggle to buy tickets in English doesn't help. Then the train to Legnica is late. He almost misses the connection, which would mean a long wait and the uncertainty whether his ticket is still good. Luckily he catches it in time and has the entire car to himself. Most of the trip passes lonely, snow covered meadows, interspersed by stops at several small stations before the train slows to a halt at Rogoznica. It is exactly like the picture on the website. He is the only passenger to disembark.

The dingy station is empty save for a clerk at a keyboard in another room. Raymond exits at the back, pauses to re-read the directions he copied for the three kilometre walk. Snow and ice hinder his footing. His first steps are slow, until he gets used to it. The road leads past a park into a village. Several cars go by, his self-consciousness increases. An echo of the look of Kayla's grandmother is ever present in his mind; the fear of it recurring in this place puts him on edge.

Once in the nearly empty village, this feeling is replaced by a desire to get to his destination due to a chilling cold wind. The bark of a large dog echoes ominously under the grey sky. The forecasted sunshine is late. He ambles around a church, then up a road that exits the village and inclines slightly to parallel a ridge. No sidewalk. Raymond has to cross the slushy road often to avoid the splashes of cars from both directions.

At last the sun breaks the clouds as he reaches the quarry, and then the concentration camp. A horrible place in a tranquil setting. A portable trailer inside the fence holds an office. While admission is free, he pays for a ticket to watch a short film in the museum building where, thankfully, he can warm up.

The film is interesting, but Raymond finds himself paying more attention to faces in interviews than to the translations. In the museum he uses the display cases as a mirror to compare a face to his reflection. He spots similarities but nowhere does he see anyone resembling himself enough to evoke such a reaction from Irena Slaske. He's glad to exit the museum and walk the grounds. It would be a pleasant stroll if not for its cruel history. Flat concrete slabs indicate where buildings stood. It resembles a construction site full of foundations ready for framing. A pang of guilt upon seeing a sign stating one was a Blaupunkt plant: he once owned a Blaupunkt car stereo.

At the crematorium, an ugly black metallic device brings to stark reality the mechanical, efficient brutality. At the end of the camp a fence separates the prison from a bucolic hayfield that no doubt invited escape, despite the watchtower at each corner. He turns back to enter a barracks, expecting the severe horror of the crematorium to intensify. Instead it dissolves. To Raymond, it's a building, a mostly empty one. He cannot link his emotions to the events that transpired here. He's not emotional in general, but if this doesn't upset him, what will?

This missing element—as he begins to refer to it—plagues him on the long walk back to the tiny train station. It's still cold, but sunny, and the walk actually warms him up. Only for him to freeze again during the wait. It gets worse at the next station, Jaworzyna Slaska, where there's a longer wait to transfer for the train back to Wroclaw. Slaska. The first time he becomes aware of the similarity with Kayla's name. There are many places with Slaska in their name around here. He wants to ask Lech what it means, but then he'd have to explain about Kayla's Babcia.

The younger Pole is waiting for Raymond and beckons him to a semi-circular booth occupied by a withered but sturdy man who appears asleep. A bottle of vodka and a tumbler is in front of him. Lech taps the man's shoulder. He slowly stirs awake.

"Jan, this is Raymond. He's from Canada. He's the one I told you about. The son of someone you helped."

"Canada?"

"Hello, Mr. Kowalski."

Jan rises to shake hands, his head down. When he lifts it up, he gasps and his eyes animate in a way Raymond's experienced recently, but this time with joy, not the fear and terror shown by Kayla's grandmother. Jan moves his hand towards his chest to make the sign of the cross. Lech appears surprised too, but not alarmed. Jan raises his thin arms to clasp Raymond's shoulders and pull him close for a hug. The ensuing kiss on the cheek is shocking yet oddly not inappropriate. Only then does Raymond realize Jan is blind.

"I appreciate you meeting with me, Mr. Kowalski."

"Leo. That voice. Leo. It's Leo. Of course, I know you are not Leo, not in reality, but you are him. And I insist, call me Jan."

The man says Raymond's father's name softly, happily, as if at last finding a lost ally. Could it be Jan was evil too, the real Kapo, complicit with his father's crimes? Or vice versa?

"Sit. Lech, get Leo—I mean, Raymond—a drink. I assume, Raymond, you are curious about your father."

The directness catches Raymond off guard. It's unsettling, a test even of his preparedness to hear the truth.

"Maybe you can tell me about Gross-Rosen first. You see, I was there today."

"You were? How interesting."

The ambiguous way Jan says it confuses Raymond. He's not sure what he's about to hear. He hopes the beer will calm him.

Jan fills a third of his glass with vodka while Lech heads to the bar. The old man's wizened face stares at Raymond. There is a warmth in it that's touching. They sit simultaneously and wait for Lech to return with Raymond's beer.

"I was merely a boy when the Germans invaded my village and arrested me. They took me to Gross-Rosen to be a slave in a quarry. The same quarry you would have passed today."

Hearing Jan's firsthand anecdotes of forced labour, hunger, and desperation not only disturbs Raymond more than the ones from the film at the camp, it brings those stories to life. As his empathy grows, so does an urge to return to Gross-Rosen to see the film and displays again. Along with this is a feeling of relief: nothing Jan says confirms Kayla's grandmother's assertions that, as heatedly as they came out, are nevertheless hearsay. In fact Jan hasn't mentioned any women. Raymond needs to ask to be sure but is hesitant to interrupt. The vodka bottle is almost empty after Jan fills his glass to the rim. Jan smiles morosely, as at a sad inside joke, but then Lech taps his arm.

"How did you meet Leo, Jan?"

"We started getting prisoners from outside Poland. Leo was a soldier in the Red Army. While their arrival made everything more cramped, it gave us a sense of hope knowing we were not abandoned. That others were fighting for us."

"Then how did you become friends?"

"We did work at the same sub-camp but our friendship was at its strongest during the death march or what they preferred to call an evacuation. They did not want us but had to take us to hide the evidence of their deeds. Possibly as hostages to obtain a favourable peace. Deluded psychopaths. So I believed until it came to me the true reason they did not just leave us. Because if they did, they would have to turn around to fight the Russians. Pure cowardice. All their bureaucracy and death marches had no purpose other than to avoid the fight at the front. They hated those poor Jews, and us as well, but not nearly as much as they feared fighting."

Lech taps Jan on the shoulder.

"Jan, please, he wants to know about Leo."

"As I said Leo and I worked together but did not know each other well until the death march when we kept each other alive. If not for him, I would be dead like so many. He too. Then came the opportunity for Leo to escape, to go back east. Of course I did not deny him this. Never did I think I would see him again, I assumed he died. Years later he sent a letter to ask my help to let his wife and unborn child escape the Soviets. It was not easy but I was happy to do it."

"My mother has told me. She's very thankful."

"Poor Leo."

The story fills Raymond with a sentimental sense of pride, one in which he's tempted to indulge. But he came for more and there's a sense Jan is leaving out a lot.

"Were there women at the camp too?"

Jan looks up as if someone slapped him. He downs the rest of his tumbler and slams down the glass on the table. He takes a deep breath, pours another glass, then takes a gentle sip. Lech and Raymond exchange glances. Just as Lech is about to tap he old man again, Jan lifts his head. A teardrop rolls down one eye.

"There was a woman. Horrible woman. She caused this."

Jan points at his eyes and Raymond asks about it.

"No, that I cannot speak of. Instead, I will tell you about my friend, Frantiszek. It involves your father too."

Frantiszek was a childhood friend of Jan's. They were like brothers and did everything together, including getting arrested and sent to Gross-Rosen to work at the quarry all day, and then construct the camp in the evening. They witnessed Gross-Rosen transform from nothing to a significant labour pool for the SS. The growing population necessitated functionaries—Kapos—to act as supervisors. These were recruited amongst prisoners and given powers that corrupted some, leading to the abuse of other prisoners. The abuses were gleefully encouraged by SS officers who selected the lowest sort of prisoner for these roles. Beatings became commonplace as did starving anyone who resisted, or just to send a message.

Frantiszek was an exception. His troubled past and prison record gave him the green triangle badge, not the red one given to Jan as a political prisoner. The SS loved to recruit criminals as Kapos but didn't know Frantiszek had reformed. Jan convinced his friend to act the part of an evil Kapo in front of the SS, which he did convincingly. Frantiszek's prisoners didn't begrudge his extra food or regular clothes because he treated them well when alone. They would even volunteer for a beating if an SS officer was around to keep up the charade.

"Until that selection day."

It appears as if Jan is falling into another gloom once his last drop of vodka goes down. Lech hesitantly offers to get another bottle and is visibly relieved when Jan asks for coffee. Instead of going to the bar, Lech signals to the bartender who arrives with a cup of coffee. To Raymond it seems this is a regular pattern.

"Go on Jan, talk about the woman. What was her name?"

"There were no women in the main camp, not that I saw."

"But Jan, you just told our new friend—"

"Irena. Her name was Irena."

Because of the way Jan pronounces it, with the first syllable as a double "e" and the second sounding like "rain", hearing the name doesn't register for Raymond at first, but then hits him as Jan resumes his story, with a sharp image of a feeble old woman in her scooter.

"There was a selection. As usual, it frightened us. You never know if this is to be the one sending you to Birkenau. We were stronger, better workers—me, Frantiszek, a few others—so if we are selected together, we feel okay. We boarded a truck to a sub-camp about an hour away. I don't remember which, there were over a hundred, but this one had mostly women. We get off the truck, about two dozen of us, to face a line of officers and some female Kapos. Suddenly, Frantiszek clutches my arm and says, 'Jan, there's Irena, my Irena,' referring to the fiancée he had left behind, a girl he thought he had lost forever.

"So what does the fool do? In front of SS officers? He rushes to hug the woman, Irena, who is also wearing the armband of a Kapo. An SS officer pulls him back, kicks him. Instead of yelling at Frantsizek, he laughs at Irena, a good looking girl, but rotted.

"'This? This is your Polish man?' She is quiet. The SS officer pulls up Frantiszek roughly, strips off his armband. 'She is to be your Kapo here.' Irena betrays a tiny painful reaction that only I see—I never told Frantiszek.

"The officer then leaves but we know he is still watching, to test her. She is cold and efficient and passes with flying colours. In my opinion. Frantiszek, my poor delusional friend, chooses to see it differently. When we are told the trucks are unavailable and we are to stay and not go back to Gross-Rosen, Frantiszek is happy. But I know it is a bad thing."

Jan finishes his coffee and asks for more vodka. Lech signals to the bartender who brings a new bottle and fresh tumbler. The younger man otherwise is as riveted as Raymond.

Jan goes on to say that from then on Frantiszek became the target of not only the SS officer's torment, but also his estranged fiancée. They would steal his food and let him starve until just before he became a *Muselmann*, stumbling about, then give him enough to restore him, only to do so again. Like an experiment. Through it all Frantiszek foolishly retained faith that Irena was only obeying orders to keep herself alive out of a hope for their future together. Jan thought it was hogwash but there was no convincing his friend otherwise.

"He was lost. I have never seen anything so pitiful."

Jan pauses. Not even a tough, unsentimental man like him can keep his voice from cracking. The pauses are more frequent as he describes the traumatic, pathetic love triangle in which the more Frantiszek suffered, the firmer his faith in Irena grew. This faith impacted the German, though, whose petty jealousy grew in proportion to this faith. It peaked one night when a group of men, including a boyhood friend of Jan and Frantiszek, tried to escape along with three other prisoners. They were caught and sentenced to hang. All prisoners were forced to watch to deter future attempts. SS officers slung nooses over the cloaked heads of the men who stood on small chairs, while Irena's SS officer slowly approached, as if preparing to kick them away.

"But he didn't kick. Instead, he demanded a volunteer, one of us, to do the job. When no one came forward, he approached Irena. 'Who is it to be?' he said. Without hesitation, she pointed to Frantiszek. I am certain they prearranged this but that didn't make it any less awful. A guard shoved my friend towards the gallows with his rifle and prodded him until at last Frantiszek did it for each man. My friend's sobs amused the guard, and the SS officer. They mocked Frantiszek, calling him a *Stuhlfuhrer* or Chair Fuhrer. My friend was a toy for them. For Irena too."

"Couldn't Frantiszek have exposed this affair with a Jew?"

"Yes, Lech, the officer might have received punishment, but the one asking the question would certainly be killed. Not even Frantiszek with his broken heart wanted to be killed. It is likely too he feared Irena would suffer the most. It was about this time that Leo joined us at the sub-camp to replace one of the failed escapees. Your father, I am afraid Raymond, made the mistake of talking to me, a friend of Frantiszek."

Jan slumps, overcome with grief. Or guilt. For Raymond, all this strikes him how opposite it is to what he was told by Kayla about her grandmother. Only one version can be true. Is Kayla's Babcia lying? He wants to believe that, but it's risky to do so.

"Then came June 11. A day I always — you think I drink a lot now. Be here on June 11 and . . ."

"What's June 11, Jan?"

"Irena's birthday."

Jan describes how the SS officer, whose name Jan seems to intentionally avoid saying, gave Irena a whip for a birthday gift, how the evil in her eyes gleamed as she took Leo aside before he sat to eat. She ate his food, taking it as a birthday gift for her, then spat it out, before asking him to guess her age. Leo flashed his hand four times with all five fingers out. Twenty.

"'Liar. You think I am an old hag. You think I am forty. For that, one lash for each year.' I will never forget that shrill voice."

A deep sigh followed by sudden silence from Jan. Raymond uses the moment to replay Irena's words in his mind, imagining himself in a small unit on the sixth floor of his condo building. He flinches at the word "lash" and then taps Jan's shoulder.

"Jan, what happened on evacuation?"

"Death march. Always say what a thing truly is."

Another pauses before Jan goes on to describe how he and Leo walked side by side in a column, looking for ways to escape in the cold and deep snow. Jan hoped Frantiszek was behind them but feared he was near Irena who was never far from the SS officer. Each evening Jan or Leo ventured forward while the other went to the rear to check on Frantiszek. It was risky. They never knew who or what might betray them or give them away. It took little to provoke a bullet to reduce the numbers. The two men learned to be stealthy and when to abort. Often they did not see Frantiszek until roll call at daybreak.

"One day Leo went forward while I fell back to the rear. It was dark but by then the smell of individuals was a better guide than sight. They became used to us doing this and learned how best to let us through. Any disruption could go bad for anyone. It made the trek go efficiently. Leo and I met again in an hour but neither of us saw Frantiszek. Leo told me he didn't see Irena or her SS man either. Since they always kept near the front, this was unusual. We were exhausted but risked another search, this time me going forward, Leo to the rear. That was the last time I saw your father. Or the despicable lovers."

"What happened?"

"The next morning we were told of an escape, and the death of an SS officer. I contained my joy at this news, and it was only a brief joy. Other officers went into the nearby woods while we waited. We heard gunshots, then silence, before they returned with smug faces to announce the escaped prisoners were dead. To punish us for their lost comrade, they took twenty prisoners, shot them, and made the rest of us dig a grave for their bodies."

"But my father . . ."

Lech raises his eyebrows.

"Imagine my shock when I received a letter from Leo asking me to help, and then a week later your mother showed up, right here in this bar with a copy of the same letter."

"*Tak*, I know what you think, Lech. How could a suspicious blind old man trust a strange woman? I will tell you. For one, I was not fully blind yet. But even if I had been, I could tell she was the girl Leo talked of so much, the girl whose vow to marry him when he returned kept him alive. It was sweet and touched even a hard man like me, this infatuation of a teenager. But his naive hope had a power in the circumstances that is difficult to describe. Not like Frantiszek's, that was purely delusional. For Leo, the possibility would remain until it was proven wrong. And it did come true."

Jan pauses until Leo stops shaking his head.

"Of course, I made her tell me things only Leo could know. So I helped her—and you, her son—get to North America."

"So Jan, she must have said what happened on the escape."

"No, Lech. Leo would not talk about those days to her and he begged me to keep quiet about them too. Which was sad and stupid because I am sure that attitude is what got him arrested and what killed him."

Raymond's beer glass has been empty a while, as have the others' drinks, except for Jan's bottle. Lech gathers them to take to the bar. He helps the bartender, leaving Raymond alone with his father's friend who is busy refilling his tumbler. Raymond thinks of Kayla's Babcia, and an accusation that can only make sense if she is the same Irena as the woman in the love triangle, and accused him as an act of defence.

"If my father wasn't killed, isn't it possible the Irena woman, and Frantiszek, survived?"

"No, it is not possible."

"How can you be so certain?"

"Tell me, what about Irena interests you so?"

"Nothing. Or I don't know anything."

"Then I am at a loss as to your interest in the woman."

The question frightens Raymond. Instinct directs him to be discrete but he clumsily implies his mother told him.

"Leo would never have told your mother."

"She's a very intuitive woman."

"I am sure I do not believe you, but I will not pursue it."

Jan reaches for Raymond's hand, pats it, and smiles grimly, as if he's long ago surpassed that sentiment.

There is a commotion as a rowdy group of German tourists enter and sit in the booth directly behind them. Lech, joined by the bartender, approaches the new patrons and speaks to them in a civilized manner. They persuade the Germans to move to a table further in the bar. Jan bears a stoic expression on his face as this goes on, but a weak one. It cannot conceal a fear identical to the fear that shocked Raymond in his condo lobby months ago, when he first saw Irena. Then suddenly Jan's face bursts alive with a renewed vigour in the form of a crooked smile.

Raymond's drunk on exiting the bar. He can't remember how he said goodbye, who paid the bill, or the emotions he felt upon exiting, all gone. Including what he yearns for: a palpable sadness for what his father and Jan and Frantiszek experienced. He can grasp it intellectually, not emotionally. Is he numb to it? Cold-hearted? The hateful crimes of the Nazis are self-evident, but his detachment from the physical events, the absence of a material threat, makes them almost too fantastic. His instinctive empathy yields to a clinical perspective that pierces through to see these murderous Nazis as Jan sees them: cowardly, petty. It was misfortune for his father, Jan, and others to be born during an epochal perfect storm that created such a brutal but efficient bureaucracy as destructive as it was de-humanizing.

Similar thoughts percolate within Raymond on the train to Krakow the next day, hindering efforts to ward off his hangover with some rest.

Auschwitz, a true factory built for the mass killing of Jews, is a stark contrast to Gross-Rosen, where prisoners survived as long as they withstood the conditions and the SS determination to work them to death. Auschwitz was hopeless, and few were fooled by its cruelly ironic welcome gate.

Raymond spends much of his time there scanning the walls of portraits taken by the Soviets after liberating Auschwitz and Birkenau. The sheer number of photographs along with the vast mounds of shoes, suitcases, human hair, indicate the immense scale of the operation. Two photos Raymond stares at for a long time, ones that could be Leo. Others watch as he does this, just as he watches them do so for people they identify, the narrow corridor promoting a solemnly unhurried flow.

At one point, a woman steps in front of Raymond, dabbing a tissue at her eye with one hand, while her other hand clutches the wrist of a reluctant boy wearing a yarmulke. She yanks at him and points at a photo.

"There, David, that's your grandmother, your Babcia."

Babcia. Grandmother in Polish. Instead of the empathy he was seeking, his loathing grows for Kayla's Babcia. True, there is no hard evidence, but it's near impossible she isn't the Irena described by Jan. The real Kapo. Accusing Raymond of being the son of a Kapo was a defence mechanism. However, she has Kayla fooled. What will he say to Kayla? Or his mother?

He only goes to L'viv as a concession to his mother who felt it would be nice for Raymond to visit the city of his heritage. He regrets it upon finding himself in a stuffy train compartment he shares with two older men, a couple, and a young man. One of the men keeps altering positions, getting close, resting his shoe-less feet next to Raymond. The other old man is only slightly better, treating the seats as a divan once the young man starts taking phone calls outside the compartment. The couple proves to be clever in persuading the conductor to find another seat for them. At least the scenery is pleasant, enhanced by several deer sightings amidst snow fields and a dramatic police takedown outside with a dog searching for something.

Thankfully at Rzeszow the oldest man gets off. He struggles with his luggage and asks for Raymond's help. His goodbye is given in a sweet, classy way that impresses Raymond. The free space is filled by another couple, forcing the other man to sit up all the way to the border at Przemysl.

After a currency exchange, Raymond looks for the platform, which is separated from the local ones. He climbs stairs to find himself amongst a large crowd caged behind a blue mesh fence, the connecting train already there beyond it. A delay ensues as uniformed men usher out incomers, one car at a time, shuttling them to a gate blocked by desks occupied by customs officials.

While waiting, he is reminded of an image at Auschwitz, a photo of Jews corralled at a railway platform, with their bags, ignorant of the fate awaiting them: instant death via Auschwitz or slavery in a labour camp like Gross-Rosen. How anxious they might have been to get to a destination, unaware that the longer the delay, the longer their life. All Raymond can do is imagine it; his world is insulated from such outcomes.

Yet the growing impatience of the crowd seems to ignite an internal rage on behalf of Jan and his father for the lies of Irena. Even towards himself in the form of a shameful guilt at having stayed ignorant of these events all his life. He can rationalize his guilt by an all-in-good-time argument—he's here, isn't he?—and redirect his contempt at a woman in a condo two floors down in his building, a grandmother whose guilt is tangible and who is deceiving a wonderful girl.

As he waits, contemplating Jews watching over their bags chalked with their names, under an impression they will reunite with them if separated, he falls into a confusing melancholy due to an increasingly pervasive notion: Irena, before she became what she became, likely experienced a similar predicament.

-2 -1 G **M** 2 3 4 5 6 7 8 9 10 11 PH R

"Give me a chance to do the minutes again. I've studied recent ones from Gary, I'm sure I'll—what are you grinning at, Ned?"

"If it ain't broke, don't fix it, right?"

"It might be best if we just continue as we're doing."

"But Stacie, I'm the secretary of the board. It's my role."

"True, but the fact is, Gary doesn't have the time to try and train you again. Right, Gary?"

"Sorry, Dennis, maybe another time."

"Then when? Soon it'll be summer and you're not around as much. After that is the AGM. Now is the best time. Right guys? Stacie? You all shrug as if you don't care."

"We do care, we just have a lot on our plates. Can we move on to the WiFi? You have info for us, Gary?"

"I do. ForageX is getting itchy since they don't know what's going on. I listen to their pitch every week but there's nothing I can tell them. I've heard reports they're talking to residents and selling themselves directly. Which means more resistance if we go with someone else."

"Well, that's just great. Do you have an update, Ned?"

"Not really."

"Surprise, surprise."

"No thanks to you, Nigel."

"Okay, that's got to stop, you two. Here at the meetings and in your caustic emails. What if you accidentally send one to the wrong person? We can't let that out, right Gary?"

"Absolutely, Stacie. Internal issues are common, but when it comes to the residents, the board must appear united."

"Speaking of other people . . ."

"Yes, Lorie."

"Ned and I have talked and . . . you tell them, Ned."

"We were wondering, maybe we should involve Raymond again. He seems to have a good sense of — what's wrong, Gary?"

"It's just, involving non-board or management people in a board matter, it's not something I'd recommend."

"But we've gotten nowhere. Nigel's off in some fantasy land acting as if we've got years when it's only months now."

"It's not a fantasy land. It's already available and happening all over the world. We need a grander vision, not a stopgap that will only require us to do this all over again in a few years."

"I'd love to see something grand. But you need to do more for the committee, put some real time into it."

"About that, I'm afraid my work commitments will make it difficult for me to continue working on that."

"So you're quitting the committee?"

"Don't put words in my mouth, Ned. All I'm saying is don't count on me for any dedicated work."

"So you're quitting?"

"No, because I'll still contribute in a consultative fashion."

"Doesn't do me and Lorie much good. Gary?"

"Me? Oh no, I've got too much to deal with day to day. And you have taken this on as a board matter."

"Gary's right, he should focus on the day-to-day. Remember that new condo management software is being installed soon. It will keep Gary busy learning it and loading it with documents. As he recovers them from his corrupted laptop."

"But Stacie, we're kind of in a jam. We can't rely on Nigel."

"Not too sure about that, relying on Nigel, I mean, but you do have a point. About this owner. Maybe we can bring him in slowly—"

"I still don't think you should."

"It's all right, Gary, I'm sure Ned and Lorie will keep it all in line. Right, Lorie?"

"Yes, I think so. We have to, right?"

March

The Committee Redux

Had a feeling this would be a wasted trip, had a feeling that once again he'd messed up. Eleven to one. Two hour window to snake an entire line from the penthouse to the first floor. Is he kidding? Four hours minimum, six hours is better, in case it uncovers problems that can be or need to be fixed immediately. It's like he hasn't managed a building like this. But I know he has and this hasn't been a problem before. He's getting sloppy, maybe he's bored. I've seen it with other managers and I'll see it again. What a nuisance. Now I need to tell him it couldn't be done and he'll have to schedule another outage. No doubt he'll give a look of impatience, as if it's my fault. A symptom of complacency: the more you screw up, the more it's someone else's fault. Except that the true symptom is the blindness to it. I'd be pissed if I lived here, having my water shut down twice in a month due to the carelessness of a property manager. Hope I don't encounter any of – oh crap, elevator's stopping. Maybe whoever it is won't say anything.

Playing pool on his own is a desultory way to pass time, a way to ward off the gloom that beset Raymond upon his return from Europe. The gloom that belies his feelings for Kayla are real, the more it lingers after not seeing her once in the weeks since. He often dares himself to go or even loiter in places where he might run into her, only to exacerbate the feeling, and his anxiety. Like the pool room, or his next destination, the lobby, to check his mail for the third time today, in the off chance of catching Kayla and Buster going out for or returning from a walk.

The elevator door opens while Raymond is brushing chalk off his fingers. He almost runs into a service man who's wearing a uniform sporting a plumbing company logo.

"Hey there. Is the water back on?"

"It was never off. He scheduled it wrong. Not enough time to get the work done. It'll have to shut down again."

"He? You mean, Gary?"

"Gary, that's right, that's his name."

At the ground floor, the service man heads to Gary's office, while Raymond checks his mailbox. Only junk, which he tosses into the blue bin before pausing to listen. He can't make out any words but the service man sounds exasperated. Not unlike how Raymond must have sounded talking to Gary about the bicycle room. It's a sort of comfort he's not the only one.

"Hey, Raymond, how are you?"

Raymond waves at Elle—he's never heard her surname but knows she's Parisian—holding court with two women in front of the lobby fireplace. Only an utter recluse could not be aware of Elle. Her ubiquitous, amiable presence illuminates the entire building. The ladies giggle at something she says. Elle then goes to Raymond and comments on how she hasn't seen him around. He's in no mood for explanations and only nods.

While the impact of listening to Jan has subsided, it remains dormant like a volcano, ready to erupt any time he might spot a blue scooter. What will he do if that happens? Or should he take control like Australia does with wildfires? Set it off deliberately by confronting Irena in her suite? No, can't go there again.

Ideally, it will erupt naturally. Or not at all. As was the case with his mother, when he waited for her to bring up his trip but then decided to dilute the details—just as he withheld telling Jan about Irena—and embellish his excursion to L'viv. A lovely city, he took plenty of photos, but felt no connection to it. Not to the degree his mother still does. What's interesting is that after he left her he got the sense it was his mother who opted for that discretion by being unusually tolerant of his vague account. As if holding back until he's ready in some way.

Unlike Terri, who was annoyed at him for leaving abruptly. At first he resented the implication he was on call to her since no progress had been made on the project funding. But when he met her for lunch, she apologized and revealed her issue wasn't professional but personal. All reconciliation attempts failed and divorce proceedings are underway. She needs a friend.

He presses the elevator button but no door opens. One is on his floor, the eighth, while the other appears to be on service.

Where is Kayla? Is she avoiding him? He desperately wants to share what he found out, watch her reaction. He's rehearsed explanations, speculated responses for various moods, and how he might adapt what he says based on mood or body language. Whatever it takes to make things right by her, even if it nullifies all romance, is worth the effort: his anger isn't with her. What he fears is the longer it takes to happen, the more time he has to nurture resentment into hatred, the more likely impatience will prod him to confront the real Kapo. He must resist such actions as long as possible.

At last an elevator arrives. Raymond hears a bark just as he presses eight. Buster. Unconsciously his finger presses the door close button. Coward. Isn't it better to face her now rather than return to the condo and brood about it? No logical argument to counter that, only the raw impulse favouring retreat. He grabs a can of Coke and settles in at his desktop. The first email is from Ned Esposito. They intend to resurrect the WiFi committee. It's an invitation to rejoin.

Isn't it too late?

Maybe not. Scrolling down unveils an email sent by Nigel Khan, the director whose persuasive promise to address it two years ago got him elected, but whose inability or unwillingness to fulfill the promise triggered Raymond's volunteering. But the note indicates he has been working — wait, the phrasing — oh, he is a slippery one.

Raymond scrolls down to the original email from ForageX to Gary, asking to present to their WiFi offering to the board. It's not the first time they've tried to set something up apparently. Unanswered. Then a follow-up two weeks later sent directly to the board. Still no response from Gary, or the board. Instead, another follow-up from ForageX, an apology for emailing the board directly, promising to restrict future contact to Gary. All leading to Nigel's response to the board, and Gary, in which he calls ForageX desperate, then chastises them, behind their back, for not offering it three years earlier. Anyone not reading his words closely might infer Nigel, as Raymond did initially, had taken the initiative. Only the wording — "if the vendor had taken us seriously with real intent to keep us as a client, why did they not approach us with this when I talked about it back then?" — is a clever way of making it sound as if he solicited an offer when in truth he only talked. An illusion of doing. It seems the WiFi situation has deteriorated much farther than feared.

At least Nigel points out action items, albeit simplistic ones, and supports resurrecting the committee. He is completely out to lunch thinking a formal request for proposal is still an option. That ship sailed in December under the tailwind of a low-key approach.

A second email shows up: Nigel's response to Ned's request for participation time. Nigel claims he's busy and can only act in an advisory role.

Dump him, Raymond thinks, filled with an urge to help out Ned. Lorie too, who appears willing to put in the effort Nigel can't or won't. Nigel is a consultant, through and through, of the type Raymond has suffered far too often via the blind allegiance to "experts" paid by IT directors and their superiors. Here is his chance to nip a similar situation in the bud before it irrevocably derails everything. Raymond sends an affirmative reply.

A few days pass and Raymond hears nothing from Ned but then his inbox fills with emails containing various attachments.

There is an amusing exchange based on an announcement from ForageX about hardware upgrades in which they instruct residents to direct questions to the property manager. This was forwarded to the board by Gary with a rebuke to inform Gary if the board intends to offer up his services. That leads to several bewildered responses from the board. Can't blame Gary for his reaction, considering he knows zilch about the WiFi. Though he apparently knew enough to advise against the owner sessions in December as part of that dubious low-key approach.

The real issue is managing a vendor that, due to its control of the condo website and its users, has direct access to owners. Availing themselves of this opportunity is indeed a sign of their desperation, as Nigel puts it, but Raymond can't blame them if the board hasn't even listened to them. What would you expect them to do if they have a contract expiring in six months and no word from the client?

The attachments make this more confounding, particularly one in which the condo lawyer gives an opinion that the wiring for the WiFi likely is the property of ForageX, as they installed it when the contract commenced; however, there's no document explicitly stating this. The lawyer adds his opinion it's unlikely the vendor would expend the effort to extricate the cable should they be replaced. Makes sense. In fact it's more likely for them to leave it there as bait, in case another vendor fails, or to hinder their competitor.

What doesn't make sense is the contract. Raymond received a copy prior to December but didn't peruse it then. Now he sees it references a schedule of equipment that presumably specifies equipment ownership, including the wiring. Not there. Nor is it among the myriad of other attachments. There's also a reference to a schedule identifying performance criteria the vendor must meet. Not there. So how has this vendor been managed?

It's a lot to digest but it is something concrete to work with, enough to fuel Raymond's desire to pitch in. He again summons his project management skills to draft a framework on which he can first get them organized, then steered in the direction of a solution. He'll accomplish in a few hours what Nigel had more than two years to get done.

GENERAL APPROACH:

Is a formal RFQ still viable? It's a complex process entailing reviews, sign-offs, input from numerous people. An informal approach might be warranted, even interviewing vendors individually, discussing our WiFi needs and, if fortunate, finding one with a viable solution at an acceptable price that we can adopt immediately.

VENDOR MANAGEMENT:

This pussyfooting around ForageX is counter-productive. Best to deal with this vendor directly and candidly, sooner not later. Soliciting bids and not including them is not as big a deal as it's been made out to be. If it is, let them bid, let them know they've got more to prove. It can help reduce the awkwardness if we need to remove their presence and will make for a graceful exit, from both sides, avoiding friction. This is to our advantage. As is negotiating month-to-month extensions of the existing contract, as a tenant might do at the end of a lease, as a fallback in case of delays.

MISSING INFO / PITFALLS:

Without the current contract schedules — which are essential for other reasons, such as framing inquiries to other vendors and being able to evaluate them — we are in a weak position, relying only on anecdotal information. Not having them will hamper the process. If they are legitimately lost, ask ForageX to provide an itemized list or inventory of what they claim they own onsite. We'll need this at some point, anyway.

Additionally, as our issues with them are anecdotal, as far as I can tell, let's conduct a survey of user satisfaction, issues, experiences, etc. to see if the problems are as prevalent as we think. Let me restate: the fear of ForageX catching wind of our intent and causing trouble is a red herring; it's merely something to manage.

ROLES / RESPONSIBILITIES:

1. Core Team (Ned, Lorie, Nigel, Raymond):
- Manage process end to end
- Write, distribute, evaluate RFQ or alternate bid document
- Vendor recommendation

2. Property Management (Omnirez, Gary):
- Consult on bidding process through selection
- Communicate updates to owners as needed
- Coordinate impacts (i.e. outages) to residents as needed
- Vendor management (as per other suppliers)

3. Board of Directors:
- Act as Steering Committee
- Consult during RFQ process through selection
- Possibly participate in vendor evaluations
- Provide approvals, including final vendor selection
- Vendor negotiation
- Ongoing vendor monitoring

SCHEDULE: Daunting but doable:

- Now/March: Identify candidate vendors; define problem
- April: Vendor response period + vendor Q&A session.
- May: Response evaluation and selection
- June/July: Vendor development and testing
- August: Implementation and testing
- September: Handover; ForageX de-commissioning
- October: Feedback / Assessment, possibly at AGM

In truth, all this ought to have been done over a year ago; it was what Raymond expected from Nigel and his big talk. That it didn't happen creates a fear this is beyond their capacity, and too much to handle, particularly this late in the game.

Those concerns are partially offset by the effort Ned puts in to draft a survey. Taking the opportunity to consult owners and exhibit tangible progress beyond the platitudes found in their AGM reports. This step puts Raymond in a good frame of mind to meet Ned and Lorie at the bar.

But when the elevator opens onto the lobby, the exit at the front entrance is blocked by a scooter with Kayla's grandmother sitting in it. She is looking away from the elevators towards the main street. Raymond's inclined to keep behind her and exit via the rear entrance. But the indignation from Poland, dormant all this time, compels him to confront the woman, to call her a liar, a Kapo, and even threaten to report her and make it public.

The obligation to see Ned and Lorie holds him back, freezes him, though not the inner voice persisting in saying he must do it, this is his chance, he can't suppress the burden. He takes a step just as the old woman reaches for a magazine. Her effort is weak as she grabs a hold of it, tries to pull it close, then drops it and emits a helpless sigh. One that arrests Raymond's steps: he no longer sees the Kapo, only a frail, elderly woman.

He retreats to exit via the back door. A fear of seeing Kayla, especially in this frame of mind, prompts Raymond to scan his surroundings before strolling to the bar. Clear. Sunshine and a soft spring breeze restore his good mood. Except one thing nags at him: Why does he keep avoiding her when he's pining for her company?

Hence, she becomes a distraction during his conversation with Ned and Lorie. They don't notice because Ned is similarly distracted by an attractive young waitress while Lorie is content to enjoy a glass of red wine from the bottle she and Ned share. Her attention to the young man is odd, the way she fawns over him. Is it like a mother, a love interest? Hard to tell. Even odder is it's not awkward, nor uncomfortable; in fact it's kind of sweet. There is a solid bond between them.

"That Dennis is utterly useless, I tell you."

"Now Ned, I've told you, be kind. Everyone has their values and their faults. Forgive him, Raymond, he's young."

"He does nothing other than bake those awful cookies. And I'm approaching thirty, Lorie, for crying out loud."

"What's Dennis's role on the board?"

"He's the secretary."

"The one who does the minutes, keeps track of corporate records and documents, et cetera?"

"Hardly."

"Wait a minute, he doesn't do the minutes?"

"Gary does those, just like at the AGM."

"I can't believe you let an outsider control the minutes?"

Both board members shrug their confirmation.

This is a big red flag. When he was project manager, unless a project could afford an assistant, Raymond would always take minutes himself. He would never consider letting a consultant, let alone a vendor, do so. Whoever controls the minutes controls a lot. You need someone trustworthy to keep them well, and do so honestly in the interests of owners. Not a vendor. It's not that vendors are inherently untrustworthy — though many are — it's that their priorities can easily produce a conflict of interest.

It's hard to decide what's more troubling: that they allow it, or that they don't see the danger. Clearly they cannot grasp the risk; otherwise why wouldn't another board member to do the task if Dennis is incapable? Raymond wants to lecture them on this point but senses it would be a waste of his breath. Instead, fishing, he brings up finding it odd for Lorie to nominate Ned at the last AGM.

"I'll be honest, I didn't vote for you because of that."

"That's silly. Why?"

"Because she's on the board, it looked funny, right Lorie?"

"A little, yes."

"You didn't look comfortable nominating him."

Lorie concedes a nod, that's all. Ned's wry smile shows he's genuinely perplexed.

"What does it matter who nominates who?"

"Because it looks like you're a clique."

"Nonsense, there's no clique. Can't be."

"You agree with Ned about that, Lorie?"

"I suppose. Next AGM three of us are up for election. That's a majority, so that cancels out the idea of a clique."

"But I'm safe because I got in for two years. Lorie, you'll be safe because everyone likes you. This is a great chance to get out Dennis and Nigel. What's the matter, Lorie?"

"Now I get what Gary meant saying it worried him that we could end up with a rogue board."

"I heard him say it but I don't know what it means."

"Just three new people with their own ideas, I guess."

"You worry too much, Lorie."

Raymond watches their exchange, sensing another issue he ought to be aware of, but is unable to pin down. The discussion ends, giving no further clue. It's tempting to poke at it, but he instead asks about Nigel's role on the committee.

"Waste of time, Ray. He's promised to provide contacts for a long time, for candidates. Nothing yet. Even Gary's reached out to contacts at the cable company and has said he'd be willing to set up sessions for us with the other vendors."

Raymond manages to contain his frown. They still lack the urgency, even after all the delays and stalling. His plan depends on Ned and Lorie buying in, on their commitment to control the others. He's seen so many projects fail from no backing, from no support, either due to incompetence, political agendas, or both. Without the authority to implement his ideas, they're doomed. Lorie's and Gary's rogue board concern sounds scary, but is it? Isn't it just as likely such a change would be healthy?

Why, oh why did he not insist on taking the reins way back in November? Would they have let him? Ned seems to be in his element and liking to be in charge. Perhaps that's the deal with these directors, the desire to be one regardless of the ability or self-awareness to excel as one. Raymond is developing doubts about Lorie now who also seems out of her depth.

"As far as Nigel, goes, Lorie and I don't know."

"This feels like it's getting complex."

Raymond wants to lash out at Lorie for saying that, to point out it's complex because the board sat on its ass. But there's no value in that, not for these two who, bless them, are trying.

"It is complicated, but in our case, failure may be an option."

They both look at Raymond, their interest piquing when he explains they can buy time if they negotiate an extension clause to the current contract, time to be used to do this right.

"They're anxious to talk with you. If you give them a chance to make an offer they'll likely be accommodating extending on a month to month basis, like a tenant with a lease."

Their enthusiastic response cheers Raymond, but only for a moment before the true implication of it comes to mind.

By taking this option, they will concede failure. The positive feeling accompanying Raymond to the bar is gone. In its place, a sense of futility. It doesn't hold him back from enhancing his framework back in his suite by putting it in a PowerPoint deck to present his approach as simply as possible.

As he works on this over the next few days, Raymond turns into an online spectator of nasty back and forth emails exposing the full depth of the conflict between Ned and Nigel, the latter consistently deflecting Ned's attempts to get Nigel to contribute anything of substance. The consultant tactic of asking questions to thwart progress is in full force. Yet the impotence of a board president whose "we're-on-the-clock-guys" interjections seem to be ignored are as bad, if not worse. Lorie chimes in occasionally as peacemaker for a brief truce. Dennis is, to paraphrase Ned, a non-entity. Gary's cable company query generates a boilerplate bulk order brochure quoting high prices and demanding long commitments. Another series of emails — it's now an impromptu board meeting — argue specifics of a survey Ned is writing. Each director pipes in with an opinion, delaying the issuing of it, costing more time.

Miraculously, a draft gets approved and it just needs to get distributed:

> Your Board is analyzing ways to improve our WiFi service and you can help by taking a few minutes to complete this survey. Your input will be valuable to us in assessing both our current WiFi habits and identifying areas where the service can be improved. Once filled out, please drop off your completed forms at the Management Office where they will be treated as confidential. Thank you in advance.

One day, while sorting through the emails, he comes upon one from Kayla, sent while he was in Poland. One sentence:

"I did not mean it and thought you would have seen that."

Was her anger that day in her suite for her grandmother's benefit alone? Raymond escapes to the balcony. Dark clouds are approaching but it's still warm. A feeling comes over him that if he stays there, Kayla and Buster will eventually stroll by.

Cars enter and leave the parking lot. Couples depart for and return from walks to the lake. A stray cat roams the grounds in search of prey or amusement. There's Elle, talking to an old lady with an aging Labrador on a short leash. Raymond hasn't seen her before but she seems to fit in. Farther out, waves of vehicles emerge from the train station parking lot to clog the main street, creating long lines of homebound commuters at the traffic light. The thumping of loud stereos or rumbling trucks occasionally disturbs what is otherwise a quietly pleasant early spring day. Darkness descends quickly, but Daylight Savings Time will fix that soon. As if to offer an early sample, clouds are breaking up, patches of sky revealing a bluish-white moon. An auspicious vista, stoking a feeling she'll show up soon.

Only the feeling is false; there is no sign of her.

He tries to compose a response to Kayla's email. It's difficult putting the proper words together; they all sound ridiculous. The problem is how upset he is with her grandmother and he can't get past the notion Kayla is guilty by association. Meaning any plea on his part to reconnect will be founded on falsity until they address the big lie. And if they do, any such plea would likely fail.

-2 -1 G **M** 2 3 4 5 6 7 8 9 10 11 PH R

"There are valid points in what he presents."

"Of course, Lorie, this is rudimentary project management."

"The kind you were going to provide but no longer have the time for, leaving it to me to pick up the slack?"

"Do you even understand it, Ned?"

"All right, Nigel. Yes, Lorie, there are valid points. Like this survey idea. I saw your draft, Ned. Is it ready to go out?"

"You bet."

"Then just send it to Gary who can —"

"Sorry, Stacie, but I'll be on my holiday next week. I won't be able to distribute it and take in the responses."

"Can't you show your backup how to do it?"

"I suppose so. But I need to remind you all announcements go through a single email that can be seen by ForageX. Do you want them to know about this?"

"Right, I keep forgetting. Ned, I still like the survey idea so maybe we can think of — yes, Lorie?"

"How about we print copies and drop them off at the doors of all the suites? I don't mind doing that. Then give them — how long will you be gone, Gary?"

"A week."

"Give them a week to fill out and drop off at the property management office. That work for you?"

"Residents may still tell ForageX about it."

"At least it won't be immediate."

"Okay. I'm just collecting them, right, not anything else?"

"That's right. Lorie and I will collect them from you once it's over next week and do the tabulating."

"Okay, works for me. I'll inform my backup. Though I'm not sure how much a survey will help you guys."

"At the very least it'll show progress. Yes, Ned?"

"Everyone needs to get back to me with vendor contacts so I can start setting up appointments for us to talk to them. Gary, you can get ForageX, plus I think you had another one?"

"The cable company. Which I forwarded to Ned already."

"Is that it, Gary? It's just a bulk sales brochure with pricing that's hardly competitive."

"It's what they gave me."

"Don't forget too, Ned, they want a seven-year commitment to get the best price. As treasurer, I may take a stand on that."

"And I'm still waiting on you, Nigel."

"Here."

"What's this?"

"The name and number of a contact."

"Never heard of them."

"They're new, up and coming, eager to make a deal, I bet."

"How do you know of them, Nigel?"

"Consulted on a minor project for them once, nothing big. But it's better if I let you initiate contact."

"Just the one? I thought you knew the market?"

"I have a full time job, a full time business."

"Okay, I'm glad to see we are making headway. Anything else? Just good news, if possible? Gary?"

"The snaking of the water line got done, as scheduled."

"Great. Hope we don't have to do it again for some time."

"Given the faulty building design for that particular section, it ought to be budgeted as a distinct item."

"Lorie, we talked about that with Sheila and Gary. Doing so would highlight the issue. It's best to keep it under wraps."

"Are you sure that's wise?"

"Some owners are always looking to make a fuss."

"But if it comes up frequently, people will notice anyway."

"Not really. There's always a way to, you know, categorize expenses and keep within the accounting rules."

"Let's pray it doesn't come up frequently and that everyone keeps their pipes clean. I think that about wraps—yes, Lorie?"

"There is the matter of Elle and this year's rooftop picnic. In addition to the potluck, she recommends the board spring for a few bucks for hot dogs, burgers, that sort of thing. She'll work the grill, and it's BYOB. I think it's a good idea."

"Is it something I'd have to go to?"

"It would be good for the president to be there, for all of us to be there, but no one will take roll call."

"How about me?"

"You'd be more than welcome, Gary, it's up to you. We can figure where it comes from in the budget later."

"Let's do it then, unless there are any objections."

"All right, but as board members be careful what you let out in conversations. Some owners are alert to the slightest slips."

"Like who, Gary?"

"Dennis, we need to wrap up. Gary, can you issue minutes from today before you go on vacation?"

"I'll try, but I can't promise anything, Stacie."

"Of course. And do enjoy your time off."

April

The Death of the Committee

That was, like, surprisingly pleasant. Here I am, like, a renter, literally a second class citizen next to those who own their units, afraid, like, well not afraid but hesitant to talk to the property manager about the side door. I get why they want it closed, there's, like, a sign saying so, but, like, is it a big deal to take my dog for a pee and, like, leave it open a few minutes? No point going all the way to the elevator if, like, I'm only on the fifth floor. When I said this to Gary for sure I thought he'd side with that owner. But, like, he agreed with me it was no big deal, as long as I, like, made sure it got closed. Maybe it was saying it was the guy with the French accent complaining that did it. I suspect Gary doesn't care for him much. Or, like, many owners for that matter. Best of all I now, like, don't need to call my landlord. In the future I can go to Gary. For anything. He's, like, sweet . . . what is this at the door? A survey? About the WiFi? Is that, like, for me or my landlord? Is it mandatory? I suppose I can fill it out since, like, I am the one who uses

118

it. Only six questions, easy enough. How do I rate my satisfaction of the WiFi? Pretty slow, so, like, less than average. What do I use it for? Check email, surfing, videos — like, yeah, tons of vids — games. Social Media, Facebook? Oh yeah, like, all the time. Do I use another service provider? How would I know? Areas for improvement. Serious? Got to be speed. Also reliability. Cause, like, literally, it's down three, four times a week. That's it? Pretty skimpy. Hmm, asking for a suite number. I'd better leave that blank.

-2 -1 **G** M 2 3 4 5 6 7 8 9 10 11 PH R

Each time an elevator door opens, Raymond's heart races at the possibility Kayla and Buster will emerge. It keeps him alert as he waits for Lorie and Ned to join him for the walk to the bar.

That part is enjoyable, socializing with his neighbours, even listening to their awkward gossiping about the board members. The business part is what grates. Ned and Lorie are with Stacie at the moment. Instinct warns him the process is about to shift from a practical approach to a political one.

A man emerges from the elevator, wearing a robe, holding a piece of paper — the survey — in his hand. He slides it under the closed property management office door quick enough to catch the same elevator back upstairs. Is the man a renter or owner?

For some reason, the board didn't distribute the survey via email, but hand delivered it, dropping it off at residents' doors, when it's owners' feedback that's needed. If the communication between owner and tenant is strong, it's fine. Otherwise owners leasing their suites won't see it, won't have their voices heard. And how many tenants will just ignore it? That may or may not prove significant in the results.

The board has initiated vendor contacts but sessions have not been arranged yet. There is a continual back and forth about scope that's proving a hindrance now that Nigel's unrealistic demands have reached the board president's ear. Ned and Lorie are with Stacie now working to get her back on track, Raymond hopes. Just as he hopes his revised framework gives them the ammunition to do manage such complications.

The elevator door opens and out walks a smiling Ned, with Lorie right behind him.

"Hey there, Ray, ready to go?"

"Yeah."

"Great. We just had a terrific meeting with Stacie."

The words terrify him in the manner of "sick" being slang for good. An omen they're lost. Which is confirmed at the bar by Ned and Lorie paying scant notice to Raymond's plan. They don't get it, won't ever get it. That what is a matter of course to Raymond is beyond Ned's capacity is not as shocking as Lorie's behaviour. She seems to grasp certain aspects, but is too weak to assert her view, and so is the true letdown.

A glimmer of hope arises when Ned shares raw data from the survey to which just over half the residents responded. They are damning to ForageX. To begin, thirty percent don't even use a service that's part of their condo fees. Of those who do, more than half are displeased. From that, it could be inferred the two-thirds vote required to terminate the service was attainable and worth testing at one time.

Raymond doesn't even bother mentioning it. In his suite, he analyzes the numbers further and forwards the results to Ned with the faint hope they'll trigger something in him.

Raymond modifies his framework to incorporate the survey results to fit into the fewer than six months before the ForageX contract ends. Given the situation, it's more key than ever they contain interference and scope by establishing explicit roles and responsibilities, as well as formalize communication lines. His strategy: detach the tactical needs defined in the contract from the strategic wishes of a certain board member such that both are addressed, just not with the same urgency.

Also, it must be an auditable process. No solution can hope to satisfy all, but if there is a good record to make it clear how a solution came about, it can be shown it wasn't a whim based on vendor promises or running out of time; in other words, it must be defendable. Nonetheless, a point comes when reality sets in and Raymond realizes it's likely a waste of time. But he enjoys the work. If he can stave off the idea of failure, the effort will be worth it. Even if only as a template for future bid situations.

1. DEFINE THE PROBLEM

1.1 - Current Situation (ForageX)
- Contract expires end of September; no renewal terms
- Recent survey indicates:
 > 73% use ForageX; 26% use independent; 1% use both
 > Of the 73% that use ForageX:
  >> 65% find speed poor or average
  >> 63% find service reliability poor or average
  >> 60% find technical support poor or average

1.2 - Objectives
- Reduce cost of service by a minimum of 10%
- Increase flexibility by limiting contract to < 3 years
- Improve user speed score to 75% satisfied or better
- Improve service reliability score to 90% satisfied or better
- Improve tech support score of 75% satisfied or better

1.3 - Scope in Terms of Function
- Wired Internet in suites using existing wiring
- Individual Private WiFi in suites
- Public WiFi in defined common areas
- Technical support for all components

1.4 - Scope in Terms of Users / Stakeholders
- Owners pay for WiFi in condo fees
- Residents use in suite WiFi; require tech support
- Others use common WiFi; common password?
- Property Management oversees and pays WiFi vendor
- WiFi Vendor supplies, maintains equipment and software
- WiFi Vendor provides technical support to Residents
- WiFi Vendor provides reporting (usage, performance, etc.)

1.5 - Special Considerations (Strategy to Address)
- Ensure solution follows condo declaration (Only consider WiFi-only offerings; no bundling)
- Ensure privacy, especially during any conversion (Define privacy policy for vendors to comply with)
- Ensure improvement in service levels and support (Institute periodic surveys to score solution)
- Ensure vendor can deliver offer promises (Test before payment; apply probation period.)

2. IDENTIFY THE SOLUTION

2.1 - Solicit Vendor Proposals
- Assess vendors, long list of candidates, find contacts
- Shortlist 3-5 from whom to solicit bids
- Share our requirements (i.e. Scope/Objectives above)

2.2 - Define Vendor Evaluation Criteria
- Tie to objectives identified above
- Include scoring on:
  > Promised performance
  > Confidence in ability to achieve promise
  > Experience and references (from actual implementations)
  > Technical support quality, availability
  > Security and Privacy processes and guarantees
  > Quality of submitted offers (clarity, completeness, etc.)
- Highest score not automatic win for vendor
- Identify evaluators and specify weight of their scores

2.3 - Collect Vendor Bids
- Sort tangible elements to enable side-by-side comparison:
  > Pricing
  > Specifications and Solution Complexity
  > Support / Service Level Agreement (SLA)
  > Contract Terms / Conditions
  > Privacy Considerations
  > Vendor Reliability, History, Experience

2.4 - Perform Vendor Scoring
- Document scoring results against evaluation criteria
- Document what parties participated in scoring
- Determine recommendation
- Review and validate scoring

2.5 - Make Vendor Recommendation
- Analyze scores ==> core team recommendation
- Board to verify core team recommendation
- Record decision rationale, esp. if not highest scorer
- Notify all vendors of decisions as needed
- Initiate negotiations
- Announce to owners

3. IMPLEMENT

3.1 - Infrastructure and Performance Details
- AKA infamous missing ForageX contract schedules
- Define and catalogue hardware needs for all building areas
- Define and catalogue software elements
- Define performance specifications and criteria / SLA
- Define measurement processes
  > Quantitative via system reporting
  > Qualitative via survey

3.2 - Planning
- Define steps to implement solution, how it will operate
- Identify notification needs
- Identify training and education needs
- Identify impacts to Property Management
- No surprises via clear communication
- Smooth transition

3.3 - Execute
- Create and distribute manuals, guides, etc.
- List operating instructions
- Perform vendor testing
- Perform onsite testing
- Detail activities for installation
- Notify owners / residents; arrange suite access
- Perform installation

3.4 - Post Implementation
- Warranty
- Handover to Property Management for operation
- Vendor assumes ongoing support / SLA in effect
- End of Core Team effort

APPENDIX - PARAMETERS

A.1 - Urgency
- Five months until contract expiry
- Unclear tendering process compels tactical approach
- Need more info from vendors and users
- Need to clarify roles

A.2 - Assumptions
- *Window for formal RFQ closed*
- *Tactical solution to ensure continuity of service*
- *Chosen solution will be managed by selected vendor*
- *Condo website and other software managed separately*

A.3 – Role of Core Team (Ned, Lorie, Nigel?, Raymond)
- *Manage process through implementation*
- *Analyze information from vendors, owners, etc.*
- *Document and recommend solution*
- *Oversee implementation of solution*
- *Apprise via status reports*

A.4 - Role of Property Management (Omnirez)
- *Communicate impacts of options considered*
- *Contribute to vendor selection and negotiation*
- *Support onsite implementation*
- *Facilitate communications to residents / owners*
- *Assume vendor management upon completion*

A.5 - Role of Board of Directors
- *Sign off on major milestones in timely manner*
- *Approve final vendor recommendation*
- *Participate in vendor negotiation process*
- *Communicate ongoing progress to owners*
- *Communicate impacts to owners*

A.6 - Communications Plan
- *Email exchanges and impromptu meetings unofficial (i.e. no decisions to be derived from them)*
- *Weekly Core Team meetings; more as needed*
- *Status Reports distributed (frequency TBD)*
- *Monthly Board of Directors status update*
- *Meetings with potential vendors as necessary*
- *Halt non-support related contacts with ForageX*

A.7 - High Level Plan
- *Information gathering and analysis (April-May)*
- *Vendor evaluations and make selection (May-June)*
- *Vendor negotiations and kick off (June-July)*
- *Development and Implementation (July)*
- *Testing (Vendor and Onsite) (August)*
- *Conversion and handover (September)*

A.8 - Potential Outcomes and Risks
- No decision ==> loss of service
- Status quo ==> no savings; AGM fail
- Continue with ForageX ==> poor service; survey fail
- Higher cost offer ==> AGM fail
- New vendor ==> risk of service disruptions
- Audit-ability

A.9 - Opportunity
- Use survey as springboard for regular feedback
- Instil trust from owners and residents
- Create foundation for future tendering situations

A.10 - Next Steps
- Communicate survey results (Thank participants; share results; heads up of what's coming)
- Sit down session with ForageX, Core Team
- Sit down with other bidding vendors
- Interview survey responders to delve into issues / wishes

Raymond meets with Ned and Lorie to review this updated framework but finds it difficult to convey. Plenty of polite nods, sideways glances, glassy stares, mostly from Ned. No questions. The learning curve is too steep.

What was he thinking?

Reviewing his notes, it baffles Raymond how he could ever delude himself into thinking a process that should have started over a year ago could work now? On his own he could make it happen because he knows it well. It's pointless to push for this on the basis it can help future bid endeavours too. Because they are just as incapable of learning. What on earth possessed him to board this sinking ship? Twice?

Unless Raymond's perspective is wrong and he's needlessly complicated this situation, overanalyzed it, merely for the sake of ensuring everything goes smoothly. That he's succumbed to an occupational hazard in trying to apply professional methods when a more laissez-faire approach will suffice. Maybe they see him as too pedantic. Winging it may be the way to go for them, a more realistic way, and Raymond will have to accept planning and quality as hapless casualties not worth the effort.

Perhaps this is a lesson for Raymond about the modern IT world too, a hint his methods of the past are no longer effective and indeed could hinder progress. He may have to accept those methods, and by extension himself, are anachronisms. Adding to his misery is a memo Ned drafts for the survey results. After a brief and pointless summary, he writes this:

> As you are aware, the current contract terminates at the end of September. To ensure an optimal solution for all, the WiFi Committee has begun the process of contacting vendors that can address our needs today and into the future.
>
> The need for technology and bandwidth is growing, thus necessitating services that attain higher speeds. Along with our wish to keep an up-to-date WiFi service and to sustain property values, the Board is exploring novel solutions, including fibre optics.

A weak, vague message that sounds like a cheap version of what Nigel might say. That any possibility of "exploring novel solutions" remains viable in their minds is delusional. Raymond can't hold back responding, but only to Ned:

> The survey response needs to be stronger. I recommend 5 crisp paragraphs roughly comprising:
>
> 1. A thank you with the survey statistics.
> 2. A clarifying statement that this is not a basic contractor replacement and also that it's a service we are compelled to continue, according to the condo declaration.
> 3. Only a modest statement about future trends, including how they add a complexity factor in that we don't want to get stuck in something that will inhibit us down the road.
> 4. A reminder of the contract expiry and we are in contact with vendors, including ForageX, after which we will define the solution specifics.
> 5. A declaration of intent to keep owners posted via updates and perhaps information session(s).

The note must be simple but direct. People will see through it if we don't show focus on the immediate issue, which is ForageX, the prime subject of the survey. Also, since the survey didn't ask if owners were willing to pay more for improved services, I'd expect resistance to any plan that conceivably does so as early as next year.

As long as we keep (and show) focus, this is manageable. I'll be honest, when we met last time I feared we'd taken a step in the wrong direction, talking about fibre optics and other niceties as viable options at this late stage. Talking about it is okay if we have a tactical solution for September. But not if it redirects our energy and puts our heads back into what-if mode. That opportunity was available to you the past few years. Not anymore. Those solutions will have to wait until we're in the clear later this year.

I'm sorry if this comes off as harsh. But I believe in what I say is best for our fellow owners as much as for myself. I'm afraid we've losing sight of how dire the situation is. I would rather risk being harsh than hold back.

It is harsh and Ned does not receive it well, which troubles Raymond enough to send Ned an apology email. It helps stem any bad blood but does little otherwise.

For in subsequent days all semblance of the WiFi committee goes by the wayside. Every detail involves all board members — Gary as well — via trains of Reply All emails that can only breed confusion, reduce clarity, and obfuscate accountability.

An impromptu meeting between Raymond, Ned, and Lorie in the Social Room is meant to clear the air and set parameters for the upcoming vendor sessions. Raymond wants to challenge ForageX on the survey results, only to be told the board intends to take a low-key approach with the incumbent. Low-key.

It's December all over again. On the spot, Raymond decides he's no longer of value to this endeavour, beyond providing his expertise in dealing with vendors and, as a last contribution, he compiles talking points for those sessions.

ForageX:

- Share at high level survey results; is it a surprise to them? What could they do immediately to improve those results with current situation, both in performance and perception?
- Do they have reports or other data to corroborate or dispute? If no reports, why not?
- Since none of us were there at the time, explore how they landed a ten-year contract, who they knew?
- Engage them to discuss their recent offer and how to proceed:

    > Breakdown of offer, what's different from current solution and what's the same?

    > What is impact to users in terms of software, hardware, resets, outages, etc? Are they installing new equipment?

    > What do they propose for 1st and 2nd level support?
- Discuss existing contract:

    > How user data (ids/passwords) are managed and protected?

    > If we do not go with them, what specifically do they need to do to exit and how long would it take?
- Discuss option of month-to-month continuation just in case we find we need more time
- Discuss next steps / next meeting as it is unlikely ForageX will have all the answers at this one

Other Vendors:

- Review Our Requirements (provide separately beforehand)

    > WiFi for all suites + common areas (roof, Social Room, etc.)

    > Technical Support provided by vendor, not property manager

    > Utilize existing infrastructure; minimal in-suite installations

    > Billing to condo corporation, not individual suites

    > WiFi only, no bundling, though they may offer other services to individuals and bill separately
- Get Them To Specify:

    > Hardware, software requirements for communications room or other common areas

    > Hardware / software requirements for suites?

    > Individual setups (i.e. registration, software setup)?

    > Individual privacy, security assurances

    > Technical support process and Service Level Agreement

    > Experience with similar buildings, references

As the meetings are arranged and it becomes clear all board members will attend—even Dennis—Raymond decides to skip them, leaving the board to its own devices. He sees the potential for disaster and opts for plausible deniability. In doing this, he acknowledges the death of the WiFi committee. He'll no longer participate, but is still willing to advise.

A few days later Raymond joins Ned and Lorie at the bar to discuss the ForageX session. No meeting minutes or agenda to review—unlike the November committee kickoff meeting—just a diagram of the vendor's previous proposal on a single sheet of paper. With scribbled notes strewn throughout, notes that could only make sense to the writer who penned them.

Nonetheless it sounds like a decent proposal based on how Ned and Lorie describe it. A bonus is ForageX's offer to waive charges for the current platform after the existing contract ends, until their new solution is in place, guaranteeing continuity of service and a smooth transition. It could save tens of thousands of dollars if the implementation creeps into next year. Which it undoubtedly will. Ironically the delays could pay off financially and in some way salvage their efforts.

However, the appeal in terms of pricing and specifications is countered by a lack of details. It is troubling how credulous Ned and Lorie are with promises from a vendor that performed as poorly as it did in their survey.

Most disturbing is the revelation of Nigel's behaviour. How he grilled ForageX on technical aspects of their solution before abruptly exiting after he got answers.

"Didn't Nigel say he worked with them once?"

"Yeah. A minor project, he said."

"Don't you see? That's a conflict of interest. The way you've described it, it could be inferred he attended solely to probe for confidential information. ForageX could interpret it that way."

Their reactions indicate the message got through in fact, not in essence.

At home, Raymond searches online for the company Nigel provided, who the board plans to meet next week. They have a barebones website with an announcement of a recent marketing hiring. A search brings up the woman's personal website, which includes a résumé. Raymond pulls his AGM documents to find Nigel's résumé. Sure enough, there's a common employer, and both attended the same university. Could be a coincidence but one that's hard to ignore when he notices Nigel removed all the dates from his résumé. Why would he feel the need to do that?

Even if it falls on deaf ears, he has to fire a final email salvo:

Ned and Lorie, I had a revelation last night, culminating in two major issues to be addressed by the board with urgency:

1) Survey Says: Convene Owners' Meeting:
- If you study the survey:
> *26% don't use it, would likely vote to terminate it.*
> *48% (65% of the other 74%) finds it poor or average.*
> *That adds up to 74% who might vote to terminate.*

- With these numbers it may not be too late to give owners an opportunity to weigh in, possibly cancel the service, as it is feasible that two-thirds would opt to do so.

- I recommend convening an owner's meeting ASAP to present the choices and vote. Without that mandate, it would be negligent to unilaterally take such a decision.

2) Potential Conflict of Interest:
- From your description of the talk with ForageX, a board member who earlier shared an affiliation with a candidate vendor, asked proprietary technical questions.

- If the affiliation was disclosed to ForageX, no issue; if not, one could infer the board member was probing on behalf of a competitor and the abrupt exit could look suspicious.

- If we opt for a competitor, ForageX could conceivably sue the corporation based on appearances.

- I do not know if there is a conflict, for I have no evidence, only what you two told me. But even the appearance of a conflict is problematic. I urge you to drop this vendor from the running, at least until all doubt is cleared.

- As to the board member, I'll refrain from recommending any action, except to say that board members ought to take responsibility for the impacts of their actions.

Raymond does not expect a reply, nor does he seek one, nor does he want one, nor does he get one. It's oddly and startlingly liberating in that now he can tend to other parts of his life.

It seems life is cooperating as a day after sending the note, Terri asks to meet him for dinner.

-2 -1 G **M** 2 3 4 5 6 7 8 9 10 11 PH R

"Owners should be owners; vendors should be vendors. Or else my job becomes more difficult."

"No room for people like Alice to help?"

"Lorie, once you mix the two it's hard to keep track of who's doing what. There could be insurance impacts too."

"I suppose."

"You're a nice lady Lorie, everyone likes you. But as a board member, you ought to listen to Gary, and Sheila, and heed their advice in such matters. They're the experts."

"I know, I see your point. As to the landscaper, I studied the contract and I'm struggling to see the savings."

"They're there. Five percent signing incentive bonus, on the first year, which covers most of the client setup fee. Regular cost on the subsequent two years. Pretty standard."

"Client setup?"

"What's that, Nigel?"

"I asked about client setup."

"Yes, we had to do the same with the other contract."

"I don't remember seeing anything about that."

"It's there, Lorie. You can be sure those guys were about to increase their rates. The savings are there, in a roundabout way. Along with a more reliable service and a better reputation."

"Were the other guys really that bad, Gary? I have to admit, I don't look at the grounds much."

"They were getting sloppy. Alice isn't the only one to make noise about it. Their contract clearly states they must provide a minimum of four people when they're here. The last two visits, there've only been three."

"So that's why we're switching?"

"One of the reasons."

"Geez, they've been with us for how long, Lorie? I believe it was one of the first contracts I voted to approve when I first got elected to the board."

"At least eight years."

"Eight years ought to buy them some benefit of the doubt. Couldn't you just monitor it, Gary?"

"I could . . . but the contract is due. The other firm is highly reliable. I know, because they're at my other site. They can start immediately so this is the opportune time to get them."

"Well that does sound good, let's jump on it . . . right, Lorie, there should be a vote. All in favour raise your hands . . . okay, that's unanimous then."

"I'll get that new contract ready for signing."

"Satisfied, Lorie? I am."

"Sure, Stacie."

"Yes, Ned."

"Question for Gary. When do you plan to send out the WiFi survey results memo I sent you?"

"You still want me to?"

"We had the meeting with them so there's no surprise."

"I'll get around to it."

"Loved seeing their faces when we showed how poorly they were doing."

"Bet you did, Nigel."

"I think my questions showed them we're not dummies."

"It did get a bit awkward. Glad we decided to not come at them hard. Our low-key approach was harsh enough."

"I don't agree, Stacie, I think we were too soft."

"Maybe, Nigel, but what would be the point?"

"To keep them honest?"

"They at least have something. Only it doesn't sound like its the full fibre optic to the suites solution I was looking for."

"Only the phone company can do that."

"The phone company is out of the running, right Ned?"

"They're not chomping at the bit."

"How come?"

"We're small potatoes."

"Can't believe in such a modern building that fibre optic is still unavailable. Oh well, it's a start."

"It's available to the building, Stacie, not individual suites."

"I see."

"I'm still not convinced ForageX can deliver even if they say they have something. We have to look at other options."

"Like the contact you gave us, Nigel?"

"Precisely."

"What's the matter, Ned, Lorie. You two look a little funny."

"Stacie, it might be best if Nigel not participate anymore."

"What are you talking about?"

"It has to do with that matter I mentioned to you, Stacie."

"Oh, right. Let's take this offline."

"What matter?"

"Nigel, let's you and I discuss it after. Anything else, before we wrap up?"

"I have some news, of a personal nature, for you, Lorie."

"Oh."

"Your friend Irena, the lady with the blue scooter? Omnirez just hired her granddaughter, Kayla. Sheila is rather impressed with her so far."

"That's terrific. Is she working on our account?"

"That'd be a conflict of interest. Besides, Sheila sees a great potential for her to become a full-fledged property manager. So Kayla is taking classes while performing administrative work at another Omnirez site."

"Then who's looking after her grandmother?"

"There's a professional who comes in. She's not doing well."

"Irena didn't say anything to me when I last saw her. How do you know this, Gary?"

"From Bruce. He has to let the aid worker in and escort her up to the suite."

May

The Retreat

Helps to have supportive folks like Arlene. Makes it pleasant to assist them with their WiFi problems. Comforting too to see she was equally shocked by the survey results. Arlene wants us to stay, afraid of a replacement. Unfortunately, the writing's on the wall, can't be clearer than those results. Or can it? Still confused after that meeting. Here I was expecting, after over a year playing along and working through Gary, to get an opportunity to present our platform to the board, only to be ambushed with that survey. Thought for sure it was the end for us. Then it got weird, still not sure what it meant. Suddenly they got nice. Except for Nigel whose grilling caught me off guard, but I think I handled him well. Unless something I said caused him to go, that his emergency was just an excuse. Hope not, though I was glad to see him go. He and Ned not getting along provides a glimmer of hope. Ned didn't balk at the price increase and our offer to not charge until the new one is in place went over extremely well. Would be tough to lose this client, but with people like Arlene on our side, even if they're as in the dark as we are, we can stay, possibly without forfeiting revenue. Ned and Lorie are trusting, wouldn't be hard to negotiate a contract in our favour. As long as we don't get greedy. Five bucks more per month per suite is about right. For now. Once the new infrastructure is in place, we can acquire other clients in the area. Now that I think of it, why do we need to forfeit revenue if it goes into the new year, next spring? That's what, six months? Their stalling is what prevented us from making it happen in sooner. Give them a deadline, that's what we'll do. And a commitment. If they sign up in the next two weeks, for five years, we'll honour the free window, or part of it. There we are, green lights, Arlene up and running. She recognizes the pattern. She's so appreciative. She'll be fine. We'll be fine.

-2 -1 G M 2 3 4 5 **6** 7 8 9 10 11 PH R

He's lost the six pounds he gained over Christmas. And a ton of anxiety since parting with Ned and Lorie and their floundering effort to deal with the WiFi. Raymond can lose more anxiety by skipping the sixth floor on his stair climbing, floor-crossing, power walks. The sixth floor is a test, in which he dares himself to knock on a certain door. He never does. Is that passing a test? Or failing? A cute conundrum to distract the monotony of going up and down grey stairwells, two steps at a time as Dr. Mason challenged, on rainy days when he can't get outside. Oddly he's never encountered a soul on the sixth floor. Countless people on other floors. Initially that was awkward. Then word spread of a youthful senior traversing hallways, in a Blue Jays headband. If he sees people now, especially older ones, he's rewarded with a kind greeting, as if they consider his presence added security. A few expressed a desire to join him, though no one has yet.

Raymond opens the exit door to continue his ascent to the top. He's almost exhausted by the time he reaches the tenth and his pace slows, his mind drifts. He almost knocks down Alice Greenberg as she exits the elevator. She's in another world too, not stopping to chat as normal. She fumbles for her keys.

"Everything all right, Alice?"

"You know, I wish I could help. I'm good at it."

She tells Raymond about the landscaping at the back, how it's been neglected lately.

"I used to have a garden, a good-sized one, at my house."

"Who won't let you? And why?"

"Gary. Something about it being the vendor's responsibility. I guess they don't want us stepping on their toes. But they aren't doing a good job, at least not lately. I can help. I want to help."

"Maybe Gary took your offer as a criticism."

"But that's silly."

Raymond would have thought so too, prior to dealing with the board and the property manager. But Gary's defensiveness seems to be his character. Poor Alice. All she desires is a chance to get outside, till some soil, plant some seeds, be active as she enjoys the pleasant spring weather. He can empathize with her but can offer little more. Nevertheless, she thanks him for being a good listener, before leaving him to continue his walk/climb.

Raymond pauses in the stairwell. Alice's situation is similar to his in both volunteering personal time at no cost for the good of the condominium. Only to have their efforts thwarted by an uninspired property manager holding far too much sway over a swayable board. A distinction for which he is envious of Alice is her rejection was instant; whereas his was drawn out over six months. In two stages.

He takes the stairs all the way down to the main floor and exits through a side door only to be blinded by a bright sun and wrapped in a humid heat. The parking lot is dry. He circles the building to enter via the front door, intent on lecturing Gary on Alice's behalf, albeit unsure what he'll say or how he'll bring it up. No matter, naturally the office door is closed. It's not lunch hour; it should be open. He checks the hours posted on the door in case they've changed again, but no, the property manager should be here. Or at least a note.

"Gary must have stepped out."

Elle is sitting in a leather chair, poking fingers at a tablet.

"Hi Elle. You waiting for him too?"

"Uh huh. He should be back soon enough."

"So who's minding the fort?"

"The superintendent is around somewhere."

"But what about these hours?"

"Guess he calls his own shots."

Indeed, Raymond thinks. Elle asks if he intends to go to the rooftop picnic, adding she's waiting for Gary to finalize details. Raymond's uniformly pleasant recent encounters with people in the building makes the idea appealing. He'd prefer to forget the WiFi committee failure but that ain't gonna happen; this may be a subtle way to see how much the owners care.

"I'll try. I mean, yes, I'll make it."

"Great."

Before taking a shower, Raymond sends an email to André du Bois, finding the address in Ned's original note, and asks if André can spare time to share why he backed out, what he saw in Ned or the situation that Raymond couldn't see.

Several days pass with no reply. Not as much a surprise as the sense of emptiness it creates within Raymond, exposing his dejection, how badly he desires an ally.

He's taken to spending more time on the balcony, where he can relax and look out towards the noisy, busy street, observing cars and trucks zip by or slow to line up at the intersection. Or look right to a calming lake to watch sailboats or the occasional cargo ship. Until it's spoiled by absurd speculations such as the notion of André with Kayla. Where is she?

A daily pattern evolves to combat his boredom after waking up: check email; breakfast (coffee, juice, banana, two slices of whole wheat toast with jam, or a bowl of Shreddies), preferably eaten on the balcony, otherwise in front of the TV, indulging in urban stresses that no longer impact his life; brushing his teeth; washing dishes; making the bed, tidying up the kitchen, then playing computer solitaire until it gets tedious. That leaves the rest of his day free to cycle, walk or swim a few laps. If he's in an industrious mood, he'll take on housecleaning, dropping his trash down the chute, taking his recycling to the basement (choosing an extended route to avoid seeing Kayla's Civic in his parking space) and of course his power walks up and down and the building. In many ways this is the lifestyle he imagined his retirement would be. Except for the dullness.

Perhaps that's why, despite his involvement with the WiFi committee having terminated, he remains fixated on it. The way it ended — the inevitability of a preventable failure — continues to plague Raymond, recently manifesting in a hyper-alertness to external noises. Any barking dog, honking car, train horn, siren, revving motorbike, beep-beep of a truck in reverse, starting car, lawnmower, yell from a neighbour, disrupts his day, sends him to the balcony to investigate the source.

It's yet another morning — albeit an hour later from sleeping in — as he takes his coffee and slightly burnt toast to the balcony where the sun still glows red behind the distant trees as it rises. Not high enough yet to blind him, which keeps it cool. A small animal scurries amongst the weeds in an undeveloped property across the way, disturbing some robins. One of the birds lands on his balcony rail but doesn't seem to notice Raymond, or his food. A crunchy bite of toast sends it away, leaving Raymond in solitude again. It remains quiet until he hears a scaly snip.

He looks out over the front garden where Alice, wearing a pair of oversize garden gloves, deftly cuts away at hedges with pruning shears. The noise from two pickup trucks slowing at the driveway entrance breaks her concentration. Alice's look of dismay at recognizing the landscapers is visible eight floors up. The trucks presumptuously occupy two and three parking spots respectively. Alice collects her tools and retreats inside.

When the motors shut off, Ned's voice comes through, then Lorie's. Raymond stands up and looks around, locating them at the front entrance walking towards Ned's car. Ned's blond curls blow in the breeze. The car pulls out and has to manoeuvre past a truck. They do spend an inordinate amount of time together.

Ned's car slows as another enters. Each driver rolls down a window. The conversation is brief, cordial before Ned drives off and the other car parks in a visitor's spot. The driver gets out. By the bald patch it's easy to identify Gary as he reaches in the back seat for a binder, which he clutches against his chest while he walks, as if it contains sensitive condo secrets. A glance at his oven clock: nine-thirty-nine. Did Lorie and Ned chastise Gary for his lateness? Hardly. By the rapid nods from Ned, it's more likely he and Lorie were the ones taking direction.

As if seeing Ned and Lorie isn't enough to sour Raymond's morning, seeing them with Gary stirs something that nagged at him for a long time: that the recent issues over the WiFi, along with Alice's frustrations, are symptoms of a deeper concern: the hegemony this man has over board members, vendors, owners, every facet of the condo to the finest detail, not least of which is the minutes. Enough to make the board ineffective. The absurd red herring threat of ForageX sabotaging its client that killed the WiFi committee ought to have highlighted this point. Raymond didn't see it well enough to object and yielded to their knowing better. Leaving him vulnerable to re-board this capsizing ship when it would have been wiser to stay on the blissfully ignorant shore with the other owners. Not let it become the obsession it's become, consuming his far too ample free time.

He's convinced the decision to forego information sessions in December doomed the effort, made it a waste of time. What an opportunity lost for the board to get a sense how owners felt, as well as demonstrate to owners the board is capable of action. It would have given the WiFi committee, and the board, a clear mandate to proceed with confidence and spot potential impacts ahead of time. Then if the process led to a contentious decision, they would have the rationale to defend it. Nigel's unrealistic ideas could be in sync with owners' wishes. If they were willing to wait it out, Raymond would have supported that, knowing his efforts would correspond to expectations. Now the board is doomed to be blind to any reaction.

The horn of a freight train sounds, amplified by the wind, to resonate in Raymond's ear to recall a memory from his odyssey to Europe. It was at the border town in Poland where he stood with a hundred or so others with boxes, bags, and suitcases in a myriad of styles, corralled behind mesh fences, waiting to board the train to L'viv. Uncertain what would happen next, as people disembarked from the inbound train, one car at a time, escorted by armed personnel to a makeshift customs office.

There the passengers approached a desk where an official pointed them left or right. The recollection is superimposed by his memory of Auschwitz and how that left and right decision determined if a prisoner was to live or die.

"You shut that door on purpose, I don't have my key."

"That door is supposed to be kept closed."

"Gary said I could leave it open."

"He would never say that, it's an emergency exit."

"I have an email from him saying so."

Raymond looks down. Two women he sees frequently, one a jogger wiping her brow, the other holding her tiny dachshund in her arms, face each other, about eight feet apart. The younger woman with the dog is in pyjamas. It looks like she's locked out. Why didn't she take her keys? More importantly, if her claim is true, why did Gary say she could prop the emergency side door open? The buzz of a small motor drowns out their voices. It also seems to end the argument too as the women separate.

By plugging in headphones to his laptop, Raymond mutes the subsequent noises issued by weed whackers, lawnmowers, leaf blowers, while still observing and admiring the energy of the youngsters tackling the landscaping, pausing occasionally to check their phones or listen to instructions from a supervisor.

An email comes in. From the phone company sales rep Ned found. The note makes clear they will not bid on the WiFi. What they can do is to put their building at the front of the line for the program to install fibre optic lines directly to each suites. As the program is focused on the city, it could take years to get out this way. But they'll make an exception and install it now, under the proviso that for ten years they can match all competitor offers using those lines. Raymond's impressed with Ned for this win. Personal feelings aside, Raymond's happy for him.

It puts Raymond in a good mood and, with the sun shining, the wind calm, he'll forego the dishes for a power walk. He rises to take in a last breath of freshly cut lawn. The workers are still at it except for one who is talking to Gary casually. The young man turns and Raymond notices a resemblance in their profiles. Could they be related? Uncle and nephew? Father and son? A case of nepotism?

A call from Terri interrupts his thoughts before his paranoia goes too far. She was to call him a few weeks ago but he's heard nothing until now. Her voice sounds calm on the surface but he suspects she's making an effort not to sound frantic.

She doesn't disclose what it's about and just says she wants to meet for dinner that evening. Her tone is hard to decipher. It might be personal, might be work. He suggests meeting her at a restaurant near the library where Raymond can go early to find books about blockchain. Until then he'll watch online videos on the subject and risk falling asleep.

He's still a little dozy when it's time to leave. He catches the elevator but forgets to press a button. The door closes, the car remains still. He presses a button and the elevator descends, but stops at the sixth floor. A woman he's never seen gets on and presses G, which is when he realizes he pressed P2 by mistake. Two people are waiting in the lobby for an elevator going up. Raymond decides to continue to avoid explaining.

He exits into the parking garage and wanders to his parking spot. There he finds a nearly new white Corolla. Kayla's car is a Civic, at least ten years old. Did she trade up? Raymond returns to the lobby where Bruce waves hello.

"Bruce, you know Kayla Slaske, right?"

"Irena's granddaughter? Of course."

"There's another car in the spot I'm renting her."

"Yeah, yeah, that's Cindy's car."

"Cindy?"

The property management office door opens and out walks Gary who pays no attention to Bruce or Raymond.

"Afternoon, Gary."

"Oh. Hi Bruce."

Gary rushes off.

"Does he have a meeting or something?"

"How would I know?"

"Right. So who is Cindy?"

Bruce tells him that Cindy is the personal care worker hired to look after Kayla's grandmother while Kayla is on a course out of town. Raymond is miffed at first but quickly determines that she pays for the spot, it's not his business what car she parks in it. Bruce then tells him the old woman is dying. It's annoying to Raymond how Bruce is well informed about Kayla. Then again, his negligence in ignoring her email probably justifies it.

"By the way, did Kayla say what kind of course?"

"She's learning to be a property manager. A board member got Omnirez to help her out."

"Omnirez? She's working for them?"

"All I know is they recommended the course to help her get her licence."

"Out of town?"

"Yes, I forget where. Couple of hours away, I think."

Even though Kayla's talked about it before, the actuality of her becoming a property manager puzzles Raymond. In a way, it seems a betrayal, the loss of an ally to the other side. Which is silly, because if that's what she wants to do — and she did before he got a whiff of that world — that's her business too.

Nonetheless, the notion rattles in his head enough to inhibit making sense of the blockchain books at the library. He defers signing them out, not wanting to seem presumptuous to Terri.

Good thing because their dinner is not about work. This is immediately evident on seeing Terri in a tight skirt and wearing more makeup than usual. The grey in her hair is now chestnut. And it looks restyled. With emotion, she again chastises him for leaving for Europe without word, clarifying it's not because of the project, but because she needs a friend.

"I'm getting that divorce."

With that opening, she spills the details, and their dinner is a long one. She picks up the tab and with a smile says she hopes to see Raymond soon, to let him talk about his trip, realizing she dominated their dinner with her own woes. Then she adds:

"I may have good news about the project then too."

It's a pleasant evening so he suggests then insists that Terri leave her car where it is to walk back to his condo to give her a chance to sober up. A wise move because he frequently needs to put an arm around her to keep her balanced.

Once inside, she's lucid, strolling around the condo, peering into both bedrooms, both bathrooms, and laundry closet, before putting her hands on the kitchen island to survey his home as a general might survey a conquered city.

"Nice place for a retirement, Raymond. What have you got to drink here?"

"The date's finalized for the picnic? Second Wednesday in June? I can send out the notice?"

"You can, Gary. By the way, will you be joining us?"

"I'm at my other site on Wednesdays."

"Right, I'll probably skip it too."

"Me as well."

"Come on, Nigel, Stacie, it would be nice to have the full board represented."

"Relax, Dennis, I'm confident you and Lorie will adequately carry the load for us. And Ned."

"Gee thanks, Nigel."

"Guys, come on."

"By the way, what'll you say, Ned, if they ask if you picked a vendor yet for the WiFi?"

"Come to the picnic if you want my response."

"Funny. I think it's silly I'm no longer involved as I can offer the best technical perspective, as you saw at that session, now that your owner has faded into the background."

"Thanks to you, Nigel."

"I thought you said he quit on you."

"He did, but you didn't help matters."

"You worry too much about what Tibbett said."

"No, Nigel, Ned's right. You shouldn't have acted that way at the meeting with ForageX. It didn't look good."

"That's crazy. Clearly I was the only one able to determine if what they're selling isn't bull. Whether they can deliver or not."

"Be that as it may, you can't be part of this process anymore. But don't think we don't appreciate your efforts to this point."

"Fine. Just tell me if my contact is still in the running."

"Come to the picnic and find out."

"Ned, Nigel is still part of the board and has a right to know where things stand, even if he no longer has a vote."

"We've ruled out the cable and phone companies, that's it."

"Really? Why is that?"

"Because we're small potatoes, Dennis. Nigel, as you know, we're having a follow-up with your contact next week."

"Thanks, Lorie. I understand your concern, Stacie, but I still need to be there. So let me know when—what's so funny, Ned?"

"Nothing."

"Look, you guys, your bickering gets us nowhere. As Sheila and Gary always remind us we must appear united as a board."

"We know that. We are."

"It would be easier if we were so in the boardroom too. That includes the e-mail boardroom. Let me remind you our position is not that Raymond quit on us, regardless of what any of you might want to think, but that his plan is untenable."

"Why is that, Stacie?"

"Because, Dennis, his proposal explicitly cut out myself and Gary, which made it a non-starter."

"Well said. Always keep your property manager involved."

"Let's talk about the fibre optic offer. It sounds good."

"I agree, Ned, I've been itching for fibre optic to the suites for a long time. My brother has it in the city, it's great."

"But it doesn't address your current concern, right?"

"No, Gary, it doesn't."

"Not only that, it involves coordinating entry into the suites over the summer, possibly."

"About fifteen minutes per suite, that's all."

"Too much for some people. Especially for a feature most if not all will not use, at least not right away. Plus fifteen minutes times one hundred fifty suites, we're talking dozens of hours of them taking up my time and the superintendent's time."

"What do you advise then, Gary?"

"Not confusing folks with something unrelated to the WiFi."

"Not even if some expressed interest? Like you, Stacie?"

"It pains me to say it, because I've wanted it for a while, but it's in our best interest if we not proceed with this, not now."

"They are making an exception for us, it's time limited."

"Exception. So they say."

"Come on, Nigel, you know as well as me there's a big push for this. Who knows how long it'll take to finish the city. Could be years before they come our way."

"What if they hear we didn't capitalize on an opportunity to enhance the value of their units while we had it?"

144

"I'm not disagreeing with you, Ned. But summer is coming and time is running short for the WiFi. Concentrate on that. If it means missing an opportunity, so be it. We'll keep it between us. What they don't know won't annoy them, right Gary?"

"Absolutely, Stacie."

"What is it now, Ned?"

"I should probably add that the offer was sent to Raymond Tibbett as well. So he is aware of it."

"If he makes an issue of it, we'll come up with something."

"Right, Ned, right."

June

The Rooftop Picnic

-2 -1 G M 2 3 4 5 6 7 8 9 **10** 11 PH R

People used to say: Alice Greenberg has the greenest lawns with the prettiest flowers, that her house was a true green burg, ha. Now here is this Gary fellow dismissing me as usual with a "why would you want to do that?" as if pitching in to help is a sin. Raymond has it all wrong. Gary isn't taking my offer as criticism, he isn't hurt by it, no, he's protecting his crappy landscaping company. I love it here but oh how I miss my old bungalow garden, miss toiling in the soil. Why shouldn't I indulge in an old hobby, help out my own little way like that nice accountant fellow encouraged us to do at the AGM? Without having to run for the board, like Lorie, who can never stop meddling in little fixes. Me, I could never run for the board, my skills are in gardening. The skills to make the surroundings as lovely as our elegant building. So many ideas, each time I look out my balcony on which I'm running out of space. Rules are rules I suppose. Maybe it's a union thing, some clause in their contract that doesn't allow intervention by owners, even if those owners can do a better job. Sadly, this new company is no better than the previous guys. Negligent. Missing spots the previous guys didn't miss. Those flower beds need attention if the tulips have any chance of lasting even another week. Oh dear. I want to do it now. Maybe if I get up early on the weekend.

The silence about the WiFi, with just over three months to go, is bewildering. Raymond admits it still gets to him, particularly on rainy days when he's stuck in his suite and the exhaustion from his power walks, which at one time provided a respite for his anxiety, prove no longer effective. Occasionally he mentally wills the board to succeed; more often he finds himself hoping for a colossal failure to embarrass them to the point owners step in to say: enough is enough.

Why bother? Why care? Truth is, he does care, he can't help it. Whether it's out of wounded pride or genuine concern for his fellow owners isn't relevant anymore; a cloud hangs over him, darkening his mood with few breaks. The option of selling his condo and leaving arises from time to time but is quickly shot down by the reality he wants to live here and his pride will not allow himself to be chased out. So what does he do? Go for one of the three board seats up for grabs? Maybe.

Of course, he'll have to socialize to ensure the best chance of getting elected. No better time to start than today, June 11, the date of Elle's rooftop picnic. The date strikes him as familiar but he is unable to connect it to anything.

Just before the elevator door opens to the roof, he reminds himself of his strategy. While it would be tempting to expose all the WiFi failings to everyone, he intends to contain his feelings on that topic and instead be free, easy, friendly. He opens the beer can he took with him, takes a sip, and walks through a couple of doors to a stunningly bright sun, so bright it almost forces him to go back for sunglasses. But his eyes adapt quickly and the glare diminishes once he steps onto the patio stones. To his right are two men, neither of whom he knows. They glance at Raymond and return to their conversation.

Raymond meanders through several people to the barbecue where he finds Lorie and Ned aiding Elle, who is quite adept at handling a grill. A warm greeting cements Raymond's resolve to play nice. Lorie gets him a bun, as Ned points to a table with condiments, napkins, paper plates, and plastic utensils.

"So how's it going with the WiFi?"

"Oh, Ray, it's just Romper Room."

Someone calls for Ned before Raymond can ask what that means. Lorie presents a plate to Elle who expertly flips a burger and does a last check. Far across the water, two faded greyish bars rise vertically out of the water. Niagara Falls. Elle takes the plated burger away, leaving Lorie alone to tend the grill.

"You two are struggling, aren't you?"

"Hey, it's Ned's baby."

Selling him out already. They're in over their heads but only Lorie seems aware of it. Such a shame. The mood overall is too pleasant to spoil; any lingering inclination to expose this fiasco to his fellow owners vanishes.

Gary then shows up, declares he broke away from his other condo to make an appearance. Hmm, Raymond thinks, does he do the reverse too? That might explain his early departures and late arrivals, though not necessarily excuse them. The guy bugs Raymond and he wishes it weren't so. Hard to imagine how he garners so much deference from Ned and Lorie. Gary is smiling and unusually talkative today, charming even. Raymond asks about the other building he manages, its location, how the two compare. Gary tells him they're similar, both just over a decade old, both with twelve residential floors and a roof patio.

"Same builder?"

"No, theirs didn't have as many issues."

The conversation is relaxed, without any trace of the tension Raymond would have expected.

"So Gary, I hear you're worried after this AGM we'll end up with a rogue board?"

"What do you mean?"

"I guess, with three seats up, the majority could change."

"I never—what concern is it of mine? I work with whoever is elected to the board."

"I imagine there's certain types who—"

"Excuse me."

Gary abruptly shifts his attention to Lorie. Raymond smiles, now itching to prod the property manager about the landscape worker he saw Gary talk to. That seems fishier after this. He lets the temptation pass, remembering his plan; besides, it would be impossible to not come across as goading.

Raymond steps away to socialize, though the few people he knows are locked into little groups. Elle approaches. Being the great connector she is, Elle pulls Raymond into a group of three older men. To Raymond's surprise, Stacie, the board president, joins in, followed by Dennis. He may be getting paranoid but he senses they're trying to read him, trick him into revealing what he might be up to. It would be great if they challenged him with a direct question. But they only discuss mundane matters. This, oddly, is more infuriating. Is he the only owner who cares about the WiFi or how the condo is run? It would appear so.

Several loud sirens break up conversations to draw a crowd to the balcony from where they can see two cruisers blocking in a pickup truck on the street below. The tension is palpable as two policemen warily approach the truck, hands ready at their guns. Only the driver surrenders without a fuss, draining the drama from the onlookers who disperse back to their groups or into the building. Soon only about a dozen remain. But then an influx of new arrivals restores the liveliness.

Raymond's drawn to two attractive young women holding court, surrounded by several seniors. Such a gap in the building demographics. It apparently doesn't faze the girls who describe how they find everyone friendly here, pointing out they feel as if they are equal to owners, adding they would never have been invited to this gathering at their previous condo rental. The thin blonde teaches at a Montessori school while the brunette is an office supervisor. The older folks are clearly charmed by youth.

Raymond comes across Alice Greenberg talking to Marjorie Gibbons, a lady from the third floor, who seems stressed.

"You don't have issues with your pipes backing up, Alice?"

"Not that I can recall."

"It just keeps happening. And I keep having to get Gary to call a plumber to snake the line. At least he doesn't resist me the way he used to."

"That is odd. How often?"

"Twice a year. At least. Harold thinks it's a design flaw from the beginning. Gary denies it, says that's silly."

"Gary wasn't here when the building was built. Why don't you ask Lorie?"

"I have but she's acting strange lately, unhelpful, telling me to take it up with management."

The ladies' conversation pushes Raymond's buttons. Deflect and deny, deflect and deny. Even Lorie, likeable Lorie, is now a party to it. Raymond looks towards the barbecue, the treasurer is watching him. Not him, behind him. Lorie hands the tongs to Elle, then rushes to the door to stand in front of the entrance.

"How nice, it's Irena. It's her birthday today, you know? My goodness, she'll roast in that long-sleeve blouse."

"You know why she always wears sleeves."

"Oh yes, of course. What a survivor. She should be proud."

"At least she won't get sunburnt."

The two women chuckle respectfully. Their exchange sends Raymond's heart racing.

Lorie holds the door while others guide the scooter carrying the old woman up over the lip. Right behind is Kayla carrying a square box, no doubt with a cake inside. Lorie guides them to a clear space by the barbecue, far from Raymond. Kayla glances his way. A slight stutter in her step indicates she noticed him.

He moves aside to clear a path for Alice and Marjorie to go to their friend, hoping Kayla comes to take their place, if only to briefly acknowledge his presence. Instead, Kayla stays with her Babcia, with Lorie, with Alice and Marjorie and others who join in to sing an indistinct version of *Happy Birthday* before sharing cake. At this point Kayla turns her back to Raymond. It makes him nauseous to fight a losing battle to stay put.

He is merely inches behind Kayla once they finish the song. He waits for Irena to blow out a single candle. During the light clapping he leans down to whisper in her ear:

"Happy Birthday, Kapo Irena. I bring you a special wish on behalf of Jan, Frantiszek, and my father, Leo for a safe voyage to hell for you and your SS officer boyfriend."

The woman's muscles tense up but she doesn't turn around. With an internal rush of righteousness, it's enough to know his words and tone conveyed the desired effect. He leaves.

However, once inside and descending the stairs, his feeling of moral superiority does an about face. The impact of what he just did hits him like a baseball bat smacking a piñata, releasing a bounty of guilt. His steps slow. He agonizingly replays his irrevocable words. It seems to take forever to get inside his suite and to slump into the easy chair with a beer he barely sips.

A light on his phone is flashing, a voicemail message from Terri. He deletes it, but then wonders if it was an update on the project, perhaps even a contract. However, there's nothing in his email, other than a note from a strange account.

It's from Lech. Apparently Jan is dying, with only months to live. Is the universe intent on persecuting Raymond, choosing to connect Irena's birthday to Jan's imminent death? His response to Lech is a terse note of gratitude for sharing the news. He can't think of anything else to say.

He's not sure if it's minutes or hours he's been dozing when a sharp police-type rapping at his door startles him into spilling some beer. He goes to answer but looks in the peephole first. It's Kayla. He opens the door and she bursts in.

"What did you say to her? To Babcia?"

"She didn't tell you?"

"She won't tell me, she's too upset at what you said."

"Would you like a beer?"

"No, I would not like a beer."

"Just to calm you down while I explain."

The offer is genuine but he's stalling, Raymond knows, not only to come up with an explanation, but also because it thrills him that she's in his suite after so long. Only the feeling clearly isn't mutual.

"What. Did. You. Say. Huh?"

"All right, but at least please sit down, and let me give a full explanation."

"No, I want to know your words. Your exact words."

In a way, this is better, even though his uncertainty of how these specific words came to him makes them confusing. Unless Kayla knows and has known all along. If true, that could reveal much. He repeats what he said verbatim, the harsh words that have rattled in his head the past hour, feeling a release doing so.

Kayla's reaction is not confusion, nor a confession, nor even sadness, but a combination that shows she gets the gist of it.

"You're claiming it's your father who's the victim and that my Babcia is the — is that what your saying?"

"Precisely."

"And how do figure that?"

"I don't figure it. I discovered it, on my trip to Poland."

"Poland? That's where you went? Without a word?"

Her surprise is genuine. Raymond spots anger coming back in her moist eyes. Or is it hurt? He tries to explain he left out of shame for his past, to face the truth. She's buying none of it.

"You twisted the lies you found into a story to throw at us. I can't believe you would do that to an old woman, a dying old woman, on one of her last birthdays."

The tears activate the guilt within Raymond, but that guilt quickly turns to anger. He is right; she is wrong. She's being lied to but can't or won't even fathom the possibility. Blind faith is leading Kayla down a misguided path. It pisses him off enough to not feel sorry for her, but not enough to lash back. It would do more harm, especially if he blurted out his next thought: that Irena's death is long overdue.

Kayla leaves, without pulling the door closed behind her. It gets stuck on the mat to stay open. His phone rings. It's Terri.

"Where've you been? I've been calling all day."

"It's been a challenging day."

"You sound terrible. Is everything all right?"

"Terri, it's my turn to need a friend."

"I'll be there in an hour."

"No, I didn't meant that . . ."

"I'm bringing champagne and a bit of news I guarantee will cheer you. Raymond, my long-time friend, we have something to celebrate."

"Warned you that picnic would be a minefield."

"What are you talking about? I thought it went splendidly. I though Elle did a terrific job and everyone had a terrific time."

"I have to agree with Dennis on this one, Gary, it was much more pleasant than I expected. Did someone say something that bothered you?"

"Forget about it."

"No, Gary, let's hear it."

"All right. It was Raymond Tibbett."

"What about him?"

"From whom did he get the notion about a rogue board?"

"Rogue board? What do you — yes, Lorie?"

"It might have been me. Or did you say something, Ned?"

"It was you, Lorie. I remember Raymond had a strange look when you said it. I think it was when the three of us were at the bar to talk about the survey."

"Then I'm sorry, Gary."

"How often have I said, never quote my words, particularly what I say at board meetings. That's for directors, not residents. For board matters, even casual, offhand comments must be kept confidential. Only share what we agree to share."

"You're right. But at the time Raymond was still with us."

"Turns out he never was with you was he? Which shows the risk of involving non-board members."

"Again, I'm sorry, but is it really such a big deal? Stacie?"

"Don't get upset, Lorie, we'll deal with it."

"I don't want to come down hard on you. Just that it's not in your interest to remind anyone three of you are up for election. It could inspire others to become candidates."

"It's okay, Gary, you're right. Lorie's a big girl. I'll be up for election too. Though I'm president and think I'm well regarded, I'd be more comfortable with less competition."

"I'm not upset. Consider it a lesson learned."

"All right. Lesson learned. For all of us, I hope."

"Now I do have a concern over this software contract. Gary, since Omnirez is a partner of this firm, maybe you can help."

153

"That's more Sheila's territory, but what's the issue, Lorie?"

"They want us to pay up front for the full five years. I'm not comfortable with that."

"The partnership Omnirez has with them protects you. It's why we are on the contract too. A five year term is reasonable."

"Maybe, but they want the full amount up front. We can't afford it, not unless we liquidate a GIC."

"They want us to pay for five years in advance?"

"That's right, Stacie."

"Okay, I'm with Lorie, maybe we should hold off."

"But that would mean continuing to use the ForageX site to store our notices and using outdated methods to book the Social Room, guest suite, manage parcels, service requests, and so on."

"Good point, Nigel, we don't want that."

"We can work out an arrangement to use one of our bulk licences. Then we'll bill you monthly at a marginally better rate, which we get because of the business we do at other buildings."

"Kind of like leasing, right Gary?"

"Kind of, Stacie, but without interest."

"Sounds good. Will that work for you, Lorie?"

"I suppose."

"Nigel, you have something?"

"I would like to understand it better. Does putting it under Omnirez introduce any restrictions?"

"Well, it would make Omnirez their direct client, the ones who administer it."

"Which is no different than what you do now, right Gary?"

"Hold on Ned, we don't do anything now, so it wouldn't be exactly the same, would it?"

"You're right, not exactly the same. I'll get Sheila to sit down with you, she can explain it better than I can. Keep in mind, the longer it takes to sign the contract, the longer we continue using the site built by ForageX, as Nigel pointed out."

"More like slapped together. It's so ugly."

"We all agree on that, Nigel."

"Lorie, can you work this out with Gary and Sheila?"

"Absolutely, Stacie."

"Thanks."

"And everyone, let's avoid engaging this Raymond Tibbett in anything other than small talk. Lorie. Ned."

"He's off the committee for good, as far as I'm concerned. Is that sufficient? Gary, you're shaking your head."

"Raymond is the type to stir up things."

"Ignore him, gotcha—yes, yes I know, but be pleasant."

"Always be pleasant, even if it becomes difficult. But I think the one who has to be most careful is you, Lorie."

"I know, Gary, I know."

July

The Reconciliation

-2 -1 G M **2** 3 4 5 6 7 8 9 10 11 PH R

Okay, place not in too bad a shape. No tears in the furniture and the appliances appear to be in working order. A few scuff marks on the walls. I can get Angela to let her girls to do their magic – the benefit of dating the owner of a mobile maid service – and in a day or two I'll be able to rent it out again. Plenty of demand for the building, think I'll bump it up a couple of hundred bucks. That should filter out sketchier applicants. Wait, what's this mess in the bedroom? Did Justin and his girlfriend have a fight before leaving? Okay, just a stack of papers, I don't mind that. Of course one flies away; why do I keep trying to pick up things while I have my phone in hand? This is weird. Oh, it's that WiFi survey. Now it makes sense. The actual survey was dropped off by hand for Justin, while the results were emailed to me. Actually, that makes no sense. If this is from the board why don't I, the owner paying for the WiFi, the one who elects them, get the survey? Instead of a tenant who might simply ignore it? Makes me wonder what else I've missed, what else has been decided or ignored on my behalf by one of my tenants. Can't blame Justin, he probably thought I got it. Can't expect my tenants to let me know about every little event. Isn't that what I have a board of directors for? Maybe I ought to start attending those AGM meetings again. Reminds me, got to print off one of the updated rules packages for whoever will rent it next.

-2 -1 G M 2 3 4 5 6 7 **8** 9 10 11 PH R

The first meeting with Stan and his developers does not require Raymond to commute downtown because the developers are in Vancouver. It's a dubious arrangement to Raymond, who is not used to developers developing far from their team leaders. As a contractor, it's wise to keep such concerns private and focus on putting forth a positive impression. Which is difficult with the fire alarm ringing out, triggering reactions from thousands of kilometres away.

"What the hell is that, Raymond?"

"Damn it. Sorry, everyone. Just the monthly test. It's over."

"What the hell was that, Raymond? Is there an emergency?"

The analog voice startles him, though not as much as seeing Terri's pale, naked shoulders nudging out over his bath towel, another towel wrapped around her hair. He panics but manages to press the mute button with one hand while the other is at his lips, shushing her. Thank God it's not a videoconference.

"I'm on a call with Stan and his team."

Why she finds this funny is beyond him, but her laughter has a way of softening the echoing ringing in his ears.

"Thank God, that was awful. Is there a fire?"

"No, it's the monthly test. It's over. Do keep quiet."

Terri looks at her wrist, but it's bare, so she goes back to the bedroom to collect her watch and puts it on while he continues the call. He jumps when she starts massaging his shoulders.

"Stan, I don't recall it working that way. I'll check it out after the meeting and get back to you by end of day."

"Can't believe I slept in. You got any coffee?"

"What's that Raymond, what did you say?"

"Sorry guys, excuse me a moment."

He presses mute, then ushers Terri to the kitchen. He pours a cup for her, refills his own. He repeats the need to keep quiet; she laughs again.

"Relax, Raymond, they'd never guess it was me. Besides, it might impress them to think you're a stud."

"But that's not . . . and we didn't . . ."

"I know, I know, but let them assume otherwise."

"I should get back to — hey, shouldn't you be on this call?"

"Yes, probably, but I trust Stan. And I trust you."

She goes to get dressed. It's quiet in his office and Raymond checks to see if the connection is still there. It is but Stan and the others are silent, perhaps on mute, perhaps gossiping. It makes Raymond chuckle as he's reminded of one of the Elvis Costello songs they listened to last night.

There's a sound from outside. A bark? That bark? He wants to check, but can't disrupt the meeting again.

"Hey everyone, I'm back. Sorry about that. Just the monthly fire alarm test. It's over."

The silence breaks. Someone expresses relief the fire threat wasn't real; apparently they were waiting for Raymond. Other than that, it's a good start and the kickoff goes as Stan predicted it would. It's been a long time since Raymond's worked with people this engaged on a project.

He hangs up and the quiet fills with traffic sounds coming through the open screen door to his balcony. Along with a tiny yelp that's either an echo or his imagination. He finds Terri still there, relaxing in his suede recliner, sipping coffee as her bare legs stretch out on the matching ottoman.

"Nice morning sun here. How'd the meeting go?"

"Good. Except this blockchain stuff is way over my head."

"You'll figure it out before I do. Who knows, maybe I'll coax you out of retirement. You know, our health benefits cover the little blue pills."

"Ha ha. Guess I was kind of nervous. Sorry about that."

"Oh my God, don't be. I'm only kidding, please don't think I expect anything. You're a comfort in this difficult period for me

158

and if that's all it ends up being, so be it. It's more important to have an empathetic friend with a safe haven than sex."

"Terri, the work helps me out too, so I hope you continue to consider this a safe haven."

"All right then. On that note, I'll take my leave. I'm looking forward to the walk back to my car."

"You remember where it is?"

"Near the library, like before. I'll find it."

He escorts Terri to the foyer where she slips into her purple sandals. Their hug isn't too awkward before he opens the door. A piece of paper floats in the air before landing in the hallway. Terri picks it up.

"'Please meet me at the BBQ at eleven?' Signed, K. I'm sorry, this is personal, I thought it was junk."

"It's okay."

Raymond takes the paper and reads it. The question mark is curious. Either Kayla's anger has vanished or settled enough to talk. He recalls the ambulance that came last week, without any alarms. Was it for her grandmother? Did her Babcia die or go to the hospital? If she died, did she leave her lies behind?

"Who's K? And quite a flourishing capital at that? Definitely a woman. Maybe a lack of blue pills wasn't the issue?"

Terri laughs teasingly, pre-empting any reaction, perhaps to ensure there is no doubt she's kidding. She gives him a peck on the cheek and walks to the elevator without looking back.

That Kayla wants to talk is a good sign. He checks the time, unsure when it was he heard the bark. Meet at eleven? How can she be sure he'd see the note in time?

The rooftop is eerily empty and looks bigger with the tables and everything cleared, no remnants of last month's picnic. The barbecue is shut, a wooden scraper swaying from a rope. He's at the same spot where he whispered in the old woman's ear. Why would Kayla want to meet here?

He waits several minutes, pacing along the railing, looking out across the lake. Sailboats glide by. A slow cargo ship makes its way to Hamilton, or Niagara to navigate the Welland Canal, farther off. Its pace mesmerizes Raymond. He ought to come up here more often to relax.

A deep sigh startles him. Raymond twists to see Kayla, her thick black hair a lovely mess, her eyes red. From tears? How long she's been standing there he can't say, but it's evident she's been waiting for him to turn her way by how she puts her arms around him and holds him.

"I'm so sorry, Ray."

He's at a loss for words. This isn't what he expected. All his thoughts while taking the elevator up focused on defending his position. All that has to be expunged before he can say a word. It's fine as Kayla seems content to hold him. She's thinner.

"I'm so sorry. I'm so ashamed. I'm so — "

"Hey, relax."

"I'm really ashamed, but I still love her, I miss her."

"So she is . . . Ir — your grandmother, is she gone?"

"Please just hold me."

The embrace fills Raymond with a warm, pleasant sensation he hasn't experienced in months. Years. It's so natural, so caring. With Terri there's awkwardness; with Kayla it's natural.

His greatest fear right now is for the roof door to open and for someone to emerge to spoil their moment. Though the true danger of spoiling lies not in an inadvertent intrusion but in his impulse to kiss her. At this, she recoils. Firmly, not harshly.

"What's wrong?"

"Oh no, Ray, oh no. That can never be. Not now."

He wants to protest but then gets a metaphorical rebuke in the form of his cargo ship now having sailed from sight. Still, he can't admit defeat so readily and gives her an appealing look.

"Oh, Ray, if you can't see that . . ."

He can't see it. His emotions, his gut, mess with his mind, inhibit it from getting past basic logic: this girl just lost the most important person in her life, while also discovering the horrors the dead woman perpetrated. The logic is less convincing in his heart than in his mind. If they are to have a chance, he will have to wait, he will have to be less than truthful.

"I can see it. But we can remain friends?"

"Oh, most definitely."

Her first smile is followed by a shorter but happier embrace that makes Raymond breathe a sigh of relief. That sigh gets him past his gut to realize that while Kayla may know the truth, she hasn't processed it. That will take time. He has to concede there is enough doubt about what actually happened in the past—for isn't Raymond somewhat blindly believing Jan too?—that Kayla may hold doubts that need confirming or at least time to settle.

"Do you mean it, that you can see it?"

"It's not easy, but yes."

"Okay, good."

Then she tells him about her grandmother dying and a note she left, a blanket *mea culpa* confessing she did terrible things in the war and to not dispute any accusations by Raymond. It's too pat, too unspecific, insincere even. Does Irena actually bear guilt for her actions? It may sound crazy but the thought crosses his mind that she engineered her own end as a dare to Raymond to expose her. He vows to not reveal what he learned from Jan until Kayla asks. He lets a moment of silence pass.

"I've missed seeing you and Buster around."

"You know I was away for another reason."

"I heard you were taking a course."

"Yep. When you took off abruptly to Poland, I needed to get away too. You know my Babcia was friends with the treasurer, Lorie, and she was able to get me a job with Omnirez."

"Our property management company?"

"Even better, they're training me to be a property manager. Maybe soon I'll be looking after a building just like this one."

"I see."

Raymond's heart sinks. She has no clue why it bothers him. Why would she? If only she was there as a sounding board last month during those frustrating times, if only he'd never met her grandmother. Then she'd understand how this news might feel like a betrayal.

"You don't look happy for me."

"It's not that."

But it is that, he realizes, as he shares with her the end of the WiFi committee. His efforts to remain objective only clutter the telling. At least he doesn't come across as self-pitying. And it is a comfort to have such an ardent listener who gives a sense she is on his side and can empathize with his message.

"Kayla, I think the real problem is Gary, and how he seems to be able to twist these directors around at will."

"Of course it is. At one of my classes, there was a discussion about such situations. Lorie and Ned need to be stronger."

"Amen."

"So what's going on with the WiFi now?"

"Who knows?"

"Look, if I were the property manager, I'd know when to get out of the way and when to insert myself."

Raymond smiles at the naïveté, which he finds charming.

"Does Lorie know you and I are . . . friends?"

"She wasn't looking, no one was, when you spoke to Babcia. You were gone so quickly. Why?"

"How close are you with her?"

"She was Babcia's friend, not mine, but she helped get me a job with — wait a minute, all this about Gary and the board, are you up to something?"

"Kayla, I'm glad we're talking again. I hope we can see each other more often. You were my only friend in the building."

"Are."

"What do you mean?"

"I didn't tell you? Babcia's will allows me to stay in her suite as long as I want. She left the property to my parents but they can't sell it until I leave or stop paying rent. So we can hang out as much as we want. Discretely, of course."

That's great, Raymond wants to say, because it is great. Had they been anywhere other than the roof where his verbal assault on her grandmother took place, he would say it. It's irrelevant that Kayla appears willing to forgive him — otherwise why ask to meet on the roof? — he will always be ashamed about it when he's up here.

"I'm not a favourite of the board now. I wouldn't want your relationship with them to be tainted by me."

"I thought your issues were with Gary?"

He has to give details of the past few months leading up to the picnic. What makes it a challenge is her expression is hard to read: he isn't sure if Kayla's amused or bored. She doesn't ask any questions and lets him relate his story, then grins.

"Maybe I can help you, maybe I'll be your spy."

Raymond laughs but then she tells him her grandmother never cared for Gary and she especially hated how he got Lorie to perform tasks the property manager or superintendent ought to perform, such as putting up notices in elevators or even the one time helping rearrange Gary's office."

"I thought Lorie enjoyed doing stuff like that."

"But why make such a big deal of it? Have some dignity, be proud of your role, which is treasurer, not custodian. Babcia got incensed at that, at Lorie doing what Gary should do. One time she told him how Gary was rude to her friend, Alice."

"I know Alice."

"Alice just wants to plant flowers and stuff but Gary gets all official on her and rejects her. Guess whose side Lorie was on?"

"I know."

"Yeah. You may have your issues with the board, but many have them with Gary. Except my grandmother who he seemed to treat like royalty, despite her opinion of him."

Kayla's intensity startles Raymond, largely because her tone is soft, tender. There's a calculating mind there. Yet he enjoys it. As if it were scripted, he sees something below and points.

"Kayla, see that girl, in the pyjamas, walking her dog?"

"Ah, Melissa, with Casey. He and Buster play."

Raymond describes the altercation between Melissa and the woman about the side door, how Melissa claimed Gary allowed her to prop it open. Kayla shakes her head.

"So she was lying about the permission?"

"No, I believe Melissa. It sounds like something Gary would do. It's no secret that he prefers renters over owners."

"Melissa is a renter?"

"Yes. I'm glad you told me about this."

"Are you going to tell on him? Wait, you want his job?"

"What a thought, Ray."

"That'd be great if you could."

"Another thing, I no longer need your parking spot. I sold the van with the lift because now I can use Babcia's spot."

Losing the extra cash doesn't bother Raymond, as he has an income, and it makes it easier to keep their friendship discrete.

They agree to limit how often and at what locations they see each other, and to act casually indifferent if others are around. Meaning no games of pool or meetings on the roof. No walking the dog together. He won't visit her suite — nor does he care to — as Lorie occasionally drops by to check on Kayla. All that leaves is for her to visit him at quieter hours. Even that's risky because Buster has to come; if he doesn't, his barking due to loneliness will upset her neighbours.

An evening routine develops in which Kayla takes Buster for his walk/run that, since she started intensifying it to lose weight, exhausts the aging pet. They start around seven-thirty, at which time Raymond steps onto his balcony. Her route is the same each time so after he waves he knows they'll be back in an hour to hang out, to watch television or talk. Once in a while, on weekends, they share a bottle of wine or a few beers, but only so much to ensure their relationship remains platonic.

Raymond feared he would become impatient for romance between them but that isn't the case. His new career phase is a pleasant distraction, almost an echo of his early days. His role to translate or deconstruct legacy code crafted years ago into a sort of pseudo code is fun, bringing to mind the occasional nostalgic anecdote to share with Terri. Stan and his programmers convert his output into programs, apps, objects, and other elements to be ultimately used for a blockchain being developed in concert with another organization. There's a lot of code to sift through, and plenty of archaic business rules to weed out.

Raymond can and prefers to do this at home where there is little to no risk of his curiosity about the new technology getting stoked. It helps pass the weekends when Kayla visits her family at their cottage in the Muskokas. The idea of him visiting never comes up, nor does Raymond expect it to. For all he knows, she has a boyfriend up there, or someone like a Terri. Though to call his colleague a girlfriend would be grossly overstating things.

With Terri it's complicated. He sees her when he goes to the city, but only in brief spurts. It could be the discovery of Kayla's note keeping her distant from him or it could be something else. She will see him on weekends for an early evening date, or for a food truck or beer festival. Sometimes they hold hands or even share a kiss. Nothing more. She takes the train there and back, obviating the need for his crash pad. Of her divorce, she reveals little, just that it's convoluted.

It's a nebulous yet pleasant situation for Raymond with the two women. It can't stay like this forever. At some point he'll be forced to choose. The middle ground is safest now because each choice seems fraught with peril.

One evening Kayla shows up with an energetic Buster who, instead of laying on Raymond's ottoman, yelps happily to play. Kayla tells the dog to keep quiet and Buster obeys.

"I need to step up the routine. He's getting used to it."

"He looks in better shape. So do you."

"Thanks, hey, did you see this? Is it related to the stuff you were working on with Lorie?"

It's the memo announcing a new website for the condo with registration instructions. Raymond expected this to come, but to his fellow owners, many older and unfamiliar with computers, it arrived out of the blue. No warning, let alone training.

"Yep, I saw it. I registered already."

"So it's legit?"

"It's legit. In fact, it's pretty useful. Or will be."

In this, the board got it right. This is an improvement on the poor site developed by ForageX long ago. Raymond might have held off announcing it until it was fully loaded with documents and functions to give it substance.

"Something's bothering you about this, it's obvious. Is it that they actually succeeded at something?"

Raymond recalls seeing how the initial contract declared the client was Omnirez, not the condo, with Gary as contact.

"Ha, maybe a little. But I'm wary about the link between the website company and Omnirez."

"You want me to look into how it works?"

"You mean there is a link?"

"Yeah. Their CEO—actually his title is Principal, which is a weird one—met with Sheila just last week."

"Sheila, that name sounds familiar."

"It should. She's the one who chairs the AGMs here."

"Oh, her. Gary's boss."

"Actually, Gary's boss's boss. Just another brick in the wall of bureaucracy, right?"

"You seem to be quite astute about what's going on there."

"Those were the words Sheila used when I got promoted to be her assistant. I've impressed her so far. Best of all, I can give you the inside scoop on things."

"Well, congratulations on making an impression there too."

"Thanks, Ray, that means a lot."

-2 -1 G **M** 2 3 4 5 6 7 8 9 10 11 PH R

"What was sent is sufficient. No need to provide a manual, or a cheat sheet or anything. Let alone a training seminar like Lorie suggested. The system's intuitive."

"Do they know where to go with questions?"

"They go to the property manager, to me. But I've gotten no queries yet. Which is good because I've got more urgent matters to attend to. The same goes for all of you as well, I imagine."

"Gary's right, if he's referring to what I think you are."

"I am, Stacie, I am."

"Go ahead, please share with the others what you told me."

"Now this is still being vetted with our lawyer."

"You mean the condo lawyer or the Omnirez lawyer?"

"Nigel, let Gary finish. Seems we've come upon a solution to the issue of the number of directors up for election this year."

"Stacie, may I?"

"Sorry, Gary, didn't mean to steal your thunder."

"No worries, part of the cat's still in the bag. Okay, for the rest of you, I brought up my concern about the potential change of power in the next election with Sheila. You know, about there being three directors up for re-election. It concerned her too. So she assigned a clever staff member to scour the declaration for anything that might address the issue, some exception."

"And?"

"This person, with fresh eyes, discovered a detail you have all missed: that the election cycle has been wrong for years."

"Wrong? What do you mean, wrong?"

"Your faces are just like mine when Gary told me."

"What does it mean? What's wrong about it?"

"What it means, Dennis, is that as directors we've been short changing ourselves."

"How's that?"

"I'll let Gary continue to explain."

"Okay, as you know, there's a schedule defining the number of directors who come up for election each year. It varies."

"As does the length of the terms, which are staggered."

"Ah, but Nigel, that is only the premise you followed. That's what's wrong."

"How?"

"The staggering terms of one, two, and three years were to seed the elections initially. They only applied to the first cycle of three years. After that all director terms are three years. Forever. Check it out for yourselves, it's quite clear."

"What does that mean for us?"

"Well, Dennis, this year, instead of you being up for election alongside Lorie and Nigel, it'll only be you."

"Why only me?"

"Because you're at the end of your third year. Lorie still has one more to go and Nigel has two."

"Wait a minute, that means I wasn't supposed to go up for election last time."

"Correct, Nigel."

"So that means I'll get one more year than I expected."

"Correct, Ned."

"I'm still concerned, Gary, this seems too easy. Are you sure it's not wiser for us to consult our lawyer before we take such a decision?"

"What's the point, Stacie? You have to fix it."

"I just worry this 'fix' might look arbitrary and self-serving."

"What else would you suggest?"

"I'm not suggesting this, but others might argue we need to start it all over again. Elect a new board and re-seed."

"No one will question it when we send out the AGM notice announcing one spot instead of three."

"Isn't it possible someone could legally challenge that, based on what Stacie said?"

"And do what?"

"Sue for the board to be dissolved and to start over?"

"Nigel, if it gets that far, we'll admit our mistake and say we handled it in a way we felt was proper. You guys are all unpaid, non-professionals, in terms of this board. You'd be forgiven."

"I suppose."

"Besides, since this is a unique situation, a legal consultation may take a long time and encroach on the AGM preparation."

"And cost more money?"

"That's right, Lorie."

"I'm with Gary, let's apply the fix and let it be. Are you with me on this, Lorie?"

"Yeah."

"Nigel?"

"I'll abstain."

"Dennis?"

"I still don't see what the issue is."

"That's a yes?"

"All right, if you all feel that way, I guess I do too."

"Stacie, also note this virtually ensures no chance of a major change in the board."

"True. With the WiFi uncertainty, the last thing we need is a new voice poking around."

"Like that Raymond fellow."

"Exactly Dennis. His snide remarks are one thing. We don't need him obligating you to respond if he brings them up here. So whatever you're doing, keep it up."

"We're not doing anything, Gary."

"Precisely Ned. Don't engage him or others like him. They go away eventually. Yes Lorie?"

"This discovery about the number of board seats, should we put out some kind of announcement?"

"What for? No one will notice so the less said the better."

"Maybe something with the pre-AGM notice?"

"Trust me Lorie, it's not in your interest to flout the fact the board's been contravening the declaration this long. Or Nigel's."

"But it doesn't help me."

"Better start campaigning, Dennis."

"You'd love that, wouldn't you, Ned? To see me go."

"Just kidding, pal."

"Maybe I ought to stop doing this, free up these nights."

"If that's your choice, I won't—where are you going?"

"I think we're done and I need to think about my options."

"Good night, Dennis."

"Ned, hush."

"He'll be back, though we can live without him."

"Actually, Ned, you all need him more than you think."

"Why do you say that?"

"If only to make sure you have all board seats spoken for to deter a random vote from the audience. Attendance increases if there's uncertainty as to who will be on the board. With Dennis, you have insurance via the proxies to at least keep the devil you know and avoid adding an unpredictable element. A Tibbett for instance. Imagine dealing with him for a three-year term."

"My goodness, Gary, you're absolutely right. Ned, be nice to Dennis and encourage him to stay."

"What if we get Elle to run against him? That could work."

"If Elle declares candidacy in time for the AGM package."

"And if she isn't shy like Ned."

"What does that mean?"

"Nothing, Ned, just something we discussed last year."

"No, Nigel makes a good point. Last year wasn't a certainty for you, Ned. Thanks to Lorie's hard work you got elected."

"All right, Gary."

"And Lorie? I almost forgot. The staff member who figured it out? Kayla Slaske. The granddaughter of your friend, Irena."

"Poor Irena. May she rest in peace."

August

The Mystery of André du Bois

Finally figured out how this email thing works, finally learned how to contact Gary. Useless now. Or is it? Nothing to say they're replacing that and no way as far as I can see to do it with this new system. New system. For an eighty-five-year-old man, are there any scarier words unrelated to health? Really hate how things are dropped on us. No warning, no training, not even a guide how to use it. Is this the thing they've been talking about at the AGM? Don't think so. I think this is only software and the other is hardware – all so confusing. Computers are useful, I suppose, they let me see pictures of the grandkids, what they're up to. Would rather they'd call or visit more but I'll take what I can get. Now what's this? Says here I must register on some Internet website – Alice did warn me about like that. Thank goodness she's going to help again, though I hope she cleans her fingers; don't like the soil getting in the keyboard. But Alice is a doll. Ridiculous they don't let her help with the landscaping, although it gets wearying listening to her complain about it. Maybe I can say something on this system about that, do that thing to make a request . . . submit, that's the word. Once she shows me how, I'll submit a request on her behalf. Submit, what kind of word is that? As if asking a simple question is the same as applying for a job. Last job I had to apply and type up one of them, what do you call it? Lists where you worked and references. Google it, Gramps, Noah would say. Sorry, my boy, Gramps doesn't care for the Internet, doesn't need it, only uses it because it's the only — résumés, that's the word. Where is Alice anyway? Maybe I'll have another go at it. My fourth time? Fifth? Now where did I put that piece of paper? Here it is. Step one enter name and temporary password . . . oh, it's my suite number . . . click there. Oh, that did work. But now I have to fill in more things. Damn, maybe I'd better wait for Alice.

-2 -1 G M 2 3 4 5 6 7 **8** 9 10 11 PH R

"So whatever happened to André du Bois?"

He watches as Kayla deftly combs the debris acquired from her walk out of Buster's fur. Cute dog. But silly. Fawning for her attention. Their walks are briefer — Raymond likes to believe it's due to a desire to spend extra time with him — and Kayla has put on some of the weight she lost. When this happened before it made her prettier; now her face seems sunken as her mind is formulating a response.

"Who?"

"André, the guy from the fourth doing the renovations."

"Oh right, André. I have no idea."

"Did you know him well?"

"Ooh, do I detect a note of jealousy?"

"Not at all. I'm curious because he was supposed to be part of that WiFi committee."

Good recovery, Raymond thinks. Because it's plausible and true: he never discovered what made André abandon Ned. Was it a perceptive instinct? Was it because Raymond was involved? That would only be relevant if there was something between he and Kayla. Or if André thought there was something.

"Supposed to be?"

171

"He met with Ned once, but no word since."

"That's weird."

"I sent André an email a while back, you know, to see what was up. I got no response."

"That's even weirder. You sending him an email."

"Why? I'm interested. I care."

"I thought you were done with that business. And what did you hope to get from him?"

"You're right, I am jealous. Jealous he somehow knew not to waste his time with Ned. How did he know?"

"Oh. You're being funny."

"Is there a way for you to find out at Omnirez?"

"Find out what?"

"Where André went?"

"You're not serious, are you? That's confidential."

"I know, I'm just asking."

She finishes with Buster and collects the dirt in a dustpan to dispose in the garbage. When done, she tells Raymond how her place of work is so secretive that many documents she works on are anonymous and hard to read with all the black boxes.

"What do they call that?"

"Redacting?"

"My God, Ray, Sheila is the queen of redacting."

Kayla describes reviewing a condo declaration and finding something that made Sheila so ecstatic she bought Kayla lunch. But afterwards, Sheila transformed into Mr. Hyde.

"She turned on you?"

"Not me. Gary."

"Gary? Our property manager?"

"Yeah. He got called into her office and she reamed him out for I don't know what. It was hilarious. He's meek with her."

"So what you found had to do with this condo?"

"I told you, I don't know. But it's possible."

"You said she reamed out Gary because of it."

"I can't be sure the two things were connected."

Kayla's tone, her manner, both seem detached, aloof, almost defensive. Raymond has noticed a change in her demeanour the past few weeks, a trace of confidence marred by arrogance, not unlike the change he detected in Ned. A superiority one sees in lowly security guards granted arbitrary power. Is it paranoia to fear continued exposure to Omnirez will transform Kayla the way being on the board transformed Ned and Lorie? To a point he and Kayla drift apart as he did with the WiFi committee?

Or is it the other subject?

Whenever either one accidentally—it's always accidental—brings up Kayla's grandmother, an offhand comment by Kayla on Buster's mournful whines as he sleeps, or from Raymond on how he misses seeing Kayla's car when he goes to the basement to drop off the recycling, the conversation terminates abruptly. By turning on the television or, in this case, talking about others in the building. It's a mutual thing, they both do it. Raymond suspects it's rooted in the uncertainty of unverifiable truths each must live with. Perhaps even the elastic nature of truth itself.

It's not that Raymond doubts Jan's account, or the belief his grandfather, Leo, was a victim of cruelty from Irena and not the reverse. The falsehoods she inflicted on her granddaughter are inexcusable, unforgivable, pointless. Why go out of your way to accuse Raymond when he played no part in the events, and has no inkling of what happened? The puzzle keeps Raymond from fully condemning the old woman, or hating her. It has nothing to do with his friendship with Kayla. Of course if he hated Irena as much as Jan did there would be no friendship, only the awareness Irena did not choose her fate. For she was a victim as well, whose actions were borne out of desperation. Just as Jan's hatred survived decades, so did Irena's desperation. That's what triggered her accusation and it took his resemblance to Leo to spook it out of her.

This is a perspective Raymond knows Kayla would love for him to express outright. If he did, the chance of them moving on from the platonic stage—he cannot delude himself thinking he doesn't want that—improves. But he can't. Not yet. It would be a betrayal to Jan and, by extension, his own bloodline. That he is detached from that bloodline makes no difference. How it came to be that events from so long ago, involving people he's never heard of, should influence their personal lives, is a mystery that frightens him. Kayla too, he suspects.

Other than their reconciliation on the roof, Kayla has never acknowledged her grandmother's misdeeds, let alone expressed regret. Not that he needs her to, but it would be nice to have her declare her feelings, even if none exist. For all he knows, she has moved on. Or not. It's hard to interpret moments like this when Kayla fidgets, while staring blankly at nothing.

"Everything okay?"

"Fine, you want to know about André and me? He and I did date, for about a year, before I discovered he was engaged to a girl in Marseille. France. I discovered this after he was gone. He moved there, as far as I know."

She stares at Raymond as if daring him to probe further, as if there's an unfinished piece he needs to figure out. For the life of him he can't think why she kept this a secret. When he asks, she bolts up.

"I have to go. Come along, Buster."

"Kayla."

"Look, you want to find him, why not try Poland? You seem to have good success finding people there. Get up, Buster."

The dog, in a deep sleep minutes ago, pops up at the second command to obey his mistress. Raymond watches Kayla open the door and lead Buster out. Only the door doesn't close.

"Damn it."

They're back in his suite and she sits down again. Raymond goes to the door and looks out in the hallway. There's Lorie and Ned walking on his floor for some reason, walking his way. Are they coming to solicit his help again? He closes the door to wait. Nothing. When he opens it again and peeks out, the corridor is empty. He shuts his door and locks it.

"I don't think they saw you, if that's what's worrying you."

"What were they doing on this floor?"

Raymond goes down the hall to the elevators. One door is stuck open. He enters, presses a button, exits. The elevator jerks but doesn't shut. He returns to find Kayla gone, though Buster is still there, looking confused. He pets the dog.

"Where's your mommy?"

A toilet flushes for an answer. When Kayla emerges, he tells her about finding the elevator stuck, along with his assumption

174

they were probably going down for a board meeting and opted to take the stairs once it opened. She nods acceptingly and sits on a barstool at the kitchen island, digging for crumbs in a tube of Pringles, most of which she ate by herself earlier.

"Why do you care so much about André du Bois?"

"I don't, Kayla. But I do care about you."

"You know, there's a great opportunity for me at Omnirez. They like me there. A lot."

"I like you here. A lot."

"You know what I mean."

"It might help if you expanded on that."

"I'm moving back in with my parents."

"What?"

His surprise is feigned as deep down this is no shock. But it is disappointing. Their relationship was bound to turn one way or another. This isn't the way he hoped but is what he expected. He can't argue her point that staying at his condo could inhibit her career options at Omnirez.

"You were right before, about me wanting to take over from Gary. I think that's possible. I love the building, the location, the people, the staff. Whenever I talk to Lorie, who drops by like an aunt to check on me—it's sweet but I'm sick of it, giving me yet one more reason to leave—what was I saying?"

"Kayla, when you talk to Lorie, what?"

"Right, it sounds as if Gary's getting on her nerves too."

"I thought she was Gary's biggest fan."

"She is. I should clarify it's the owners complaining to Lorie about Gary that gets on her nerves. Lorie does nothing about it. Deep down I bet she knows Gary is the prime source of all her troubles. Take now for instance, a delightful Friday afternoon. Where do you suppose Gary is?"

"Not in his office."

"At his cottage. If you tell me you saw Gary in our building after one on a Friday in summer, I'd say you're hallucinating."

"Why don't you complain about it too? I bet she'd listen to you. Lorie, I mean."

"Nah, I'll let Gary continue digging his own grave."

"But if the board isn't willing to do anything . . ."

"They'll have to eventually, Ray. Someday, Gary's bound to make a mistake they can't ignore."

"Then you'll swoop in to save the day."

"That would be my dream. Lorie would support me. A lot of people would support me."

"I would too."

"Thanks."

"Except it would mean you'd have to live somewhere else, and that you can't risk being seen with me."

"It's not only that, Ray. My grandmother's place is gloomy. Buster's miserable. His whining is annoying. He loves it at my parents' house, more room. Since this'll let them sell the condo, my dad won't charge me rent."

It seems the more convincing her arguments are, the more sorry Raymond feels for himself. Does she realize this means it's likely they'll never see each other? She can't come to his suite if she has no plausible reason. Going to see her could be awkward and imply too much. Her feelings for him would be secondary to a burgeoning career that was just a dream a few months ago. He can't begrudge her, but that doesn't make it easier.

"So you're leaving me, just like that."

She calmly rises, walks to the door, and calls for Buster. Her balance is steady but her eyes are so intense he must look away.

"At least I'm not running off to Poland or Ukraine to dig up a case against someone dear to you."

"That's not what it was and you know it."

"Ray, I was willing to fight for you with my grandmother."

"That's not what it sounded like then."

"I only said what she wanted to hear. I thought you would see through it."

"No. I didn't see through it. I took it seriously and it hurt me a great deal. Maybe I was being dim but it became important to me to face the truth of the accusations. I had no idea I'd discover the opposite was true, so I did not go to 'make a case' as you put it. I went prepared to face my past, whatever it might be. I was as shocked as you at what I discovered. I'm glad I went because now I won't have to live my life condemned to thinking I'm the spawn of an evil man."

She is quiet, her eyes calm, as she digests his words. It's the first time they've taken the subject to this point. It's painful yet it could be what they need. Needed for some time.

"Meaning I'm the granddaughter of an evil woman."

"Meaning not living a lie."

A slight nod tells Raymond this has hit home. It's his chance to tell her he doesn't see Irena's actions as comparable to the evil of the Nazis, but as a desperate response to those actions. Only can he assume the authority to conclude this? He wasn't there. Would Jan or Leo let Irena's kin off the hook or would they seek retribution? Would they accuse Raymond of saying this because deep down he's smitten by this woman?

He says it anyway.

His words seem to have a positive effect on Kayla, based on her smile. She goes to kiss him and hug him. But when he tries to extend the kiss, she pulls back.

"I care for you, Ray, I really do, but I must go."

"We can still keep in touch, maybe see each other in the city or other places."

"No, I need to do this now. For me. But I'll be back."

Her "I'll be back" stays with Raymond all evening, giving enough peaceful comfort to sleep. But by dawn bitterness, or a devastating blast of reality, translates the promise to the pathos of that old send-off: "Don't call me, I'll call you."

Kayla's absence from his life is immediate, leading to a few interminable, deathly quiet days. The blockchain project, as he's come to call it, though it has another name, is in a lull and calls to Stan and Terri, who is acting distant too, only result in vague assurances things will pick up. Raymond's not that far removed from the IT world to not recognize the symptoms of a project facing internal resistance.

One morning, breakfasting on his balcony, a soft cool wind tempering the shining sun, Raymond gets inspired to get out for the day, take a train into the city, aimlessly walk among people. If his feet lead him to Terri's office, so be it.

Halfway there dark clouds appear. His mood darkens with regret for not checking the forecast. Rain spatters on the train all the way downtown. He uses the underground paths and heads directly to the office tower. At least he remembered his badge. It entitles him to be on the premises, yet he feels an odd anxiety, as if intruding, that transforms into a sense of foreboding on the empty elevator ride straight up to Terri's floor.

He finds her putting things into a box. He coughs to get her attention. She looks up, not at all surprised to see him. Someone walks behind Raymond, seems to slow, then moves on. Stan?

"Hello, Raymond?"

"What's going on? You moving to another floor?"

"You could say that."

Her chuckle isn't a gleeful one. What is there for him to say on a day that's clearly her last? The words of compassion in his head compete with ones itching to know how it will impact the blockchain project, his project, his income.

"Can I buy you lunch, Terri?"

"Yes."

When they emerge it's a different day. The clouds and rain accompanying him earlier are gone, replaced by an azure sky and uninhibited sun blasting warm sunshine. Raymond carries the box filled with Terri's office life and listens as she tells him not to fret over her, that she saw it coming weeks ago and had prepared herself.

"That's why I haven't heard anything lately."

"Yeah, lots going on. I apologize for not keeping you in the loop but honestly, I wasn't sure how it would play out."

"How did it play out?"

"You mean, how does this affect you?"

"Well, partly."

"Truth is, I don't know. My responsibilities are now Stan's— no, it's not like that, he's in limbo too."

They reach Terri's car, parked underneath City Hall, put her things in the trunk. She's quiet until they're back aboveground. Then Terri lets out a sigh and says all she wants is street meat. They wait in line for their dogs and are lucky when a group of kids clear a bench in a shady spot as they get their food.

Turns out part of the IT department, the part including the blockchain project with Stan and Raymond, but no longer Terri, got severed and sold to their blockchain partner, resulting in an uncertain future for Raymond's role. His contract is not hourly, but on a deliverable-by-deliverable basis, which means there is no guarantee for him or even a notice period. Another don't call us, we'll call you.

"Doesn't sound promising for me."

"I can't BS you. I don't see them going in the same direction. Stan's probably fine. As is your legacy, your computer code that I see living on another decade. At least. The truth is no one was fully invested in it, not even Stan. I could tell because everyone seemed content with adding 'blockchain' to their résumés."

"Are you adding it to yours?"

"Of course."

"Sad. But if you knew it had no chance, and the reason, why not expose it?"

"Two reasons: One, I don't have the stamina for such a fight. And two, I could be wrong."

"Look, if you'd like to come over, or I could—"

She puts up her hand, finishes her hot dog, and swallows.

"Something else I need to tell you. Should have told you a while ago. Greg and I have reconciled."

"That's great news, isn't it?"

"I think so. I hope so. We'll see."

"I wish you the best of luck."

"Likewise."

Terri hugs Raymond warmly, thanks him for being a great friend, but then begs off to get on the highway before rush hour.

She leaves him with the tourists posing for photos in front of City Hall, businessmen striding with purpose, an occasional politician pausing to speak with a constituent. A lovely day, but he's alone, he feels abandoned. Renting a car to visit his mother isn't an option; she's on a trip to Las Vegas and to see the Grand Canyon with friends from her home.

He thinks it can't get worse, but it can. For when Raymond arrives home and finds no message from Stan about the project, he decides to go for a power walk.

Whether it's a subconscious masochistic element at play, or just coincidence, he experiences an extreme sadness when he crosses the sixth floor and sees the door to Kayla's suite is wide open. Inside, two men are packing items in boxes while another is loading Irena's large chair furniture onto a dolly.

"Excuse me, is the owner, or occupant here?"

"No."

"Then who let you in?"

"The superintendent."

Just like that, she's gone. Maybe this is how she felt when he was in Poland, the first time she knocked on his door and got no answer. No doubt she would have asked Bruce who would not have been able to tell her where he went, just that he was gone. No, she couldn't ask Bruce, he might tell her grandmother about her asking. Then Lorie would find out they're close. All of this is so silly; couldn't they have dated like a normal couple?

Over the next weeks, with no word from Kayla, Raymond's sadness settles into a tolerable gloom. He observes her condo go on the market, then off a few days later. It's only another week before he sees an elderly couple hovering at the loading dock, directing movers. He wants to warn them the property manger sucks, the board is incompetent, and they just bought the home of a Nazi collaborator. But they look too sweet, too vulnerable. He realizes this temptation is not motivated by bitterness, but a desire to protect them. But there is a better way.

It's the first time Raymond's considered going for a seat on the board. After all, didn't Kayla say there are three seats up for election? Isn't that why Lorie made that rogue board comment, or rather quoted Gary saying so? This only occurs once in three years. What better way to attack root causes than at the source? What better way to open his neighbours' eyes to reality?

Then again, do they want their eyes opened? This couple, for instance, do they want to see difficulties? Maybe not. Maybe blissful ignorance is preferred. Perhaps that blissful ignorance is how Ned and Lorie started and, once on the board, turned into wilful blindness. Maybe the other owners are content to suffer a grouch like Gary and keep their heads in the sand. Even if that means higher condo fees. They won't know if no one tells them. It's a depressing notion but Raymond has to concede it's highly possible his realistic perspective would not be welcomed by his neighbours, let alone the board.

No, he can't fall into a pit of negativity, he has to test it, has to test how popular his views are. Three seats are up. With luck, there'll be two other owners of similar mind up for election and they'll decimate the incumbents, Stacie, Lorie, and Dennis. Aha, that's what Gary must have meant by a rogue board, and maybe Lorie was scared too when he quoted Gary. Rogue not because it does random things, but because he can't control it.

There is another potential benefit for himself. If he is on the board, Kayla won't be their property manager but she can come and go as she pleases. Furthermore, as a board member, he'd have access to documents that might clear up a lot of what he doesn't know, including the silly André du Bois mystery, before it too becomes an obsession.

-2 -1 G **M** 2 3 4 5 6 7 8 9 10 11 PH R

"Not sure why we bothered meeting, Stacie, without Gary."

"Expected Denise to show up, guess no one at Omnirez told her about our board meeting."

"Gary should have told her, she's his backup."

"He might have forgotten."

"When's Gary back from vacation? If soon, let's reschedule for then."

"No point, Dennis. When Gary gets back, we'll let him focus on sending out the pre-AGM notice and all the planning for that meeting."

"Don't forget to get Gary to leave out the part telling people how they can go up for the board this time."

"Relax Dennis, I won't. Wouldn't want to miss out on those cookies of yours."

"Thanks, Stacie, I'm glad you all like them so much. There's more where they came from. Now if there's nothing else, and if no one minds, I'm going to duck out now. See you guys."

"Goodbye, Dennis . . . good riddance, can't we replace him somehow? I've never seen anyone so useless."

"Now, Nigel, you can't fault Dennis's dedication."

"Yeah, lots of work making these cookies."

"They aren't even that great, are they, Ned?"

"Nope. They're awful."

"Terrific. The one thing that you two share an opinion on is a negative opinion of one of our board members."

"Maybe not for long, one can hope—did someone ask Elle to run yet? She's popular. She'd love it."

"You've talked to her, Ned?"

"Lorie and I have broached the subject."

"I didn't broach it, Ned, just told her what it entailed."

"Stacie, maybe you could encourage Elle."

"No, I don't want to get involved in that sort of thing. But I do know Gary has also broached the subject with a few people."

"People like Raymond?"

"No, not Raymond, Nigel. You seem to like troublemakers."

"Hey, I didn't ask him to be part of your committee."

"Tell me you're not talking about Raymond, Stacie."

"No, Raymond is the last person Gary would recommend to be on our board. He's looking for quieter folks, you know, older ones who aren't . . ."

"Troublemakers."

"For lack of a better word, yes. He's planted seeds in a few heads but they're all noncommittal. Until someone solid comes along, Dennis might be our safest option."

"Good lord."

"Sorry, Ned, that's how it is. If there's nothing else, we'll see each other next month when we finalize the WiFi motion."

"What WiFi motion?"

"Ned, you didn't share the news with Nigel?"

"What news? Nobody told me anything. Not even . . ."

"Look, Nigel, your guys made a good pitch to Lorie and me but they can't be ready in time. Sorry, pal."

"Shouldn't we discuss it first, then vote on it?"

"Vote on what? There's only one option that we can have in place in a reasonable time and not disrupt service."

"Meaning what?"

"You know what it means, Nigel. I don't like it any better than you do."

"Ned, please. I'm afraid, Nigel, it's evident there will be no solution before the contract end. At least with ForageX, we keep the WiFi going until a new solution can be implemented."

"A new unproven solution."

"True, it is unproven, but it works. You conceded as much after the meeting you probably should have skipped."

"Okay, I'll grant it works. But then the same crappy solution with the same crappy vendor will be in place indefinitely. Their ability to deliver on time is unproven too."

"Understood."

"If you're willing to hold off for a vendor your own survey confirmed was awful, why not go with the other option?"

"If you had done more back when you promised, we'd have more options."

"Ned, enough. Lorie, can you explain the other benefit?"

"Yes. Going with ForageX will save us money because they won't charge us after the current contract until the new solution is in place. That gives them an incentive to get it in fast."

"Nothing to say, Nigel? See, we're not complete idiots."

"So it's a done deal? Lorie?"

"Pretty much. All that's left is the signing."

"For how many years?"

"Still to be worked out. They want five but I won't allow us to go higher than three."

"That's a detail I'll leave to your financial talents."

"While Lorie does that, I'll prepare an announcement for the information presentations by ForageX to explain their changes. I'd say for once we're in good shape on this. Right, Stacie?"

"Works for me, Ned. Good work. Best of all, I'm pretty sure Gary will be on board."

"He is. I checked with him just before his vacation."

September

The New Contract

-2 -1 G M 2 3 4 5 6 **7** 8 9 10 11 PH R

What nonsense. Only one director position up for the board this year, according to Gary, not three. Been following everything, been waiting for a chance to join the board. Have to be one of the clique, I suppose, they control the proxies. Now that they've "fixed the glitch" like in the comedy about the office world. Fix the glitch, don't tell anyone, hope no one notices or reacts. Why not admit the error? Are they that afraid of us? It is a big deal too. But not to Gary. Don't have to specifically point it out is his response, you'll find out when the AGM notices are sent out. Not sure that's how it's supposed to work, might be worth challenging. If they've been mucking it up for years, maybe it should be a fresh start, not just extend at will. Put all five up, bet some would like that, bet that would get a majority of owners at the AGM. Only they can't know until the notice gets out. After that it'd probably have to involve a lawyer. Be interesting to see reactions when it is revealed. Doubt there'll be any. Better for me to hold off for another year when there'll be two spots up. Unless someone resigns. Or quits. Can I wait that long? Gary once said I'd make for a good director, that I'd blend in with the others. Maybe I do have a chance. On the other hand, look at Lorie. She seems to have been swallowed up in another world. We used to lament together, with her hubby, Sam, about how the board is secretive and we wanted to know more. That's why she joined, to fix that, or at least that's how it was at first for her. Maybe she wasn't truthful and meant to get inside for her own gain. When I see her now she's reserved, to the point of rudeness at times. She'll listen but what you say goes nowhere. Wouldn't let that happen to me, wouldn't turn on my neighbours. She's changed.

Stan is trying to explain the finer points of the new blockchain strategy under his management. He's refreshingly erudite and atypically patient, for a millennial, apprising Raymond of what has changed and the rationale, while under no obligation to do so. Unfortunately the message is unequivocal: we're moving on, Mr. Tibbett, we don't need your services any longer. Appended by that old obligatorily optimistic "you never know, technology is volatile, things could change" that's essentially meaningless.

For Raymond it's over. He's done with volatile once and for all, evident in how easily his attention is diverted by an email announcing the WiFi decision. Surprise, the winner is ForageX. More telling is the wording, no doubt tailored and sculpted to rationalize the choice and make the process sound rigorous:

> *The criteria used to score the vendors who responded were:*
> *- noticeable improvement in the service*
> *- ensuring increased costs are minimized*
> *- ability to implement with limited WiFi disruptions*
>
> *The Board took in bids from four vendors that we evaluated over the past months. The best of these, for our purposes, in the opinion of the Board, came from our current vendor, ForageX, and their upgraded offering.*

185

"Ensuring increased costs are minimized?" When the AGM focus for years implied a decrease, or elimination? Will others notice that? And what do they consider a formal bid?

The contract is not a surprise, less so that it's with ForageX; that's been inevitable since December. What is unusual is their stated intent to conduct information sessions. Usually they drop a service in place and leave everyone to fend for themselves, as they did with the new website and likely other things of which Raymond is unaware.

What he'd give to talk this out with Kayla.

Raymond wasn't prepared for her absence to be so absolute. He hasn't heard a single word from her since that conversation. Not a peep. Delayed punishment for his leaving for Poland suddenly? Doubtful; he's pretty sure they got past that. More likely it has to do with her being in the Omnirez world, and her fear he would criticize via smartass remarks. She'd be right. His fear is she'll transform into a Gary, nurturing a wilful blindness that deludes her into believing she's doing the opposite, forever and irrevocably corrupting her.

Moments later a follow-up note lands in his Inbox, with the dates and times for the information sessions.

This could be fun, Raymond thinks, several days later, as he descends the stairs to attend the first session. He's particularly curious to see how the other owners react to selecting the same vendor, after several years of contrary messages.

Raymond arrives on time but they began early. The room is filled with two dozen owners, some having to stand. A slide is projected on the wall next to the television, a thin man in jeans and a blazer addressing it. Raymond wedges into an open spot at the back from where he can observe everyone. On his left is Lorie, seated behind a small table. Ned is in Bermuda shorts, his chubby legs casually swinging under the ledge on which he sits clutching rolled up sheets like a baton. Or nightstick. It's not the promised handout; there doesn't appear to be one. Raymond's entrance caused a disruption because it's quiet. Ned and Lorie seem to be avoiding glancing his way. The presenter, thirtyish and affable, resumes speaking to the slide, which turns out to be the first of only three.

Three crude, utterly useless slides without substance. None of them show dates or impacts, not even a technical diagram to appease those interested in that. A kid in Grade Five could have done better. This is not at all surprising from Ned and Lorie, but it's inexcusable for a vendor unless, as is likely, Ned and Lorie, maybe Gary too, told the guy to reveal as little as possible.

It slowly comes to Raymond that this is not an information session, but an attempt to buy time. Not only did the board fail to achieve their explicit desire to replace ForageX, they failed to meet a deadline they've known about for years. It's evident the earliest implementation will be October, a best case scenario. It's more likely to drag into the new year. Raymond needs the other owners to react. Most look confused. Then Alice rises.

"I have a question."

"By all means, Alice."

She stands next to the ForageX rep, as if to address him, but then faces Ned and Lorie.

"Tell me, how is it your super-duper IT all star team ended up picking these guys?"

Yes, Raymond thinks. This is what he's wanted a long time. Ned and Lorie, your board bubble is about to burst and you are about to be held accountable for ignoring owners.

Clearly, Ned is caught off guard. Lorie's eyes remain fixed at the front, but Raymond sees her twitching, her face turning red. Raymond wants to add: Why go with a vendor you were so adamant had to go, one that did so poorly in the survey? More importantly, why tarnish six months of Raymond Tibbett's life?

Ned babbles pure nonsense, riding the line of outright lying but somehow managing not to cross it. It has to be awkward for him, though he seems to have an innate shrewdness he picked up, perhaps from Gary. Alice listens intently, arms crossed, not looking like she's buying it. Her glances alternate between Ned and Lorie and the ForageX guy who nods as he lets Ned do the talking. Raymond enjoys the spectacle, waiting for a moment to pipe in with clarifications to rile up the crowd. But his plans get abruptly quashed by Alice:

"I must say fellows, well done."

What the hell was that? he thinks, as Alice sits back down.

This is a factor Raymond had ignored. How they are friends with Lorie and Ned, having lived together in the building much longer than Raymond, some since it was built. It would nullify his assumption the desire for best solution was universal. This is not unlike his IT political naïveté that for years kept him blind to the raw human motivations impacting his efforts.

The dates come up for discussion; it's evident October is not possible. Ned offers up November—two months late—only to be contradicted by ForageX saying it's likely January, making it four months late. Raymond has to smile, ready to bet anything springtime is the earliest, six months late. Which confirms this session is not for the owners, but for the board, to buy time.

Someone inquires about other vendors. Ned says four were approached, including the cable and telephone companies. That is sort of true, but he has a lot of gall making it appear the board undertook a formal bidding process. The board didn't speak to the cable company at all to follow up on its generic bulk pricing offer; for the phone company, there was no bid and they didn't capitalize on the opportunity to enhance property values via the fibre optic to the suites offer; the company Nigel proposed was probably spoiled due to a conflict of interest; so the winner won by default because no one else was left.

Furthermore, as there's no mention of it and, as the scraggly notes from the initial ForageX meeting Ned showed at the bar, it was hardly an offer. More than likely the vendor wiggled out of the original proposal to not charge for the current service from the end of the current contract until the new service starts. Lorie and Ned let them off the hook, or let it out ForageX never had competition and that the board was the cause of a needless and avoidable delay. Raymond raises a hand but someone else asks a question he is unable to catch. However, Ned's revealing response triggers a new frustration urging him to speak out.

"We'd need to run that by Omnirez."

Yet when Raymond's mouth opens, no words come out. An instinctive realization shuts him up: this is not the forum. Even on this rare occasion, in which board members interact directly with the owners they profess to represent, without Omnirez to shield them, the only opportunity outside the AGM to express what's on his mind to his fellow owners, he cannot overcome an inherent principle from his career days: not airing one's laundry in the company of a guest, particularly a vendor. Evidently Ned is not beholden to such principles when, minutes later, he utters an outright lie in saying they received nothing from the phone company. For this, Raymond finds his voice.

"Not true, Ned, they did offer something."

"Nothing worth considering."

Raymond glares at Ned. Then Lorie states they were forced to exclude the phone company due to their insistence on a ten-year term, adding the board had learned its lesson and recently resolved to never consider ten-year contracts again.

What is a proper term maximum then? Nine years? Seven? What if a cellular company wished to rent roof space to install a tower, generating income. Would an arbitrary ten-year cap kill such an opportunity? Apparently so.

In truth, the ten years was for the phone company to have a right to match offers from other vendors, in effect shutting out competition. But it only applied to what they installed. Other vendors could still sell their products, as they can on the access provided by ForageX. Hence, those who might benefit from such an upgrade and need performance that goes beyond what ForageX can provide, are blocked out. Even those who wouldn't use it lose out on the bump in value of their condo asset such an element brings. Again, this isn't the place to say this. Besides, he'd have a difficult time explaining it.

This session, out of which he hoped to glean some perverse entertainment, has depressed him. With an audience inclined to comply with what they hear to avoid discomfort, what chance does Raymond have to get his message through? The problem isn't as simple as dealing with an incompetent board, it's about waking up and empowering owners. Perhaps a disaster is the only way for that to happen. He's in a difficult position and has no one to confide in.

A few days later an email announces the date for the next AGM meeting in November—two weeks later than usual—and announces one director seat is up for election. Usually there is a solicitation note for anyone interested in running for the board to submit résumés. Not this time. Something else is amiss. One director. Raymond recalls Lorie's fear—no, she was quoting the fear Gary had—of a rogue board because three seats were up for election. It should be three, according to the pattern.

Raymond retrieves the past AGM documents. Sure enough, it's a one-two-three year cycle. Last year two were elected, Ned and Nigel: he remembers that well. Ned won the two-year term while Nigel got a one-year term, as Nigel did the previous year when he ran unopposed. So this year it has to be three again. It doesn't matter to Raymond, he's decided not to run. But as the rogue board comment continues to gnaw away; Raymond sees a need for fresh air, a walk to the lake.

The elevator door opens into the lobby. A man is standing outside Gary's office, unhappily shaking his head.

"Of course it's a mistake. That's what I'm trying to tell you, Gary. It should say three seats are up for election."

"No. I mean your board has been misinterpreting the condo declaration for years. It clearly states elected directors' terms are to be three years. The way they've done it to this point should only have been done the first few years. That's why there's only one director position up this year. That's the mistake."

"Haven't others asked about this?"

"A few."

"So why weren't we told?"

"The board is not required to do so."

"That doesn't mean they can't, as a courtesy."

"I'm just telling you what they are required to do."

"Why are the board members such poor communicators?"

"On the contrary, in my view, this board communicates in an excellent manner."

It takes a great effort for Raymond to keep from bursting into the discussion to point out that by Gary's logic the board saying nothing is excellent. Only Gary wouldn't understand it, because to him that would probably make sense.

Sunlight beckons him to not delay his walk nor dispel the subtle odd joy at hearing another owner voicing a concern. Leave before it's spoiled by the owner's sudden retreat, as was the case with Alice at the WiFi session.

Too late. The man withdraws, clearly exasperated, sighing, and skulking to the elevator. Suddenly a giant cloud occludes the daylight beyond the doors, inhibiting Raymond's desire for fresh air. He is curious about the man. He watches the elevator light stop at the ninth floor. The sunlight is returning, but now he feels a need to verify or discredit what Gary is talking about, and heads back upstairs.

And he is right. Gary, that is, according to the declaration. These boneheads have been doing it wrong for years. Raymond, not caring that this could be turning into an outright obsession, reviews the AGM documents to see how long they've messed it up. At least four years. It's only by luck they got the recent one correct, with two directors up. This year it's one, then two again for the following two years. Unbeknownst to the owners, Lorie and Ned and Nigel just got a free pass. Though to be fair, Nigel did have to run unnecessarily last year.

Contravening the declaration is a serious matter and ought to have been disclosed upon discovery, Raymond thinks. Not revealed indirectly, even sneakily, by inference alone. Gary also said the board didn't have to reveal this discovery only to then tout them as excellent communicators.

One could derive a syllogism: A) Gary believes the board's communications are excellent; B) Gary believes this board only needs to communicate the minimum; C) therefore Gary believes excellent=minimum. The type of contradiction or little lie at the core of bureaucratic incompetence, buttressed by an instinctual, officious defiance of the type Gary deployed with that owner at the AGM who asked about the pool maintenance. An effective tactic in condominiums filled with folks who fear confrontation. A subtle bullying that's condescendingly respectful, while also intimidating. What's pathetic is the strength being conveyed is founded on fear, not malice, which makes it impossible to refute or resist with logic. Thank goodness for the drive to the airport to pick up his mother, a distraction to clear his head.

The rental is an underpowered Hyundai, but a comfortable one. He arrives at the airport just as his mother's flight from Vegas lands. Why did she need him to pick her up? Why not just take the retirement home shuttle? Once he sees her emerge through the customs doors, he recalls it was his idea to pick her up, to tell her in person about Jan dying, curious to see how she'd react or whether she even wants to know.

"How was Vegas?"

"Too hot—honey, easy on the brakes."

"Sorry, not used to this car."

"Something upsetting you?"

"A while ago I got a note from Lech. Jan's friend in Poland."

"Jan has finally died, hasn't he?"

"Not yet, but he is dying. How did you guess?"

"Just how you're talking. Leo considered Jan indestructible. Unlike himself."

"What do you mean?"

But she doesn't answer and when Raymond looks over, he sees his mother dabbing her eyes with a tissue. His mother, who he's seen cry perhaps three times: at his university graduation, on his wedding day, and now. Her first sorrowful tears, at least that he's witnessed. And she thinks Jan is indestructible.

His mother hates talking in cars so he decides to hold off his questions. But she likes to hear the details of his trip to Poland, particularly the visit with Jan. She only interrupts to correct his pronunciation a few times. When she does, he notices the slight accent she's always had but to which he's never paid attention. Not even the death march shocks her. In fact, it seems she's mentally accumulating and organizing things to tell him.

At the retirement home she's warmly greeted by her friends but shoos them off to usher Raymond into her room. She takes a teapot down from a shelf, starts to boil water. A search of her cupboards for snacks yields nothing, but a foray into the shared kitchen is rewarded with a small pound cake. Raymond doesn't need tea, doesn't need cake, nothing except for his mother to tell him what it is she wants to tell him. Yet he allows her to fret over these details, sensing she's gathering her thoughts. At last, the tea gets poured, the cake set out, the ambience relaxed by the soft jazz music she likes to play.

"I'm sure you can tell dear, listening to you talk about Jan affected me on the drive. I never would have guessed you could garner so much from your trip."

192

"But you didn't ask either."

"I wanted it to come out naturally before I . . ."

"Before you what?"

"Before I told you what Leo—your father—told me. Because Jan is wrong, Leo shared a lot with me."

The tea keeps Raymond steady when his mother mentions Irena's SS officer who has a name, Kurt. He was a coward, but a clever one who sensed what might happen after the evacuation. He had no qualms about abandoning his duties to disappear.

Kurt and Irena—it's odd to hear his mother say her name as Jan said it—hatched an escape plan using poor Frantiszek, and only Frantiszek, until Leo showed as they broke away and were about to enter a forest. They had to bring Leo along. Amongst the trees Kurt strangled Frantiszek to death. He then forced Leo to mutilate the emaciated body of Jan's friend to pass for that of a decently fed SS officer, then dress it in Kurt's uniform. As he did this Kurt put on the dead man's rags. Irena watched with a frightened tension that made Leo wonder about her.

"Wonder what, Mom?"

"It only lasted a moment, but a moment that haunted Leo until his dying day."

"Can you describe it? Do you remember it?"

"I can, but only because the look on Leo's face in describing the terror he saw in her expressed more than his words."

"Go on."

"Well, this Kurt fellow gave Irena his gun while he switched clothes. She held it clumsily, almost tempting Leo to take it. Her eyes caught his, he read them and they spoke to him: Save me. He went to grab the gun, but she pulled back. They struggled in silence and her strength matched his because she had eaten. It was a stalemate until Kurt noticed and forced Leo to release his grip. From then on she returned to her cruel self. However, that exchange, no matter how brief, tapped into his innate empathy, made him see her as the harshest victim of the SS officer, that her behaviour was borne out of a primal need to survive, how the hate within her was unnatural, fabricated. He pitied her, but still regretted not killing her and the Nazi. That haunted Leo for the rest of his life with guilt for Jan, who he could never again face himself. Oh, it's all horrific. Even after all these years, this being the first time I've shared this story with anyone other than your father. Ronald, I mean."

"It's okay."

"I wish I could describe that look in words."

"No need. I can imagine it. If this is too upsetting . . ."

"No, let me finish."

After this, they forced Leo to lead them to Auschwitz where they mingled in with other prisoners to await rescue from the Russians. Kurt had to get rid of the gun. Leo always assumed it was Irena who didn't let Kurt kill him. Regardless, they released Leo to rejoin the Soviet army. It was not a joyous reunion as the Soviets were sceptical of his ability to escape and doubted what he told them.

After the war, the Soviets remained suspicious because Leo never told a consistent story about the death and mutilation of the German officer. Worse was the shame he felt for not killing Irena and Kurt. Then he found out Jan had survived. That news made him happy, naturally, but exacerbated his guilt. He could never summon the courage to tell Jan.

"Tell him what?"

"That Kurt and Irena might have survived too."

Raymond pours more tea and gives his mother a moment, a moment he needs himself to register her words. Only a moment because he knows this already. But for her it must be difficult to unload what he ought to have let her unload long ago. He taps at his mother's arm.

"Better late than never."

"I'm glad you're here son."

"Me too."

"Before his final arrest, when it was clear he would be sent to Siberia, he managed to get me to Poland and told me to find Jan, but made me swear to never tell Jan any of this. That's why I lied about why I didn't ask. It wasn't because I was waiting for you to ask, but to honour my word to Leo."

She says this with emotion and then rises. She heads to her kitchenette. Raymond thinks his mother is going for a tissue but then sees her reach in a tiny cupboard and pull out a bottle of vodka. She grabs two small glasses, puts them on the table, and fills both glasses halfway, hands one to Raymond.

As he reaches for the glass, she grabs his hand.

"Now Raymond, you have heard from Jan, you have heard from me. It is time you tell me everything that's going on."

-2 -1 G **M** 2 3 4 5 6 7 8 9 10 11 PH R

"Everyone, I'm struggling with the minutes."

"Can't read your own notes, Gary? Don't feel bad. Happens to me all the time."

"It's not that, Ned. They're ten months old. With everything that's happened, particularly on the WiFi front, you might want to find a way to reword some of this. That's why I sent them to you late last week, so you could review them."

"Want me to help? After all, I am the board secretary."

"Dennis, Gary's talking about last year's AGM minutes."

"Oh, okay. I thought it was unusual we got them three days ago instead of this morning."

"Haven't had time to read them."

"Me neither."

"How about you, Stacie?"

"Sorry, just glanced at them. Thought you were unusually efficient this month, Gary. Guess we can review them now."

"Except that'll take at least an extra hour. I want to get to my winemaking group."

"Let's just focus on the problem ones. Which are they?"

"That's just it, Stacie, there are quite a few, and I really need to get going."

"Is there a particular area of concern?"

"Mostly the WiFi. The way it actually went doesn't line up with what I wrote."

"For instance?"

"For instance the new WiFi contract. Instead of reducing the costs, it costs more. Especially when combined with the cost of the new website that ForageX used to operate."

"Okay, first off, the new contract doesn't take effect until the fall and the AGM only covers to the year-end in June, correct?"

"That's true, good thinking Stacie."

"Sheila has taught me a few things."

"We can leave that out if it comes up and defer it for anyone who asks. Sheila can manage that in the meeting. Now I tried to keep up with what was said between André du Bois, Raymond Tibbet, Nigel, and others. It doesn't make much sense anymore."

"Let me deal with those. I'll use your notes and my memory and figure out how to express them in the minutes."

"Are you sure, Ned?"

"The WiFi is my baby, right? It's the least I can do. It will be easy with André's words, since he's no longer here. The others will be harder but I'll figure it out."

"I'll reword mine myself, Ned."

"As you wish, Nigel."

"Is this proper? As secretary, should I be concerned?"

"Don't worry about it, Dennis."

"But Ned, you don't want to say —"

"When do you need this, Gary?"

"If you can get it to me tomorrow. Appreciate the help."

"You bet."

"Great. That's the biggest issue. I was thinking to state in the minutes there were no floor nominations last year. No need to remind them it was Lorie who nominated Ned."

"What's the big deal? Everyone knows Lorie and I are great friends. It would be natural."

"Maybe, if Lorie wasn't such a well regarded director."

"Ned, dear, I would prefer it that way myself, okay?"

"Sure, Lorie. I just don't —"

"What about André du Bois, who nominated himself?"

"He's gone, remember."

"So?"

"Meaning he won't read it."

"Right."

"Okay, let's do that. While we're at it, Gary, it'll look better if we indicate I provided a president's report."

"Okay. And I agree, it will."

"You didn't provide one?"

"No, just Lorie did."

"I've had pushback about the number of director positions up for election. Joseph from seven in particular. He planned to go up and was disappointed to see only a single spot available. Eric from nine also commented, but I doubt he intends to run."

"Huh, I really didn't think anyone would notice."

"Does that mean I might have competition?"

"Always a possibility. The important thing is he did not like how it came out, that it should have been clearer or told before the AGM notice. We may need to address it."

"Hmm, I was hoping it would kind of slide by, yes Ned?"

"Did Raymond say anything?"

"No? Haven't heard much from him lately."

"Okay, but I agree with Gary, we need to address this. Ned, since you're—"

"Sure thing, Stacie. I'll come up with some wording we can put someplace."

"Keep it brief, Ned, no need to make it bigger than needed."

"Short but sweet. Go make your wine. Save some for us."

"Just a minute, Ned. Gary, there's still a couple of matters I would like to dispense with."

"Can you make it quick, Lorie?"

"I'll try. So at the WiFi session, I indicated the board decided to ban ten-year contracts, though we haven't done it officially."

"We'll do it next meeting, okay? I'll make a note to add it to the agenda. Speaking of contracts, Lorie, we should mention the issue with the ForageX one."

"I thought it was ready to sign."

"Almost, Stacie, it's just ForageX is set on a five-year term, not the three-year one we proposed."

"We've got to get this signed."

"I know. We will. But to keep them at three years we'll need to forego the grace period, extend the existing contract. It means we keep paying them until the new one's in place."

"Do what you have to."

October

The Service Request

What's happened to Lorie? The nice lady, the one who actually talks to us owners at the AGM, the one who makes you think the board might actually give a damn? Why would she defend Gary like that? I mean, to contradict me and be so adamant a window washing note was sent out and distributed on the new site, when it clearly wasn't. Not just to my face but also when I asked her to tell me when she saw it sent, since it's not on the list of notices I see. Maybe you've got a different view, a director's view. Deleted your email? Sure Lorie, but why not sign on and tell me the date on the list in the system you see? Conveniently left that out, didn't you? Instead, you brush me off, tell me to take it up with management. Bet I'll get a prompt and clear response there — not. But Lorie, that won't alter the fact you reacted defensively to an offhand comment. Sad, so sad. The one I voted for, the one I respected, trusted, being obstinate like Gary, emulating his automatic rejection of inquiries without checking. Then to cover for the property manager. It isn't right. I'll definitely see what Gary has to say, see what bull he'll come up with, but it really gets exhausting. Maybe I should give up. Elevator's taking a long time too so . . . oh, here it is. Someone on it. Having second thoughts. Guess I'll go to the lobby anyway; otherwise I'll look crazy. Wouldn't you know it, office door's closed, and within management hours. Another issue with your golden property manager you shut your eyes to, Lorie. That Gary sure has a plum setup here, coming and going as he pleases, accountable to no one. Certainly not to this board. Can you blame him for taking advantage? With people like Lorie sucking up to him, protecting him? Pretty clear to see who's in charge around here. Who's the boss, and who are the flunkeys.

-2 -1 **G** M 2 3 4 5 6 7 8 9 10 11 PH R

The fellow he just shared the elevator with looks agitated after knocking on the management office door, which is closed again, meaning Gary left early. Again. Raymond takes a deep breath to help ignore it and certainly not linger on it.

The man spots Raymond and approaches to ask if he saw a window cleaning notice. Raymond recalls ropes rapping against his windows, jarring him awake earlier in the day, followed by the shock of facing a suds-covered window, a wiping squeegee in the hand of a man on a scaffold.

"That's right, there was no announcement."

"That's what I said to Lorie the other day. She was adamant one was sent."

"Pretty sure she's wrong—wait, Lorie? Not Gary?"

"That's right."

"And she didn't believe you?"

"Nope. It kind of irked me so I looked it up. Nothing on the website. I didn't care for her deflecting it either."

"What do you mean?"

"Telling me it's a management problem. Anyhoo, that's why I came down, to ask Gary. I'd let it go but Lorie's reaction bugs me. I came to see if she was lying."

"I'm Raymond Tibbett, by the way, I'm on the eighth floor."

"Oh, Monty Wilkes, just below you on six."

"Well, Monty, it could be a flaw with the website."

"But you said you didn't get it either."

"That's true. Maybe it's both of us. You could open a trouble ticket using the service request function, say you never got it, ask when it was sent. Easier than talking to Gary, and there will be a record of it."

"How do I do that?"

"It's right on the website."

"Haven't used it. Been waiting for some instructions."

"Don't hold your breath."

"Do you know how to do it, Ray?"

"It's not hard. You'll figure it out."

"Ah, maybe I'll just let it go."

"No, you shouldn't let it go. I'll help you."

Raymond bites his lip. What the hell is he doing, urging this poor fellow to enter the rabbit hole he just left? Then offering to go back into it himself to boot?

Monty's contented grin eliminates all hope of rescinding his offer. They exchange email addresses with Raymond promising to assist Monty if he encounters trouble raising the request. But after parting, Raymond's regret vanishes. Such a request will be a nuisance to Gary. And Lorie. Best of all, it will originate from someone other than himself.

What transpired between Lorie and Monty, who it seems also once respected Lorie, is troubling. If Raymond had not seen Lorie's readiness to throw Ned under the bus over the WiFi firsthand, he'd doubt Monty. Now it's easy to imagine the slim, tall woman cowering defiantly while warding off the query.

The kilometre long stroll to the lake is unusually lonesome. Pleasurably so. No cars, no bikes, no walkers or joggers; it's as if the neighbourhood collectively chose to give Raymond space to enjoy some privacy. Or another 9/11 is occurring and everyone but Raymond is aware of it and watching it on their televisions. Whatever it is, he's grateful every step along the wide multi-use path, all the way to the lighthouse at the end of the pier. A thick haze obscures the city skyscrapers but profiles of the fat nuclear plant silos are visible.

Then he closes his eyes to let his face absorb the sun.

"Well, hello."

He doesn't recognize the speaker's voice, assumes it's one of his neighbours. It's the bark that makes him turn around. Buster runs up and Raymond pets the dog as Kayla watches. She looks smart in a business suit; navy is a good colour for her. Though it can't hide that she's gained weight; if anything, it emphasizes it. Her face looks more haggard but her luscious hair ensures it retains some appeal. Should he hug her? Kayla seems uncertain too. He motions for them to take a seat on a bench.

"Didn't think I'd see you again."

"Don't be so dramatic, Ray, I'd have come by sooner or later. So you're walking down this way these days?"

Raymond smiles. Is she fishing for him to admit he's doing so in hopes of running into her? It's not true, but he doubts she would believe his denial.

"I might ask you the same."

"I have to come here at least twice a week or Buster gets all weird. It's so out of the way. At least they're good about letting me bring my dog to the office."

Raymond wants to ask why she doesn't call on him on these visits but finds the potential explanation discomfiting.

"Things going well at Omnirez?"

"Spectacular. I'm close to getting my graduated licence."

"Really?"

"Why, were you hoping I'd fail?"

"Of course not."

"They're giving me a property management apprentice role next month to make it happen. Best part is that building is less than two blocks from my parents', meaning I can walk. My car's in rough shape these days."

"So Buster won't be able to come here then."

"It's something I'd have to figure out sooner or later."

"I'm sure you will. Congratulations."

He means it. He wishes success for Kayla, notwithstanding his personal feelings about a certain colleague of hers. Kayla's wise but appreciative grin conveys she is no longer the trusting, naive woman of a few months ago. She has grown, in many ways, and it's reflected in a more confident mien.

"Seems like you're settling in there well."

"Uh huh."

Buster tries to jump on Raymond's lap. He's getting fat and needs help to lift him up. Buster always resisted help but has no choice now. Once he nestles in, he rests his head to sleep. Kayla digs into her purse to retrieve a Kit Kat bar. She offers Raymond a piece, he declines. She tells Raymond how she's made inroads at Omnirez.

"The owner's taken a shine to me."

"And what's he like? Or she?"

"Can't say. I've only seen him, never met him."

"That's weird. Is he being a secret admirer?"

"Stop that. He's got to be ninety-five. He rides a scooter. But his mind is shrewd. He's old school, his interest in me is purely professional."

"According to Sheila."

"Yes. But he does get Sheila to challenge me with situations that involve actual clients. I figure them all out. She even admits he thinks I'm smarter than her, but isn't jealous or anything."

"What do they think about Gary?"

She laughs.

"They consider him useful, like a loyal dog, in a good way."

Seeing her enthusiasm reminds Raymond how much he has missed her. Even after the talk with his mother about Leo, his father, and the war that confirmed for Raymond Jan's Irena was indeed Kayla's Babcia. A hateful woman adored by a Kayla who remains oblivious. And Irena's death ensures Kayla will remain oblivious; at least she won't hear it from Raymond.

Only that means bearing that awareness on his own, which would be crushing if their friendship once again developed into more. But as long as he continues to grasp this, they can bolster the friendship and keep it uncomplicated.

"Kayla, why don't we have a nice dinner out sometime, just as friends, of course."

She stares at him, her eyes and mouth screwed in a strange, unappealing expression. It's possibly the first time he's seen her lose her poise. She reaches for another Kit Kat, then puts it back, lets out a sigh, and grabs his shoulder. Buster stirs.

"It's nice of you to ask, Ray, but no. If you asked me months ago, maybe. Now I have a career. I can't afford to take time off. I have to spend all my free time preparing for . . . things are, well, different now, aren't they?"

"Of course, I understand."

Kayla smiles, her poise restored. She impresses him further by not running away from this awkward moment, taking time for some small talk and a hug to end their reunion gracefully.

Back in the lobby, he finds Bruce sorting a tall stack of mail packages in front of the closed management office, writing out slips to put on the mailboxes.

"You still doing this manually? I thought the system — "

"Still waiting for Gary to activate that feature."

"Did he leave already?"

"He was gone when I got here twenty minutes ago."

"Tell me, Bruce, what do you think of Gary? I mean how is he to work for? He's kind of your boss, right?"

"Kind of. He treats me all right. And my colleagues. Stood up for Kathleen, the young girl with the blonde hair, some time back when a new owner got into her face."

"I recall a message about that. Is it a big issue?"

"Most are friendly. Like that girl, Kayla. Often wondered if you two would become a couple."

"Really? She moved out. So I heard."

"That's right. Sad about her grandmother. A nice lady too."

Was she? Raymond wants to ask but instead checks his mail while the coincidence of hearing Kayla's name right after seeing her haunts him. The only item, a large envelope from Omnirez.

He opens the envelope in his suite. It's the AGM package: notice letter, agenda, budget, minutes, treasurer's report and, to his surprise, a letter from Dennis declaring he's running again for election for the single board seat. There are a few other items as well, but he sets the package aside to call his mother.

One benefit of their long talk last month is they've gotten close. So close he's shopping for a used car to see her more often now that his parking spot is empty. The retirement home office informs him she is on a shopping excursion to Chicago and will be gone a few more days.

He picks up the AGM documents again and notices a note in bold on the title page acknowledging the election mistake for the number of directors to be elected this year. What made them feel a sudden need to communicate this? Was it the man and his complaint? The wording has the clumsiness of afterthought, of cover up. That said, numerous errors from past years have been corrected. Maybe they feared Raymond or Monty going forensic on them. The thought had crossed his mind.

Unfortunately, this doesn't apply to last year's minutes. It's as if over ten months words expressed last October transformed into their opposite. Raymond has no clue what Gary put in his notes — notes Dennis, if he acted as a true secretary, would have recorded — nearly a year ago. But there's no way anyone could transcribe what was said into the drivel presented here:

"Raymond Tibbet expressed a wish that the solution reflects current and future needs while at the same time . . ."

Bastards. Twisting what he said to support their delusions. Who would do that? Not Gary, he's too lazy. Has to be Lorie, or Ned. Do they resent him that much to go so far? Raymond feels a repulsive mix of pity and disgust but suppresses an urge to fire off an email to Ned and Lorie to express his dismay. It has to be corrected but it has to be done at the AGM; he'll have to remain patient.

The contribution from André du Bois is just as bad, as is the airy-fairy brochure talk from Nigel. All fiction. They're claiming a president's report was given. If so, where is the physical copy in last year's package? The treasurer's report is there. To cap it, the minutes indicate Ned and Nigel were elected but there were no nominations from the floor. Don't they understand that to knowingly lie in the minutes — Ned and Lorie and those directly involved have to know it's a lie — equates to falsifying corporate records, hence is a crime?

Not only will Raymond have to scrutinize this document, he'll have to do it for all the ones in the past. Mining for gotchas. One factor in his favour is the paucity of communications from the board, which will make the task less laborious than it would normally. He can also count on their efforts at cleverness getting tripped up by their arrogance.

Naturally, most of his interest concerns the WiFi situation. Oddly, other than the minutes, there isn't a single reference to it, not even the tired, untruthful claim the board is investigating or working on it in Lorie's reports. Oh right, these documents only span year-end to year-end. Months before they signed the new ForageX contract. As Raymond well knows, unless the board is forced to say something, they'll say nothing.

There's another sheet, a proxy form to approve a by-law for insurance. No explanation other than a directive that all owners sign it and bring it along with them to the AGM.

"Not signing anything from you guys without explanation."

Speaking the words aloud makes him aware of the dryness of his mouth. He pours a glass of water, but then opts for a beer. The only other item of note for Raymond is a letter from Dennis indicating his intent to stand for re-election. Raymond's anger transforms into wry amusement at the idea of sticking Ned and the board with Dennis another three years.

That's right. Three years. Funny they discovered that error when they did. Rather convenient. Maybe Omnirez knew about it all along and kept it as an ace in the hole to use when needed. Not likely Gary would have discovered . . .

Kayla. It had to have been Kayla. Raymond takes his beer to the balcony, looks out, smiles. He drinks it down and returns to find an email from his new friend, or rather an email trail of a dialogue between Monty and Lorie.

"Lorie, a couple of days ago you told me there was a notice for the window washing. I do not have this notice nor do I see it on the website. Can you tell me when it was sent?"

"This is a management issue, Monty, that you should bring up with Gary. I do know it was posted on the website and in the elevators for at least a week."

"Lorie, I addressed this to you directly because it was an informal exchange between us; otherwise, I would not have done so. You didn't say what date it was sent. Was it only sent to certain people? If so, there may be a problem to be

investigated. Perhaps only those with director access got it. I saw nothing in the elevators. I've attached a screenshot of what I see on the website. I'm not sure what's the best way to communicate this to the property manager other than raising a service request. Should I do that?"

"I don't recall the date and I can't look it up because I delete those emails. Your not receiving it is a mystery as all residents should have gotten it. I'm not sure what to suggest except to contact Gary. He can tell you the specific date it went out and to whom. You can show him a printout or attach one to a service request if you want it tracked."

"Thank you for your time, Lorie, I will do that."

"Good going, Monty."

Raymond finishes his beer and gets another before checking the condo website to make sure Monty is right. He'd feel bad if it was there. It's not. If there's one thing the board got right, it's the website. He's about to encourage Monty to raise the request but the man's next email shows he's on top of it:

Gary, I ran into Lorie earlier and asked why we received no notification of the window cleaning. She assured me one was sent but I never saw anything in the elevator, nor did I get an email. Nor is it on the website. I'll attach a screenshot of what I see and a cut and paste of what Lorie told me.

Please investigate because it is a serious issue if I am being excluded from getting important messages. Had I been out I might have kept a window open, for instance, and possibly faced a puddle inside. I will be grateful for an explanation.

Also, FYI, I'm using this service request forum per Lorie's suggestion as she was unable to confirm the date it was sent. She said you could say when it went out and to whom. I'd like a copy of the email for my records. Thanks in advance for your attention to this matter, Monty Wilkes.

While it's good to catch them and have a record, the matter of Lorie's covering for Gary without proof against an owner she represents, is concerning.

Raymond suddenly recalls earlier in the day walking past a green expanse of empty soccer fields and the dreamlike desire to empty his mind of this petty nonsense to aimlessly kick a soccer ball around. If only he could let it go and do fun things like that. What is it about this toxic situation that gets him riled up? Has it become a perverse addiction?

-2 -1 G **M** 2 3 4 5 6 7 8 9 10 11 PH R

"Saw you chatting with Monty. What was that about, Lorie?"

"Nothing, Ned, he was just making an issue about the lack of a window washing notice. He claims one wasn't sent so I told him it was sent and it's on the website. I corrected him."

"Actually, it wasn't sent and it's not on the website."

"What do you mean, Gary?"

"I was busy and it slipped my mind."

"You sound like you're frustrated with me."

"It's just I keep telling you to not engage with residents so much about condo specifics."

"I think he's raising a service request about it."

"Let him. We've got more important matters to discuss with the AGM coming up next month."

"Why wasn't it sent?"

"Can we just focus on the AGM first, while Sheila is here, so we can let her go? Then we can discuss it afterwards."

"Actually, Gary, I'd like you to respond to Stacie's question."

"Right, Sheila, sorry. It's just there's not a great reason, I just slipped up."

"But you'll address it."

"Definitely."

"And ensure it doesn't happen again?"

"That's right."

"Is that acceptable to you, Stacie?"

"Sure Sheila, thanks. I'm confident Gary will resolve it."

"But this might make me look bad."

"Lorie, I'm sure Gary will handle it in a way that keeps your reputation intact. Meanwhile, it'd be wise to heed his advice to keep away from certain residents. Back to the AGM. Sheila?"

"Don't have much to add, all looks fine. That delicate matter regarding the director elections, I like how you handled it. That special note at the front of the package resolves the issue while simultaneously giving an aura of importance and transparency. Kind of a stop-the-presses feel."

"Thanks, but I thought of that, remember."

"I know, Gary, it's the presentation aspect I mean. Speaking of the election, I see only Dennis has put his name in for the one seat open. A shoo-in?"

"I hear Elle's interested."

"What? Ned, you never told me that."

"A little campaigning will be good for your soul, my dear."

"You didn't have to do any—sorry, what's that, Gary?"

"Elle hasn't submitted anything, she has no chance. I expect a low turnout this year, plenty of proxies for Dennis, likely none for Elle. Because if they only see one name . . ."

"Oh, that's right."

"Unless we hint to the proxies to write in Elle's name."

"You wouldn't dare. You guys will all vote for me, right?"

"Let's see what she has to offer."

"You're cruel, Ned."

"I'm with Gary. You have little to worry about."

"Thanks, Stacie, you're a dear. Besides, how would you all survive without my butter pecan cookies?"

November

The Tolerance of Incompetence

-2 -1 G M 2 3 4 5 6 7 8 9 10 11 **PH** R

Now what's this? Insurance proxy? Can I ignore it? Edith, how could you force me to suffer the AGM ordeal this year? Waste of time if you ask me, but of course you've stopped asking and assume I'll go because I love you. You're right. But you do need to tell me what it all is before going off to your book club. Hate these AGMs. Hate reading fiction as well, but for this I'd switch. Even if it means listening to your dowdy friends prattle on about a silly romance between gossiping. AGM will be a waste of time again, I can feel it. Not like there's a big election like that year three spots were up. Only one this year. Only one candidate too. Dennis. He doesn't need our vote. Delightful fellow, that Dennis, so unlike his partner, Tim. More pleasant, though hardly the type you see on a board. Then again, he's been a director a few years now, must be okay, if the other board members can tolerate his god-awful baking. Ugh, I can envision him prancing about the room, lobbying for votes, risking them by giving out cookies. If you want votes, Dennis, by all means do not *feed people your butter pecan cookies. The one from the rooftop picnic still lingers on my palate. Okay Edith, you're not here, I'll say it for you: I am exaggerating. Be awkward refusing if offered one. Maybe if I arrive just after it starts. Might as well skip it outright then. Who'd know? Not like anything interesting happens. The two guys who spoke up last year, they're the exception. They'll learn soon enough it's not worth the trouble, that it's smarter to dutifully absorb the twaddle shoved down our throats from the Omnirez folks, their clever responses to questions. Ah, what am I saying, of course I'll go. I'll get through it, get home — look at that, Edith baked some brownies with caramel. My, oh my, that woman can read my mind. But this insurance proxy thing? Until I know specifically what it is, what it means, I'll hold off signing it.*

-2 -1 G M 2 3 4 5 6 7 **8** 9 10 11 PH R

Gary, it's been two weeks since I put in this request. To me, it's a simple matter of looking something up. Not sure why it's taking so long. I hope you're not ignoring it. This issue is important to me and I want it resolved. Monty Wilkes.

Monty's kept Raymond apprised of the window washer saga. It inspires Raymond as he prepares for tonight's AGM, putting in the time to revise and rehearse the speech he'll give should he stand for election to the board.

The lobby is empty, save for Bruce. The street is also empty. For several minutes, all the way to the marina, Raymond fears he's gotten the date or time wrong. He relaxes once inside upon recognizing several faces. A smaller than usual crowd, at least twenty percent fewer than last year. Unfortunate.

Raymond takes a seat at the back from where he can watch all his fellow owners. The board sits at the front, stage right, the Omnirez contingent in the middle, and the accountant, Wayne, whom Raymond now mildly resents for having inspired him to get involved with Ned and Lorie, stage left. The board members look frazzled, unprepared. Especially Ned who keeps glancing away, side to side, avoiding eye contact. Or is he just arrogantly bored? It might be Raymond's imagination but the physical gap between the table and the owners' chairs seems larger this year.

Wait, Dennis is missing. No, there he is, can't miss the floral corduroys. He's chatting with owners, lobbying for their votes. It's rather charming and sincere, in a humble way that contrasts his sullen co-directors at the front. As far as Raymond knows, Dennis is the only person who's been declared as a candidate. It is tempting to abandon his plans to let the board fend with this director another three years. Elle looks anxious, maybe she has a notion to join the board. Little does she know . . .

Suddenly Dennis is to Raymond's right, addressing people in his row. Raymond's eyes turn in time for Dennis to hand him a cookie.

"I hope you'll vote for me."

"Hmm."

"Assuming you don't run."

"Guess you'll have to wait and see."

"You know it's a lot of hard work."

Of course it is, Dennis, Raymond wants to say. Instead he flashes a smile and Dennis moves to the front to take his seat.

A sudden gloom falls on Raymond when the droning voice of Sheila Mathers from Omnirez starts talking, putting his mind in autopilot as she introduces the people at the front. If he were to run, and win, his first act would be to fight to have a board member chair these AGM meetings, not an outsider. Wait, what is she saying? Raymond rises, ready to put up his hand.

". . . anyone for a motion to approve these minutes?"

"Wait."

"Yes, are you approving? Your name?"

"Raymond Tibbett. I do not approve these minutes because they contain errors that need to be addressed."

"We will get to that, but first we need to approve them."

"You're asking us to approve minutes that are in error."

"Like I said, you'll have an opportunity. For now, we need to follow the process which is to . . ."

This continues for several minutes until Raymond, speaking from the back, cannot keep up with Sheila who's calmly talking into a microphone. He relents, the motion passes. He not only loses an early battle, he's starting to lose conviction, fearing all battles will end like this. Raymond decides to forego all but two points, once granted an opportunity to protest the minutes.

The first is the outright lie no one was nominated from the floor last year, when in fact two were nominated. André du Bois and Ned. It restores his spirit when Monty, sitting three rows in front of Raymond, corroborates this. Raymond emphasizes how it was Lorie who nominated Ned, hoping it looks as suspicious to the others as it does to him that such a detail was omitted.

This must survive another bureaucratic motion / approval sequence before he can raise the second item: the misquoting of his words in the minutes from last year. No one seems to care — it's unlikely the other owners even read, let alone scrutinized, the minutes — but it's important to Raymond to press this point. It helps that he came with a pre-printed sheet of reworded text. No one objects to his changes and they successfully go through the same hoopla. Painful but worth it if only for getting Gary to promise to distribute the minutes in a few weeks.

It's a relief when Monty asks about the proxy everyone was told to sign to approve a new by-law. Raymond didn't bring his and won't sign without an explanation, though he understands the by-law's purpose: establish a baseline definition of a condo unit for insurance purposes to cover disasters affecting multiple units, to set a standard payout, leaving owners responsible for insuring all enhancements. Lorie attempts to explain but does it poorly and gives up. Gary states that since they have not yet received the two-thirds needed to pass the by-law, there will be a special meeting next month to collect signed proxies, at which time the owners can get more clarity.

A special meeting? Outside the AGM? Guess they can call one for this, but not for the WiFi. For isn't a two-thirds vote the percentage needed to cancel the WiFi, a number too daunting to Lorie? What makes it no obstacle now?

The meeting resumes. Raymond finds he is almost the sole voice in the audience, commenting frequently on points as they arise, trying to expose anything Omnirez and the board tries to hide. One odd item is a timing discrepancy between the website contract and the budget, revealing payments occurred prior to the contract start date. It's brushed aside by Lorie, but she seems perturbed at this being highlighted. It's exhausting. Though he is heartened by someone behind him mumbling how Raymond is the one who ought to represent them on the board.

There is the usual reprieve from the cheerless proceedings with Lorie's treasurer's report. At least for the others, unaware of what Raymond knows, who watch the tall woman languidly pace in front of the long table, her face belying how she relishes being centre stage. Raymond sees her for what she has become: a pompous, attention-seeking fool.

Lorie ends her report without mentioning the WiFi contract. She's not obligated to mention it because the contract signing occurred outside the period under discussion at this AGM. It bothers Raymond that no one asks. He's tempted to but feels he has spoken far too much. Also, he's consciously avoiding this particular topic until it plays out to its natural end. He finds it amusing when Lorie, about to share an inside tidbit, comments how unfortunate it is so few are in attendance to hear it. No kidding, lady, you think it might have to do with the fact we hate how the meeting is run and have lost faith?

Lorie reveals the board recently paid down a large debt and will no longer have to pay interest on that debt, saving money that could help reduce condo fees. She barely gets out the last word before receiving a reproach from Gary and Sheila to not promise that. As if the notion of spending less is impossible. It's a declaration of contempt to owners and offensive to Raymond. Worse is Lorie who, rather than responding with an optimistic, "you never know," timidly moves on.

"Effective this month, condominiums in this province are to be governed by a new act that defines and clarifies rules on how condos like ours are to be managed. For instance, directors must take a mandatory training course. All condo managers like Gary now require a licence. There are stricter rules, including specific and longer forms, defining what must be communicated. As the board and management adapts to these new rules, trust that we will inform you of these changes."

Monty told Raymond about the new condominium act two weeks ago, along with his desire it get ratified soon because it will give owners more leverage. This is the first Raymond heard about it from the board. Its being mentioned at all is a positive sign, though not how Lorie frames it:

"The new act will have little to no impact on how things run here. Except to add to the cost of assembling and mailing out more and thicker documents."

In other words: a new act crafted in the interest of owners is no more than a red tape nuisance to their representatives.

It comes time for the elections with a call for nominations from the floor. Crunch time. Raymond's heart pumps hard as he hesitates raising his hand. Only when someone nominates Elle does his choice become clear and he raises his hand too.

First Dennis, then Elle, take the microphone and state their case in a casual, rambling manner, appealing to friendship over any sort of platform or any tangible reason to elect them.

Raymond's turn. He's nervous and glad he wrote up what he wants to say, though it makes him read it like a statement rather than a spontaneously charismatic speech.

"Hello, I'm Raymond Tibbett. I'm a retired IT professional. At last year's AGM, I volunteered my expertise to assist on the WiFi issue. From November until April, I was on a committee to address the problem. At various stages, over those six months, I lobbied to involve condo owners in the process to acquire input to accurately assess needs and determine impacts to conduct a formal bidding process. My ideas and real-life experience were welcomed at first, even requested a second time, only to be eventually discarded. Months passed, with no progress, until all our options whittled down to a single, default solution that was there all along.

"A solution that, until fully operational, carries uncertainties in terms of the vendor's reliability, and can provide only a guess as to the true impacts to owners and issues that might arise.

"The decision has been made and I believe it can be made to work. Unfortunately, it's the easy part that's done. Much more lies ahead. I am still willing to help, and ensure owners are kept informed, if you elect me to the board.

"This experience has reaffirmed my belief in the need for a board that engages owners directly, and vice versa. That belief inspired me to volunteer in the first place and it is what I plan to instil in the board, if elected.

"I envision posting status updates from board meetings – or the minutes themselves. Town halls for owners to share issues and board members to share successes, face to face. Surveys to grade vendors to hire or renew using empirical data as opposed to anecdotal evidence. Our new website supports these abilities, we ought to take full advantage of it."

A glance at the directors shows them looking away. Except for Nigel, who leaves the front table to take a standing position apart from the others at the closed bar at the back.

"Furthermore, I feel it's essential to have our AGM meetings chaired by the board, not a vendor. The AGM minutes ought to be approved by the board and shared with owners as early as possible, ideally within a week, at most a month, so as to catch and correct errors promptly and accurately.

"Clear communication is the core value I bring while project management and vendor management are tangible skills I offer. Together, these can be invaluable in helping your board contain costs, sustain property values, and make documented decisions with the confidence those decisions represent the interests of all owners. Which, in the end, is the mandate of any condominium board worth its salt. Thank you."

He's shaking by the end of it but the applause exceeds the polite clapping following Elle's and Dennis's speeches, and this is reassuring. Nigel, on his way back to the front from the bar, intercepts Raymond to enthusiastically shake his hand.

"Nice speech."

Both he and Nigel retake their seats. Is it possible for them to become allies? Then Raymond feels a tap on his shoulder.

"That was great, you're a shoo-in."

But he's not a shoo-in.

Several minutes pass as the votes are counted. It comes less as a surprise, more as a relief, when Sheila announces Dennis is re-elected. Many sitting near Raymond are unhappy. For him, it would be worse if Elle had won, though she wouldn't see it that way. The blank faces at the front indicate the outcome was not in doubt for them.

"Motion to destroy ballots immediately after the meeting. Is there a second? All in favour . . . motion carried."

As the meeting progresses, Raymond feels better about how his speech was received, and that it wasn't a waste of effort. His hope is it planted seeds that will grow and ripple through to all owners, including absent ones. Sheila does her red tape thing to close the meeting, but not before Nigel paraphrases Raymond's point that more needs to be done to involve owners, especially in committees. Raymond approaches Nigel at the end.

"I'm glad you said that about involving owners more."

"Yes, something should be done about it. We should have a chat sometime, Ray. Call me, I'll try to make time for a coffee."

"Uh huh. But what's really important is for you guys on the board to run these meetings, not Omnirez."

"It's a good idea but I'm not sure that's not illegal."

"What do you mean?"

"I mean I'm pretty sure someone else has to do it."

"That makes no sense."

"Well, you can disprove me if you can show me someplace where it says we are allowed to do so."

Raymond can only smile. Sadly Nigel is still the same straw man building, work-avoiding consultant Raymond pegged him as months ago. No enemy-of-my-enemy potential ally.

Nigel joins the board members and the Omnirez contingent. What's fascinating is how their individually distinct weaknesses coalesce and congeal into a thick and unified entity impervious to any attack based on logic, common sense, or competence. It could be said incompetence is the lifeblood of bureaucracy.

Two people approach Raymond.

"It was close."

The scrutineers who counted the votes tell Raymond he did well, but the proxies cast by absentees was his undoing. No one other than Dennis had a chance as attendees were outnumbered by those proxies. Their empathy is touching. These are the sort of people he wants to help, whose eyes he wants to open. But they too are a problem, perhaps the most fundamental problem, as guilty as Raymond before his pyrrhic enlightenment, of the tolerance of incompetence.

Two weeks later, Raymond receives a memo stating that the required quota of signed insurance by-law proxies has not been met and board members will go door-to-door to collect them. So much for the special December session mentioned at the AGM; guess they opted for a low-key approach once again.

When there's a knock at his door, Raymond ignores it. He's not going to fill out the proxy. And he certainly has no desire to face Ned or Lorie or Dennis or whichever of Gary's board staff got the unlucky assignment to knock at his door.

The road to hell is paved with good intentions, as they say, and one can enjoy a pleasant outward, one-way trip riding one's own delusions. But what about the return trip? An aggregate of anger, fear, self-pity, dreams of revenge? Or an overwhelmingly misanthropic despair?

Another knock. This time Raymond gets up to look through the peephole. It's Kayla. She's holding something smaller and flatter than Buster. He opens the door.

"Hello."

"This sheet was left at your door. Some proxy."

She hands it to him and their hands touch slightly, but with no electric tingle of the kind he would have felt a year ago. They look at each other a long moment before he invites her in. She's carrying a DVD box. She lifts it and points to a bag on the floor containing a six-pack of Budweiser, a bottle of Chardonnay, and a large bag of potato chips.

"Got four hours to spare, Ray?"

-2 -1 G **M** 2 3 4 5 6 7 8 9 10 11 PH R

"Do we have enough proxies for the by-law now, Gary, or do we have to get Ned and Dennis to canvas for more?"

"I'll count them later this week. Let you know then."

"If not, I can help. My reunion got postponed. It surprises me why so many are reluctant to do so voluntarily."

"Beats me, Lorie. I want to put the issue to rest and get back to other things."

"Maybe they don't understand it."

"What's not to understand?"

"Actually Ned, Nigel has a point. When I asked some why it wasn't done before, most weren't sure what it was for."

"What did you do?"

"I tried to explain. How about you, Ned?"

"Impressed its importance and pressed them to fill it out."

"Including Raymond Tibbett?"

"Thought I'd leave him for you, Nigel. Oh, I forgot, you're too busy to help."

"It's okay, I tried Raymond, but no answer, so I just left it."

"At least Dennis is willing to pitch in."

"Look Ned, I'll say it again, I'm not here all day like you and Lorie and Dennis. I can't fraternize around the building. I need to limit my board activities to what a director does."

"Are you saying this is beneath you?"

"I'm sure Nigel is appreciative, as am I, of the work you and Lorie and Dennis have done securing the proxies. I, for one, am glad we're back on schedule with no AGM or by-laws to worry about for a while. Now Gary, let's continue."

"Actually, I'm not quite finished with the AGM."

"What is it, Gary?"

"For one thing, Raymond Tibbett left me in a quandary over the minutes. I've never had to deal with someone insisting on so many changes, never mind all the new items he brought up. It's not going to look good if I do it verbatim and I'm not sure how to sort it out."

"You can always ask—"

"Sheila? I did. She told me to work it out with you folks. Yes Ned, you have an idea."

"Do we need to do something now? Can't we wait until it's time to prepare for next year's meeting?"

"Isn't that what we do every year?"

"It is, Dennis. But people will expect something sooner since I slipped and implied that would happen."

"So? Let him wait. Let him make a fuss. We can deal with it then, if it happens."

"I think Ned's on to something."

"Thanks, Nigel. Why?"

"No, I honestly think what you said makes sense. Let's face it, we aren't sure where he's coming from. Instead of giving in to him, let him play his hand. You are rather busy, right Gary?"

"And the holidays are just around the corner."

"It's not as if this is an urgent matter."

"It may be to him."

"Yes, Dennis, but he doesn't speak for all owners. Plus, need I remind you, there is the WiFi to contend with. As president, I say we hold off. And really we're not holding off but continuing our normal practices."

"Well put, Stacie."

"Thanks, Nigel. It was an uncomfortable AGM, but let's be thankful few showed up and it was Dennis who was elected."

"That'll make life easier for me, for sure. In fact, that ought to about cover it for this evening. Yes, Lorie?"

"What about that service request, the one in which I was quoted?"

"Speaking of your quotes, I wish you hadn't said what you said at the AGM about the new condo act."

"I had to say something, I couldn't ignore it altogether."

"I'm not sure I agree with you there but even so, why point out the fact I'll need a licence?"

"Well, you will."

"Of course, just as you all will have to take the training. But was there a need to highlight it?"

"Sorry, Gary."

"This new act is enough trouble for me. I don't need owners like Raymond and Monty monitoring my career. I can see them now, pestering me about my licence."

"Again, I'm sorry, it just came out. I doubt they'll do that."

"Well, let's hope not."

"Since you bring up Monty Wilkes, can you update me on his service request?"

"It's a nuisance request."

"Be that as it may . . ."

"I'm sure you understand I've had little time to address it."

"So it's been open all this time?"

"That's right."

"No follow up to ask why it's taking so long?"

"Maybe. Haven't looked, honestly."

"I'd really like to get it resolved."

"So would I. I don't know what to say. You kind of stepped in it on that one."

"Is this the thing about the missing window washer note?"

"Yes."

"Why not just insert one in the system and make it look as if it's been there all along. What are you sneering at, Nigel?"

"Doesn't work that way. No system would allow that. Can't we figure this out later?"

"Nigel, it's my reputation."

"That's my point. Your reputation. Not ours. Stacie?"

"I have to agree with Nigel. It is something for you to figure out, Lorie. Maybe you could admit you're wrong in an email or when you see him. You're shaking your head, Gary."

"I know him, he's not persistent like Tibbett. No reason to open an avenue for him to hound you directly. I'll come up with a response, I promise. It's been several weeks, another week or two won't make a difference."

December

The Surrender to Incompetence

-2 -1 G M 2 **3** 4 5 6 7 8 9 10 11 PH R

Not that drain again. Really don't want to see Gary but may have to, reporting it on the website is too confusing. Could have brought it up at the AGM, except that gentleman kept talking. It would have been annoying but he said more of substance than all the board together. Such a shock he got beat — Dennis is sweet, but not a director — bet he would help me out with this, bet he would make sure Gary was nicer, more responsive, not always greeting you with his exasperated, "Yes, Mrs. Gibbons," followed by a chastising sigh for interrupting his day, as if he's the one with the drain acting up, not me. Not sure what to do these days, haven't been sure since Harold's passing. He'd say, don't let it bother you, just let it go. Funny how I rued he did so little, left it all to me when alive, which is true, but Hal was a rock. Or an anchor, in a grounding way, giving me the confidence to address things on my own, even if it means doing nothing and just allowing matters to work themselves out. I feel helpless now. Adrift. Letting matters go and work themselves out seems my best and only option these days. Better than getting doubly frustrated at dealing with the property manager. Don't want to end up bitter like that fellow who did all that talking at the AGM. He was some fired up, suspect he held back and had plenty more to say. Fear he had plenty more to say.

-2 -1 G M 2 3 4 5 6 7 8 9 10 11 PH **R**

That evening watching *Schindler's List* with Kayla continues to haunt Raymond. How could he have let her depart with such a notion? Then again, did he have a choice?

He looks towards the east where a red sky announces a new day. A spate of unseasonably warm weather inspired him to go to the roof after breakfast, with his coffee and laptop, to see the sun rise and breathe in a dose of fresh, early winter air. A trace of snow covering the suburban land leads to an empty marina and lake, providing a pleasant backdrop to compose a long overdue letter to Lech in Poland. The procrastination means he can include a message his mother wants to share with Jan, who is hanging on. It's difficult to write with his mind preoccupied by Kayla. He lowers the laptop screen.

Seeing her was a shock, as she must have put on at least ten more pounds since last time. Kayla used to be so self-conscious about her weight and last year would never have allowed this. Her nervous energy didn't have the same positivity. She seemed on a mission, for she asked him to again share what he learned in Poland. He did but she wasn't satisfied, as if expecting more. After silently listening to him, she inserted the DVD, opened a bag of chips and two beers, then directed Raymond to sit still to watch the movie.

Which they did, for nearly four hours, including pauses for bio breaks and to replenish their drink and food. Raymond had not seen the movie and found himself gripped by the story as much as by the sets that brought him back to Poland. To barren Gross-Rosen, sombre Auschwitz, stirring Wroclaw, before the reunion at Schindler's grave that brought tears to his eyes.

"See, I get it now."

Kayla's words frightened Raymond as he'd almost forgotten she was there. He looked at her, she was smiling, but her smile diminished upon encountering his expression and tone.

"What do you get?"

"Are you all right, Ray?"

"What do you get?"

"Maybe we should open the wine now."

"Kayla."

"Okay, okay. Didn't expect the movie to affect you so much, guess I was so concerned about me. About my Babcia, about the things you said before. You know, that she may have been . . ."

She struggled to get it out but Raymond wanted to hear it, and didn't help or push, other than to open and pour the wine. It helped Kayla relax and speak. What she said angered him to the point of numbness.

She was not willing to accept the idea her grandmother was a Kapo at the Gross-Rosen sub-camp, let alone that she did the awful things described by Jan. None if it is true in Kayla's mind. What about Babcia's admissions? Kayla believes she concocted them to clear a path for Kayla to be free with Raymond. It had to be the most pathetically absurd example of denial he'd ever heard. It took a long deep breath to settle his pounding heart.

"I'm afraid, Kayla, there's more. Much more."

"More? What do you mean, more?"

He hadn't wanted to do it but Raymond felt compelled to share what his mother told him about the evacuation, the death march, how Irena and Kurt killed Frantiszek and forced Leo to mutilate the corpse before releasing Raymond's father. Kayla's expression remained fixed and unreadable until his last words. Then she formed a crude smile.

"No, no. It's not possible. My Babcia with a Nazi?"

"Not even if it was her only chance to survive?"

"You are awful. That can't be true."

When he didn't react, she gathered her things and left, only she forgot the DVD. Possibly she was crying, but he's not sure.

Now, on the roof, he's convinced her abrupt departure was to ward off doubts about her own story. She came to him with the film intent on contradicting his version. Only he didn't give her the confirmation she sought. While he can muster sympathy for Irena for a situation she never asked for, he feels the woman took the easy way out by dying and leaving a legacy of lies that compromised Kayla's ability to accept the truth.

Her departure had a delicate eternal quality about it that he failed to identify then, but that saddens him now. Raymond has no desire to destroy her delusion—though he might have at the time—but he doesn't want their impasse to remain as unclear as it is now. Kayla might. That likely prompted her get-out-while-you're-ahead exit without leaving any way to resume contact. It won't reveal itself by looking out over the lake either.

Raymond returns to his suite to look for any hint of how to contact Kayla. Nothing. He's tempted to knock on the door at her old suite and ask if she left a forwarding address, or search around. He could ask Bruce, though that would be conspicuous. Asking Gary is of course unthinkable.

Then he spots an email from Monty, a forwarded response to the service request Monty raised about the lack of a window washer notice. Weeks ago. Gary's response:

The window washing company failed to confirm when they were going to start. They were already here that day by the time I got to the office. This miscommunication caused a big scramble to get notices put up in the elevators so as many of the residents could know before they got too far.

This explicitly contradicts Lorie's claim a note was sent, but doesn't explain why Gary didn't post the notice online. Since the window washing takes at least two days, why not do that to be thorough? What if an owner is away and left a window open, or just isn't sure? The window wouldn't get cleaned, not a disaster. But what about folks who value privacy and shut their blinds in case they don't want the washer seeing inside? No apology.

The reply of someone who got caught and who is desperate. Not a smart reply either. Now there's an official record of Lorie and Gary telling opposite stories: one is lying, if not both. Most galling is closing the service request without Monty's approval.

Raymond points this out to Monty one afternoon when they see each other at the mailboxes. But Monty has moved on.

"Raymond, my friend, I've been doing some research on the condo act, how condo boards and managers ought to work. It's been quite an education and opened my eyes to issues here. For instance, does it ever bother you that the board doesn't or can't or won't distinguish between owners and residents?"

Raymond nods encouragingly. He has noticed.

"I, for one, find it disrespectful but also problematic because the board exists to represent owners whether they reside here or not. As if the word 'owner' is off limits to them. It makes sense if Gary uses 'resident', he's responsible for the residences. For the board, the priority is owners, shareholders, as for any corporate board. If they're always in sync one is getting the shaft. Guess who in our case?"

"Yes, I see what you mean."

"Do you, Raymond? Think about it. The reality is there is no board of directors here to prioritize us owners who should be at the top. In fact, we're at the bottom, with or maybe even below tenants. We always have to adapt to vendor needs or demands. The top vendor of course being Gary and his Omnirez cohorts who set the priorities. Always in their favour."

Monty's onto something, Raymond knows, but hearing the name Omnirez distracts him with an idea: why not call Kayla at her corporate office? He doesn't need Gary for that, or Bruce, or anyone.

He excuses himself to rush to his suite where he retrieves a document bearing the Omnirez letterhead and a phone number. He starts to dial, but stops upon realizing Kayla could identify his cellular phone number. He switches to the landline, which he's sure she's never used.

"Yes, I'm looking to get in contact with Kayla Slaske."

"What is the nature of your call?"

Raymond wipes his brow from a brief surge of frustration. The woman's voice is kind, professional, not easily fooled.

"You see, I have a DVD of hers that she left at a restaurant I was at with her and some other people."

"So this is a personal matter?"

"I suppose, in a way. I don't have her home number but she said she worked as a property manager for Omnirez, that's all."

Raymond's brow sweats profusely as he extends the lie. The woman's tone doesn't crack.

"Wouldn't it be best to call the property she manages?"

He can see, despite the calm, polished, businesslike way it's given, this deflection is no different than those from Gary. This awareness comes out in his tone in the form of irritation.

"Which one?"

"I'm sorry?"

"I meant which property. She said that she worked at two of them, splitting her time. But she didn't mention the buildings."

The woman at the other end pauses for a long time. Maybe she's trying to check his number, maybe she's calling Kayla. It doesn't matter now. He's committed to getting in touch even if he has to reveal himself. Then the woman comes back, her voice as polished and kind as at the beginning.

"I hope you understand I can't give out such information."

"Sure. I'll be happy if you can pass on a message."

"Yes, of course, and what is your name?"

"Leo, it's Leo. She won't know my last name."

"All right, Leo, and what is the message?"

Now it's getting tricky. If he asks the woman to tell Kayla to drop by anytime, the woman may suggest that he instead drop it off at the Omnirez office. He decides to ask to have Kayla call the number he is calling from now. The woman obliges.

Days pass with no call. He tries again and leaves a different message. That evening, after playing pool on his own, he enters his suite and finds an envelope on the floor addressed to him. He opens it. A slip of paper falls out, a handwritten note:

"Stop calling my office, LEO! You think you're clever? You expect me to fall for your insane conclusions about Babcia being an evil person who betrayed her people to run off with a Nazi? I won't. It's all lies. You must stop spreading them. Babcia was a saint. It's you who is the troubled one. K."

It doesn't express, "I hate you," the way an old girlfriend did back in university, but the sentiment is identical. Yet its sting is not harsh, but clarifying. Watching the film was a facade, a test, no, a chance for him to buy into her delusion. To denounce the version from Jan and accept that Kayla's grandmother was a lovely woman whose only crime was to plagiarize a Hollywood film to embellish her past with sanitized sentimentalities. Never mind the raw emotion he witnessed firsthand in Jan's eyes, or the frightened guilt evident on Irena's face at the rooftop picnic. Would Kayla feel the same had she seen those?

Raymond is angry, very angry, with no outlet, leaving him to stew over this development, or rather lack of development, to try and endure yet another wall. There is one outlet. Tiny, petty, childish, but like a drinking binge, satisfying in the moment. He grabs his laptop to open a condo service request:

Hello Gary.

Monty Wilkes shared with me your exchanges about the window washing service request as it was a concern of mine as well. They confirm Lorie was misinformed and wrong in asserting an email notice was sent and posted on the website.

In the future, in such situations, I recommend not only posting in the elevators after the fact, as you say you did, but also via emails and the website. That would alert those who are at work or away and allow them to arrange to have their windows or blinds closed by someone to maintain privacy. It would prevent a situation for which an owner might hold the corporation responsible. I am opening this new request to let you formally acknowledge adopting my recommendation as part of the condo processes.

I must at the same time express dismay that it took three weeks to get a response to Monty's service request, as it appears no investigation was necessary. I can't think of a reasonable explanation for that, but if there is one, I am open to hearing it. As is Monty, I'm sure.

Not quite cathartic but the satisfaction from submitting this is somewhat of a balm. Gary and Lorie are wrong and their lies and cover-ups ought to be on record for posterity. As this is one of Gary's scheduled days onsite, it'll be fun to see the response. Will he deal with it promptly or ignore it like Monty's? Or let it fester in his head over the holidays? Raymond prefers the latter.

It's a remedy as well, allowing Raymond to detach from his thoughts of Kayla to get back to Lech's letter. It's still difficult to write as it requires some effort not to allow his anger to seep in and reveal too much about Irena. These hesitations prompt him to frequently check for a response from Gary.

An hour later Raymond checks again, and finds the service request closed. He looks at it but finds no explanation, just that it's closed. Raymond rushes to the lobby. No one is there except Gary at his desk, head down. Raymond knocks. Gary looks up, puts his head back down again, keeps it down.

"Why did you close my service request?"

"Because there's nothing to do on it."

"What about my suggestion to send out notices even when they're missed?"

"Already part of the process. It just didn't happen this time."

"Why the defensive attitude?"

"You bring it out in me, always challenging. Why can't you be like the others here?"

"I'm always challenging because your defensiveness, which I've encountered since day one, leaves me little choice. Maybe I need to escalate. But to who? The board?"

"Go ahead."

"How do I do that?"

"Send an email to the usual address."

"But if I do that, you'll see it. Do I need to contact Omnirez?"

"Do what you need to do."

Gary shrugs, taps a few keys on his laptop, but the pattern seems to have little purpose. Raymond can't see the screen. The churlishness is pathetic, unprofessional, and makes him recall a remark Lorie made at the AGM, and Monty recently alluded to, enough to take a stab in the dark.

"Gary, I'd like to see your property manager licence."

The key tapping slows but Gary doesn't look up.

"Did you hear me, Gary?"

"Put it in writing."

"What?"

"If you want to see it, submit a request in writing."

"What is your issue with me, Gary? What's your problem?"

Gary's shoulders slump as he slowly turns to Raymond, his cheeks flushed, eyes exhausted, voice guttural but intense.

"You. You're the problem. You're the only one who acts like this. Here or anywhere. I've done this thirty-two years and dealt with assholes. But none like you. Everything was fine until you accused me of rigging the board."

"Rigging the board? What are you talking about?"

"You know damn well what I'm talking about. On the roof. I wish I had a video. You stood there and accused me of trying to rig the board."

Raymond recalls the scene at the rooftop when he brought up Lorie quoting Gary's fear of a rogue board. Possibly Gary mistook rogue as rigged. Which does pose a question: has Gary rigged boards before? Raymond chooses not to pursue this, he feels bad about the misinterpretation. Too bad Gary didn't share his reaction back then. As Raymond expresses this, the tension lowers significantly.

"Gary, if it came out that way, I apologize."

"Yeah?"

"Yeah. Let's fix this between us."

Gary approaches with a relieved smile that matches the one Raymond feels inside himself. They shake hands.

"I was raw about the way the WiFi turned out at the time. It put me in an awkward position. Looking back, I regret the day I agreed to work with those guys."

"You regret it?"

"Absolutely. Had I known how inexperienced they are, how junior, yeah, I would have kept out of it."

"It's not uncommon with these boards."

"They're dreadful. Incompetent."

"Except Lorie is good, she's valuable, we need her."

"The best of the worst? They're all useless, to me."

"That's why it's wiser for you or for anyone to see me first if you have issues. It's the best way to avoid misunderstandings."

Gary's sudden transition from cornered rat to approachable, compassionate confidante startles Raymond enough to generate a corresponding transition from anxiety to relief within him. It doesn't erase his scepticism. He can't quite believe Gary, but it is enough to grant the benefit of doubt. Which is far more than he imagined could happen only minutes earlier.

"Sounds good, Gary. We'll leave the service request closed."

They shake hands again, wish each other a good weekend. Raymond's satisfied. Not for a win, he didn't win anything, but a truce, a promise of peace, at least temporarily. He knows it's a matter of days or hours or even minutes before he'll be plagued again by board nonsense. But a truce can help him process what he can't change so those things can't agitate him as before.

What about the contradiction between Lorie's claim notices were put up a week before and Gary's that he scrambled to post them that day? Or discovering Gary is required to produce his property manager's licence to whomever asks at anytime?

Drop it. Drop it. Drop it.

Raymond can continue to collect gotchas — ineptitude being a self-renewing resource — to expose the follies of the board. But what would it accomplish? Or prove?

In the end, he's better off being right, not righteous. Being at peace rather than victorious.

-2 -1 G **M** 2 3 4 5 6 7 8 9 10 11 PH R

"Which is why, as I keep telling you, it's wise to not involve the owners, not to that degree."

"Duly noted. Lesson learned. For us all, right? Lorie? Ned?

"Yes."

"Yes."

"Nigel? Dennis?"

"Yes."

"Yes."

"To be clear, that particular service request is closed?"

"Sure Lorie, it's closed. Both are closed."

"And he won't reopen it?"

"No, Lorie, he won't. I'm a hundred percent certain. Neither will Monty Wilkes."

"How can you be certain about Tibbett?"

"Glad you asked, Ned. Because of what he said to me about regretting joining your WiFi committee in the first place. Believe me, he was sincere, and not too complimentary."

"Jerk."

"You picked him."

"Shut up, Nigel."

"You shut up."

"All right, it's done, okay everyone? As I said, we've learned a lesson here to take us forward."

"Right, Stacie. No more committees."

"No, Ned, don't say it like that. This isn't about eliminating, it's about applying discretion. There may a time when we might benefit from expertise outside our group. We just need to more particular about how we do it, and what we share."

"What exactly are you saying, Stacie. Are you blaming me for Raymond?"

"No, Ned . . ."

"You brought him in, you shared more than was—"

"Enough, Nigel. Look, I need you two to stop this once and for all. I'm not blaming you, Ned, I'm not blaming anyone. If we can't be a unified board we must act as one, a unified team. Let's consider it a lesson learned. No blame required. Got it?"

"Sure."

"Nigel?"

"You bet."

"We've all made mistakes. Remember we're part time, we're on a volunteer basis. We all need to learn for ourselves why it is important to rely on Gary, on Omnirez They're experts, they've seen it all, with dozens, if not hundreds, of years of experience we ought to trust and capitalize."

"Couldn't have said it better myself, Stacie."

August

The Transition

-2 -1 G M 2 3 **4** 5 6 7 8 9 10 11 PH R

Something about that woman in Gary's office is familiar. It looked like she was settling in. A new property manager? That would be great. In her late thirties, possibly forties? I know who she reminds me of. That girl with the grandmother, Kayla, except Kayla was not so round, she took care of herself. Sweet girl, probably shouldn't have — too sweet to manage even a tame condo like this one. Wouldn't that be awkward? Maybe it is her, the black hair — never mind, figure it out soon enough. Now it's all about unpacking. The repairs I did last year were the best decision, worth the noise. Really not much to do but settle in. So lucky with the renter, place left in good shape, primed for the truck to unload this evening. Wonder if they got that WiFi business sorted out. Must have, I read no complaints. I don't need to feel bad for bailing out on Ned's committee. Nice guy but dense. Reminds me of what my boss used to say: If the first thing you say about a colleague is they're nice, avoid working with them. Must have subconsciously heeded her sage advice. May have to rethink going for a board seat if he's still on it. I suppose it might be wise to check out that rooftop picnic tonight, meet some folks, do a bit of pre-campaigning, just in case. Make a good first impression, make my face recognizable. That was part of the problem last time, no one knew me. For that matter, did they know Ned? Not sure, but the tall lady on the board who nominated him did. Suspect a lot of folks took that as an endorsement.

Voices are coming from Gary's office but the lobby is empty of people. There is a Pomeranian that looks like Buster but this one is much spryer than the poor beast that needed Raymond to lift him on his lap that sunny day last October. Ten months already. It wags its tail at Raymond but shows no sign of recognition. It's been eight months since his blow-up with Gary. It was worth it, peace being the operative word in his condo life since. Seeing a dog resembling Buster won't upset that, though it is a reminder of the ephemeral nature of peace.

That peace hasn't been uneventful, nor achieved without an occasional exertion of energy to stifle his reactions. For instance, Lorie continues to insist she saw a window washer note despite Gary admitting on record none was sent. Raymond's written Lorie off as a lost cause. After Stacie moved and resigned from the board, did they ask the AGM runner-up to fill the vacancy? No. They asked Elle. A surprise to some, not to Raymond. He is proud of his resolve to bite his tongue, even with the continual delays regarding the WiFi, just letting things roll along.

He must admit, despite the delays, the WiFi is reliable. The anticipated savings, once his contract ends, can cover the cost to operate the used Chevrolet Cruze he bought to make it easier to visit his mother, who he now sees more often. He'll wake early tomorrow for a long day to pick her up and drive them both to the airport for their big trip to Poland and Ukraine.

Raymond checks his mailbox. He discards the junk mail in the blue bin, then glances up at the cork board. A note in a large font announces the date of the rooftop picnic has moved up to this evening. In fact, it'll start in an hour. When was this posted? Never mind, it means he is able to attend. Raymond hustles to catch an elevator, its door about to shut. As he presses eight, he hears an unmistakable laugh coming from the office. Kayla.

Did Lorie invite her to the party? That's nice. Kayla did live here long enough. But it gives Raymond second thoughts about going, and third thoughts when he opens an email from Lorie, who is now board president.

> Recently, Omnirez requested the Board to oblige them in granting a temporary change of Property Manager, so as to allow Gary Lewis to perform a special assignment, which is to get a brand new condominium operating efficiently. This will last six months. Naturally, we were reluctant to grant it but did so because it will be a boost to Gary's career. And we are assured he will not be gone permanently and is accessible to our interim manager, if needed.

Special assignment.

What on earth could that mean? And what message does it convey to owners? That the person in charge of managing their investment is so esteemed by the board, they are willing to risk disrupting the operation of their home, their asset, to enhance his career? If the board truly believes in Gary's value, this has to be a highly dubious decision.

Or did Gary screw up and make some error that needs to be concealed? If so, the question for the board might be: why do you always cover for the guy? Though it is possible, if there is a performance reason, the board doesn't know. The issue may be an internal one for Omnirez.

Regardless, it sounds as if an innocent new condominium is about to inherit thirty-plus years of Gary's acquired bad habits. Maybe Gary is an infiltrating force parachuted in by Omnirez to take control of unwitting boards in their infancy, before they get too wise. Until now Raymond assumed the board always acted in concert with Omnirez; what if Lorie, Ned, and the others are genuinely ignorant of their machinations?

These days, when those old negative thoughts encroach on his day and threaten to consume it, Raymond has little trouble pausing to let them ramble on. Once in a while he tests himself, to ensure he's not merely avoiding, but has truly vanquished those demons. What better test than to socialize?

He takes a beer up the elevator and out onto the roof. There he almost crashes into Alice Greenberg, holding a tray of plastic cups filled with punch. She interrupts trying to convince Bruce a little rum won't hurt, even if he is on the job, to offer one to Raymond. He declines, raising his beer can. He wends his way past Marjorie Gibbons who is chatting with Wendell Halley and Beatrice—he can't recall her last name—the vote counters at the AGM, before manoeuvring by the charming elderly couple, the Crawfords, Arnold and Tanya. But no one from the board. Not even Elle, whose absence is particularly conspicuous. There sits Sylvia, the young woman, the renter. Guess who she's talking to? None other than Elise Adams, the owner with whom Sylvia argued about the side door last year. Seems everyone is getting along these days. It makes him wish the same for he and Kayla.

His anger with her has subsided to the point he can forgive her grandmother who, in all honesty, was as much a prisoner or victim of circumstance as Leo or Jan or Frantiszek. Time helps soften his view on the woman to accept she did what she did out of desperation, and would never have done it were it not for the actions of the Nazis, the real criminals. Sadly, he could not expect Kayla to appreciate even this and it's not what he'll say if he does see her tonight. Her mind is committed to a perception of her grandmother as a saint. Any concession Raymond might make, directly or indirectly, Kayla would either distrust or take as patronizing. He not only has learned to avoid such mistakes, he has learned to spot their approach.

"There you are. We need to get together for a chat soon."

Monty Wilkes, instigator of that contentious but ultimately peacemaking service request, slips by a couple to stand next to Raymond. Clearly he's had too much rum.

"Nice turnout, eh Raymond?"

"Sure is."

"Think Gary's departure got them all out of hiding?"

"I don't know."

"Me neither, but I bet I know why he had to leave."

"Had to?"

"I think I caused it."

"What are you saying, Monty? Think his handling of that service request, the delays and all, got him in trouble?"

"Could be they're connected. What I'm talking about is him breaking the rules in not having a proper . . ."

"Proper what? What are you talking about?"

"Stupid rum, makes me yak too much. Forget what I said."

The old Raymond within tugs at him to grill Monty, while the new one wants to let it be. Months ago this would have been no contest, the grilling would commence. Now any battle is at best an echo of one. It's surprisingly easy to acquiesce and leave Monty for Joe Gantry, the fellow Raymond overheard complain about the election error with the number of directors.

It's only small talk with Joe, however, and it dissipates upon spotting a man who appears to be André du Bois speaking with Bruce. Did André ever get Raymond's email? It was so long ago, does it matter? It would be rude to break away from Joe, who is now talking about the forecast. Raymond is unable to quell his urge to speak to André. He excuses himself from Joe. Only his hesitation takes too long; André is at the exit. It leaves Raymond alone with Bruce.

"Haven't seen that guy around much, lately."

"Who? André? He just moved back in. Was renting out his suite the past year."

"How come?"

"Says he was working for an NGO in some African country, but I heard he was in prison. Tax fraud or something."

"Really."

"At least that's the rumour."

"So, no board members here?"

"They were here earlier, for a bit, but there's an impromptu board meeting going on now. They'll be back."

Monty joins them, still tipsy, but not as bad as earlier, due no doubt to the cup of coffee in his hand.

"But you're here, Raymond."

"What do you mean?"

"I mean, you should be on the board. I'm miffed they didn't ask you to fill Stacie's spot when she quit. You clearly were our choice. I even told Lorie that, but you can guess her response."

"Oh yes."

"Look, Raymond, a few minutes ago I hinted at something."

"It's okay."

"No, you should know. While making my coffee, I sent you an email. Check it out. I took the liberty of using something you said. I hope you don't mind. At least you care."

Raymond nods absentmindedly as he glances around.

Pleasant, friendly, lovely but blissfully ignorant neighbours; who is he to risk ruining that? Who is he to point out red flags, examples of incompetence, when they are helpless to do much more than absorb the impacts? By opening doors to awareness, won't he invite in misery? He'll no longer raise trouble on their behalf or do anything but look out for himself. Instead, he'll be like them and find a new delusion — or exist delusion free — and make his existence in this building palatable enough to enjoy events like these where he can get along with his neighbours.

He finishes his beer but, instead of going back to his suite to get another, he seeks out Alice and her punch tray. She's happy to give him one; apparently they're too potent for most. It's not bad; in fact, it tastes nice and it's smooth. Marjorie joins them and distracts Alice before he can say so.

"Alice, any idea what Gary's special assignment might be? Could be good for his career."

"But is it right for his career to come ahead of our needs?"

"Good point, hadn't thought of that. I guess it depends on his replacement. I heard from Lorie he or she might join us later, give us a preview."

"Don't get me wrong, I'm not unhappy to see him go and I wouldn't have mentioned it if he was gone for good. It's just he is coming back and I guess that troubles me."

"Oh Alice. Maybe we'll get a better Gary in six months."

Raymond chuckles as he finishes the rum. The women look at him, as if expecting him to add to their conversation. He's got plenty, but it's neither his duty nor desire to enlighten them.

Is he even happy to see Gary gone or know that he possibly played a part in it? Wouldn't that be bitter icing on a crumbling, decaying cake? Alice lets out a sigh.

"I just hope Gary learns to be friendlier."

"He was friendly enough, just not helpful."

"Right, Marjorie, that's right."

"Have a lovely evening, ladies."

"You're not coming back to meet Gary's replacement?"

Raymond shakes his head and departs, bidding farewell to those he encounters on the way. He detours to the lobby to clear his mailbox to make space for the junk mail that's bound to pile up over the next three weeks.

There's nothing there. He stops at Bruce's empty desk to see if there are packages on the floor. Only one for someone named Sid. If there are others, they'd be in the closed office. Raymond knocks, waits several seconds, then turns the knob. Locked.

The elevator tings, prompting Raymond to retreat back into the lobby. The elevator door opens. Out comes Bruce, racing to the rear entrance to push the automatic open button.

"I'm sorry, Mr. Zorn, have you been waiting long?"

Raymond cannot make out the response.

Bruce comes back. He's followed by an extremely old man steering a scooter, a blue one similar to the model used by Irena. The man's face is gaunt, having lost all vibrancy, yet still retains an aura of authority.

"Right this way, Mr. Zorn. I'll escort you up."

"Thank you. And, please, call me Kurt."

Back in his suite, Raymond puts on the baseball game, then spots a letter from the condo corporation he hasn't yet filed. He reaches in the narrow cubby over the microwave, retrieves the black binder containing all his condo documents since buying the unit. Raymond fans it open on the island and inserts the document at the end. When he returns it into the cubby and pushes in, it hits an object. Raymond pulls out the binder, then grabs a chair to see what it is. It's the Barossa Shiraz bought two years ago to celebrate moving in. He ought to leave it, save it for his return, and have a beer instead while he finishes packing.

Oh, what the hell?

It's while sipping the wine, enjoying its smooth depth with notes of vanilla and blackberries, that he sits at his computer to shut it down for the next month or so. Only he is unable to keep himself from reading the email Monty mentioned. It opens with Monty describing Raymond's last encounter with Gary—when did he mention it to Monty?—that led to discovering Gary does not hold a property manager licence, and a complaint lodged by Monty with the agency that controls licences. Monty shares his full exchange with a Brenda Tripper.

To whom it may concern,

I wish to make a formal complaint regarding Gary Lewis of Omnirez, the condo management company of my building. According to the list on your website, Gary Lewis did not possess a licence while acting as condo manager here. It is my understanding a Level 2 or 3 licence has been a legal requirement for months and a lack of licence contravenes the new provincial guidelines. It came to my attention recently when a fellow owner told me about asking Gary to show his licence. Gary then told him to put the request in writing. It says in the guidelines condo mangers must show their licence for inspection whenever requested by any person.

Recently, our board president announced the board granted a request from Omnirez to temporarily release Gary for a special six-month assignment and an interim manager was to take his place. The timing seemed funny. Lo and behold, after checking your site again, Gary suddenly had one.

But it is only a level 1 licence. As I understand it, level 1 licences do not qualify one to manage condominiums solely. Oddly, I also noticed one of my closed service requests no longer show Gary as prime, but another name. As if someone discovered this discrepancy and removed Gary Lewis from our system to cover it up. All this is evident in the attached screen shots and other documents.

Good Morning Monty,

Thank you for your submission. First, let me summarize to say a condominium manager can apply to us for one of the three licences: Level 1 – Restricted; Level 2 – Graduated; Level 3 – Full. If a manager holds a Level 1 licence, they are still able to provide management services.

Also, be aware once an application is made for a licence, the applicant is deemed as holding that licence until processed and approved. Not seeing a name on our list could be due to that individual's licence being in process. Once completed, you would see their name, as you indicate is the case now.

As there is no basis for a complaint, it will be closed.

Hello Brenda,

It was my understanding a condo manager with a Limited Licence such as Gary required supervision. In the period I'm referring too, Gary was acting as sole property manager, without supervision. Are you saying that is legal?

Hello Monty,

You are correct. A condo manager with a Level 1 Restricted licence has to be supervised by one holding a Full Licence or Graduated Licence. However, the supervising manager need not be on-site at all times.

Hello Brenda,

Thank you for the further clarification. It comes as a surprise to me because this is the first I heard of Gary being under supervision during that period, and that he was, in essence, a trainee. One would think owners ought to be made aware of such a situation. But if you were to say that's a board matter, it would be hard for me to argue with you.

*Given that, I see where my complaint fell short in meeting
the strict demands of incontrovertible evidence you need
before acting on a complaint. In essence, the onus was on me
to provide the following:*

*- Proof Gary had not applied for a level 1 licence at anytime
when it was required*
*- And/or proof the manager's supervisor did not provide
enough supervision (if there is a guideline to this)*
*- And/or proof Gary performed one or more of these actions
restricted to level 2 and level 3 licences:*
  *> entered into, extended, renewed or terminated a
contract or other agreement on our behalf*
  > made expenditures over $500 from corporation funds
  *> provided anything to an owner or mortgagee the condo
corporation must legally provide*
  > signed a legal status certificate
  *> made expenditures out of, invested or otherwise made
dispositions from our reserve fund*

*It is unlikely, given the reticence of my board, I could gather
any of the above without great effort. I cannot say I'm happy
with this but do admit it has been eye-opening in terms of
how your organization operates on behalf of its true clients.*

The last snarky remark, Raymond notes, is something he'd
have put in himself before, but would exclude now, if he would
even get that far. Part of him is inclined to support Monty, but
his mind easily transitions to imagine the rolling hills and fields
around Rogoznica, peacefully incongruous against the nastiness
of the things that took place there during the war.

It's your battle, Monty, I wish you luck. I may help where I
can, but for now I am going away. In that spirit Raymond finds
it easy to ignore Monty's suggestion to review his own service
request or join in to gloat that, if nothing else, Gary's gone and
the complaint likely ensures he'll stay gone.

Instead, Raymond shuts off his computer to return to the
ball game, his glass of wine, and the immediate task at hand.

Usually a tedious chore, the sorting, folding, and pressing of clothes to fit into a new carry-on suitcase fills Raymond with anticipatory joy at the thought of summertime Poland, liberated from acrimony or fear of sinister goings-on at the condo.

-2 -1 G **M** 2 3 4 5 6 7 8 9 10 11 PH R

"One last question, Sheila. Will Gary's absence impact the AGM timing? It was later than normal last year. Stacie felt then, and I concur, we want it back to what it was, if possible."

"The timing of the AGM is a board decision, Lorie. We'll do our best to accommodate. But with an interim manager, I would anticipate holding it later this year."

"What's the latest we can hold it?"

"Technically, December 31, six months after fiscal year end."

"There you go, Elle, two free months before you're tested by a vote."

"I'd prefer much, much sooner than later, Ned."

"You know I'm kidding, Lorie."

"I recommend you schedule as early as you can, long before anyone thinks of the holidays, perhaps mid-November."

"Won't that be tight?"

"Yes, but we can make Gary available for consultation and I will make sure he attends. You'll be okay. We'll handle it. Now why don't the five of you return to your roof party. Let us ladies sort out the transition to ensure a November AGM is not only a possibility, but a certainty."

"Thanks, Sheila."

"No, thank you for letting us use the room to chat."

"Loved your cookies by the way, Dennis. Butter pecan?"

"That's right. Anything I can do to help you ease into your role, Kayla, just ask. You'll find I'm more than just a director."

"Get the door there will you . . . are they gone?"

"Already in the elevator."

"What do you think? Aren't they great? Hasn't Gary done a wonderful job with them?"

"To be honest Sheila, they're worse than I feared. They do so little, they're so slow, they seem rather docile."

"Yes."

"And I have to ask, are any of them really qualified for their roles? I mean, Dennis as board secretary?"

"That depends on how you measure. For you, Kayla, at this early point in your career, they measure up ideally."

"Measure up? To what?"

"Pliability. Condo boards are unlike other corporate boards. It's a crap shoot who gets elected, and once elected, who knows if they'll stay or quit or move. Instability makes it hard to do our work. Low turnover, even at the expense of certain qualities, is ideal. It simplifies things for us, for them. Gary did a fine job ensuring they feel they need him and each other."

"How is that good for owners not on the board?"

"Kayla, I know it sounds counter-intuitive. But the truth is, owners rarely know what's good for them and need us to guide them. It's their responsibility to elect board members and attend their AGMs. If they fail to do so then by default what is good for us is good for them."

"Question then: Why didn't I get the other assignment to let Gary stay?"

"Actually, he didn't give us much choice . . ."

"Is the rumour true that he lost his licence?"

"Where did you hear that?"

"Someone at the office joked about his 'special assignment.'"

"Well, he didn't lose his licence, he didn't have one to lose."

"What do you mean?"

"This is strictly confidential. The board can't know, though I suppose they'd be sympathetic to Gary and be discrete if they did. You see, Gary's been lax in complying with the new condo regulations."

"He seems like the type of guy who would resist."

"That's Gary. He felt it beneath him to take training with his decades of experience, not realizing he needed to absorb the new rules and new processes to break some habits. But we let it slide too long. An owner found out and lodged a complaint."

"Oh my goodness."

"Luckily the agency is on our side and gave Gary the benefit of the doubt for having applied for a licence. Except it was the restricted licence you started with."

"Meaning he could no longer sign contracts or spend over a certain amount and all that?"

"Not without supervisor approval which, once we realized the situation, fell to me. It required Gary to run back and forth between here and head office all the time. People did notice him absent a lot, but it was manageable. Only one owner continued pressing. We concluded it was best to make a change. Can't tell you how glad I am not to have to co-sign all those things."

"I appreciate you being upfront with me."

"Anyway, we have another site where Gary can be effective, where he can supervise with less scrutiny. However you're here because I believe you'll be more effective. As long as you adopt a few practices I need to share with you right away. That is why I wanted to stay to chat with you in private."

"Like what?"

"For starters, keeping minutes for all meetings."

"Isn't that Dennis's role as board secretary?"

"It's his responsibility. Nothing to say he can't delegate the task or the board delegate it for him, even against his wishes."

"They won't let him?"

"It seems so. But that's irrelevant. We, as in Omnirez, prefer to control the minutes if we can. This includes the AGM."

"I have no experience taking minutes."

"Believe me, Gary hated doing it, was bad at it. They're not hard, just dull, but as key as is having Omnirez, me, conduct the AGM. Been to any?"

"Yes."

"Did you find it dull? Overly bureaucratic? Be honest."

"Highly, it was awful. People grumbled. Sorry."

"Don't be. But really awful?"

"Yeah."

"Guess I'm not as charming as—oh never mind. My point is, bureaucracy is our friend. It induces lethargy. Lethargy ensures compliance or deters attendance, which is desirable. Minimum quorum, maximum proxies is what I like to say."

"Doesn't that create a divide between the board and owners, not to mention conflict?"

"Excellent, you catch on quickly. Conflict is good as it forces both sides to see us as intermediary. Kurt once told me: 'Sheila, don't hesitate to play them off against each other. If owners fear board members and directors fear owners, each will come to see Omnirez as their true ally. Then you can control behaviour.'"

"Control behaviour? Wow, that's, that's . . ."

"Well, that's Kurt. He's a little intense. You'll see for yourself shortly. It sounds extreme but isn't really. We don't do anything overtly. Instead we rely on little strategies. One that works quite well is to call everyone a resident to downplay ownership."

"My grandmother never liked that."

"That's my point. What it does is keep everyone equal. If an owner takes issue with it, point out, as you'll find you can with most issues, their beef is with the board, not us."

"Gary doesn't care for owners much, does he?"

"Most of his career experience is from apartment buildings. He never adjusted to the condo dynamic. Renters to him are less inclined to cause trouble or complain, more inclined to respect his authority. Also, landlord owners are primarily interested in the condo fee increases to pass on to tenants. Beyond that, they are unlikely to attend AGMs. I'm sure your head is spinning."

"These things Babcia complained about, sound deliberate."

"I must say I'm surprised your grandmother, of all people, would complain . . . look, I'm not being disingenuous in saying our methods are in the end for their benefit. If that takes some time for you to grasp, fine. Eventually you will and then you'll see how the board trusts your consistent message over random ones from owners like Raymond Tibbett."

"Raymond Tibbett?"

"You know him?"

"I — oh, is there someone at the door?"

"Good, he's here. I'll just warn you, Kurt can be direct."

"Good evening, ladies."

"Kayla, let me introduce Kurt Zorn, founder of Omnirez."

"Hello, Kayla. I'm charmed to at last meet the young lady of whom I have heard so much."

"The introduction to the board went perfectly, Kurt."

"Excellent. Now I wish to speak to Kayla alone."

"Of course. Good luck, Kayla. We'll continue tomorrow."

"Thanks."

"Good, we are alone. There is a matter I had to discuss with you in person. About the fellow on the WiFi committee?"

"Raymond Tibbett? Sheila was just— "

"So you know him? How well do you know him?"

"We played pool a few times. Harmless older guy."

"I see. You liked him? He was your lover?"

"Excuse me?"

"Did you two share secrets? Did he ask questions that were out of the ordinary? Please bear with me, it is important."

"Like I said we played pool, I kept beating him, he gave up. To be honest, I didn't know he still lived here."

"Good, because he is a troublemaker and will make trouble for you, as he did for Gary, unless you are firm with him."

"You sound as if you know him too. As if this is personal."

"Irena told me he said something that upset her once. It was with you there. Do you remember? It was on her birthday."

"You knew my Babcia?"

"Of course. For years. She never spoke of me?"

"I'm sorry, but no . . . I hope you're not offended."

"I have a thick skin. Now this man, he spoke to Irena and you were present."

"What did he say?"

"I am asking you, Kayla."

"She didn't tell you what he said?"

"Either you know it, or you don't. Answer me."

"Are you interrogating me?"

"No, no, of course not, forgive me. My old ways . . . oh my, your expression, so like Irena's. You need not be afraid of me."

"How, did, you know her?"

"During the war. We became . . . friends. She saved my life. Of course I was glad to help your career when asked."

"I thought Lorie was the one— "

"No, it was me, and to an extent, your grandmother."

"So you were a concentration camp prisoner too?"

"Yes, we met in the concentration camp."

"But you have no tattoo like Babcia."

"I did not require—no, it was because she was at Auschwitz first. There were no tattoos at the camp where we met."

"Were you with her when she escaped?"

"Ha, now I can say you are the interrogator."

"I don't mean to . . ."

"You are shaking. You look pale. Maybe it is best if we stop for now. Go to your roof party. Get some air."

"I think I may go home instead."

"That is fine. I do expect to see you in the office first thing, when you and I can continue."

"What about . . .?"

"Sheila? On meeting you and seeing for myself the potential Sheila described, I have decided to take the primary role in your development. I have big plans for you at Omnirez."

Acknowledgements

The book entitled, *A Narrow Bridge to Life: Jewish Slave Labor and Survival in the Gross-Rosen Camp System, 1940-1945*, by Bella Gutterman, proved to be of great assistance in writing the parts of the novel having to do with the concentration camps.

As always, I am deeply grateful for my wife Yolande, for being who she is, for tolerating my travails and travels as I wrote this novel, and also for reading it with care.

I am also very grateful to my sister-in-law, Marion, for being an early and excellent reader; her comments and questions proved valuable in shaping the story.

A special thank you to Frank Warman to whom I am indebted, not only for his technical support, but also his encouragement.

To contact me or learn more about my other books, please visit the website:

<u>www.peterhassebroek.com</u>